What the critics are saying...

"I cannot say enough wonderful things about this story. It is bar none the best story Ellora's Cave has to offer...I highly recommend this book, as it takes readers on a most amazing but enjoyable roller coaster ride..." ~ *Danica Favorite-McDonald, In the Library Reviews*

"*Forbidden* is definitely worthwhile reading. Vaughn's seductions and tantalizing moments will stir readers into reading more. The only bad thing is, the story ended, but with great applause." ~ *Miriam, Love Romances*

"I was thoroughly enchanted by *Forbidden*. The jealousy, heartbreak, yearning and passion of Elisa are all conveyed in this story. Our heart goes out to her –what she must endure to find her long lost son." ~ *Liz Koshy, The Best Reviews*

FORBIDDEN

Anastasia Black

FORBIDDEN
An Ellora's Cave Publication, January 2005

Ellora's Cave Publishing, Inc.
1337 Commerce Drive Suite #13
Stow, Ohio 44224

ISBN #1419950088

Cover art by: *Syneca*

Warning:

The following material contains graphic sexual content meant for mature readers. *Forbidden* has been rated *E-rotic* by a minimum of three independent reviewers.

Ellora's Cave Publishing offers three levels of Romantica™ reading entertainment: S (S-ensuous), E (E-rotic), and X (X-treme).

S-ensuous love scenes are explicit and leave nothing to the imagination.

E-rotic love scenes are explicit, leave nothing to the imagination, and are high in volume per the overall word count. In addition, some E-rated titles might contain fantasy material that some readers find objectionable, such as bondage, submission, same sex encounters, forced seductions, etc. E-rated titles are the most graphic titles we carry; it is common, for instance, for an author to use words such as "fucking", "cock", "pussy", etc., within their work of literature.

X-treme titles differ from E-rated titles only in plot premise and storyline execution. Unlike E-rated titles, stories designated with the letter X tend to contain controversial subject matter not for the faint of heart.

FORBIDDEN

Chapter One

1835, Fairleigh Hall, England

Vaughn Wardell, Viscount Rothmere, only heir of the Marquis of Fairleigh, stepped from the carriage and looked up at the three-story manor he hadn't seen in nearly two decades. Fairleigh Hall hadn't changed at all. The grounds were still immaculate, and the impressive manor rivaled any in England.

He hated the sight of it.

The years he'd spent at Fairleigh Hall had been the worst of his life. Now, at the age of twenty-nine, he had returned to this hideous heap of stone to save his future.

His gut clenched as it had when he heard the outrageous news. The thought was a despairing one: Kirkaldy, his mother's final gift, might be lost to him.

Little more than a glorified hunting lodge near Edinburgh, Kirkaldy had been his mother's only untainted possession. The days there, far from Fairleigh Hall and his father, had been the best of Vaughn's young life. At Kirkaldy, his mother had been carefree, even joyous. For that reason alone, Vaughn intended to plant himself like a weed here at Fairleigh Hall, a weed that refused to be pulled and discarded, until Kirkaldy's ownership had been determined.

Taking a deep breath, he walked up the thirteen steps to his father's home.

Vaughn had no trouble imagining the disapproval his father would convey upon his return. He'd learned years ago there was no pleasing Rufus Wardell. The only emotion Rufus had ever openly shown him had been when he'd announced Vaughn would be leaving for boarding school. A cruel smile had curled his father's lips as he'd laid out the details of what would become twelve years of purgatory, hidden behind the walls of one of the best public schools in England. Though nearly a decade had passed since he had graduated, those memories still appeared in his dreams from time to time. They would wake him in the middle of night, to cold sweat and a hurting heart, the bed sheets tangled around his legs.

The memory subsided as the door was opened. Joshua, his father's trusted valet, stared at him. "Good lord! I mean, Lord Vaughn." The valet's expression softened. "You've come home?" There was a buried hope in his tone.

Vaughn's chest tightened with fondness for the old man. While Vaughn had been growing up there had been countless occasions when he had been locked in the attic for yet another transgression. It had been Joshua who had slipped food, blankets and tallows to provide light through the long nights when not even his mother's pleadings had moved his father to release him.

Vaughn laid a hand on Joshua's shoulder. "I'm not here to stay," he said gently.

This time the disappointment in Joshua's eyes was easy to read. He stepped back, covering the emotion with formal pride. "Come in, my lord."

Vaughn handed over his coat, hat and gloves and strode through the broad entrance hall into the circular foyer that dominated the center of the building, where he halted. He turned a full circle on his heels, taking in the cold marble surfaces and massive round columns that lined the foyer in regimented pairs. They were dazzlingly lit by the glass dome on the roof that bathed the foyer in natural sunlight, showcasing the polished, untouched perfection of the green-flecked marble. The foyer was widely admired across five counties for its elegant, unusual design. Whenever his father loosened the purse strings enough to entertain, the foyer was thick with guests dotted about the floor and the stairs, tucked into the recesses between the columns, gossiping.

But while everyone had appeared to enjoy the spectacular room, Vaughn's recollection of the foyer was a bitter one that caught at his throat. His gaze lingered on the staircase that swooped in a spiral to both upper floors. His pulse skittered at the sight of the thick stone balustrade on the first floor. That was where he had stood as a frightened ten-year old, his fingers trying to dig into the cold stone, watching his mother leave in the middle of the night.

She'd promised to send for him, with as many kisses and hugs as she could manage before hurrying to escape the house. She had smelled of lavender, and her hand against his cheek had been warm and delicate.

That had been the last time he'd seen her alive.

"Your father is at dinner. Shall I announce you?" Joshua asked, startling Vaughn and bringing him back to the present.

"And ruin the surprise?" Vaughn asked, already heading toward the high-arched French doors. Taking a calming breath, he opened the double doors and stepped inside.

The room was long and dim compared to the foyer. There was a row of tall sash windows along one wall, and their limited light fell on a collection of large portraits and mediocre landscapes hanging from the picture rail on the other. Between was an ocean of expensive oriental carpets, pinned down on the edges by heavy, hand-carved buffets and occasional chairs. All of them framed the focal point of the room: a long Georgian mahogany dining table that easily seated thirty people.

There were not that many people dining this evening. In fact, there were only two. One was a woman sitting at the right of the head of the table, her back to Vaughn. This could only be his father's new fiancée, Elisa.

The woman who had ripped Kirkaldy from him.

She was to blame for all of this. It was because of her he had been forced back to Fairleigh Hall to confront Rufus.

The sight of her erect back filled him with a sudden sharp fury he hadn't suspected he held. His whole body tightened with it. She was ruining his life, taking away from him the only precious memories he owned.

Vaughn blinked, astonished at the power of the emotion that bubbled up inside him now that he was at the point of confrontation for which he had been bracing himself.

His attention was drawn to the short man sitting at the head of the table. Rufus Wardell was staring at him, his gray brows furrowing together into a frown Vaughn remembered well. Rufus' permanently red cheeks bracketed a big nose. Small muddy brown eyes sat above them. Even at sixty, Rufus' hair was thick, but it was coarse and dirty gray. With his short, rotund shape he might have appeared boyish, but because of the cruel light in his eyes and the cynical twist to his lips, Rufus looked more like a maniacal cherub.

He studied Vaughn as though he were trying to place him. And he probably was. Vaughn was over six feet tall. He was broad across the shoulders thanks to hours as an adolescent taking his frustrations out upon various professional pugilists. There was nothing of the boy who had left Fairleigh Hall so very long ago.

After an endless moment, surprise crossed Rufus' face. He'd finally recognized him. "What the hell are you doing here, boy?" Rufus asked, his rasping voice bereft of any warmth.

Though Vaughn had anticipated his reaction, it still stung. There would be no welcome here, he realized. "Thank you for the nice welcome, Father. It's a pleasure to see you, too."

It apparently disturbed Rufus Wardell not at all that this was the first return of the child he tossed out without regard nearly twenty years ago. No conscience appeared to stir him at the arrival of the son he had inexcusably wronged.

The anger squeezed Vaughn's throat and chest and nearly closed off his breath. He'd hoped there would have been some doubt, some chance of redemption, but there was none.

"Well, out with it!" Rufus glared at Vaughn. "You obviously have something on your mind, or you would not have traveled so far. Pray tell," he added with patently false politeness, "to what do I owe the pleasure of your company?"

"I'm not here to be polite, so you'd needn't extend yourself," Vaughn assured him.

"Then get out. I'm dining with the woman I intend to marry and your presence is not welcome." Rufus shot a look at Elisa, who sat in perfect stillness at the end of the table, her head bowed in imitation of a modest woman.

Vaughn's friends had been quick to advise him just how short on modesty this harlot was. He took a deep breath, trying to quell the hot tide of resentment rising in him. "It is about her that I am here," he said. He stepped around the end of the table to face Elisa, and swept into a low bow. The courtesy came automatically, as did the phrasing: "My lady, we have not had the pleasure of being introduced…"

…and then, he looked at her properly for the first time. Shock slithered through his veins, dispersing all the fury, resentment and indignation in one breathless moment.

As her large eyes glanced up at him, wide with apprehension, he stared at her, taking in her face and apparel, trying to estimate just how old she was. Blue eyes the same glorious shade as a bright summer sky stared back at him as she gave a hesitant, nervous smile. The smile drew his attention to her full, pleasantly pink lips, and the white teeth behind.

Her skin was softly touched by the sun, but flawless, and as he took her hand and bowed over it again, he noticed the cheeks bloom with hot color at his attention.

Absurdly, her coyness sent a thrill of pleasure through him.

He could not help but smile as he stepped back. She ducked her chin, unable to look at him directly. It was then he noticed the head of gleaming blonde curls the color of wheat. A silky ringlet tipped forward across her shoulder at her movement, and he resisted the temptation to brush it gently back.

She was so young…and sweetly, stunningly beautiful.

The thought occurred to him with a shock that momentarily obliterated the sting of his father's cold welcome. With it came confusion, because although he had not heard how young his father's fiancée was, Vaughn was more than familiar with the rumors of her sordid past.

This was the woman who had brought on the death of her husband by her lover's hand? All of London had been abuzz with the news.

"Boy, you've grown tall and insolent," Rufus snarled. "I didn't pay good money all those years for you to learn bad manners."

Vaughn dragged his attention back to his father. "I'm paying my respects to the future lady of this splendid home." And he turned back to Elisa once more, to study her.

"You are most welcome, Vaughn. I am pleased to meet you at last," she responded with a tiny smile. Her voice was a low contralto, soft and unexpected.

He nodded one more time, before stepping back.

He had intended to leave the room, to let his father have his intimate dinner. It would be wiser to retreat for a while and regroup his defenses now his father had shown no punches were to be pulled in the trial that lay ahead.

Instead, he lowered himself into the chair opposite his father's fiancée. "Thank you, I will have a brandy," he told Rufus, answering the question a good host would have asked.

Rufus' upper lip curled and his eyes narrowed. He looked up at the manservant standing by the door of the dining room and jerked his head. Silently, the man glided to a buffet laid with decanters and crystal to pour the drink.

Vaughn glanced at Elisa again.

She delicately cut her meat into small pieces, lifted the fork and slid a piece into her mouth. A visible pulse beat at the base of the long column of her throat.

The servant placed the brandy in front of Vaughn. Rufus began to eat again, attacking his plate with furious gusto. With every loaded forkful of food he would take a big mouthful of claret. The red liquid dribbled from the corners of his mouth as he chomped away.

Vaughn looked away, his disgust growing. Surely the man would try a bit harder in front of his intended? How could she contemplate marrying this gruesome imp? Or perhaps the money was worth it to her…

He looked back to the silent beauty on the other side of the table. He still could not believe this was the same woman of whom he'd heard tell. The gossips had spared him no detail: a bride at seventeen, wed to an aging count. A mother at nineteen and a cuckolded wife the same year. Then, swiftly, she had set about giving her husband his own set of horns. The gossips had been firm in their approval of her husband's reaction to her supposed whoring. He had taken the only honorable course of action an aggrieved husband could; he'd challenged her lover to a duel. No honor had been lost because he'd been killed. In fact, society had gathered about his grieving family and presented a solid, united front to anyone who dared to abuse the deceased lord's memory.

That had been years ago. In the aftermath, Elisa's name had quickly disappeared into shamed obscurity. No good woman or honorable gentleman would speak of her aloud in polite company. It had only been the relaxed bawdy banter around a late night card table that had alerted Vaughn to the fact Elisa had re-emerged from her exile. His card companions that night had thought it a superb jest his own father had proposed to her. Vaughn had gone along with the joke at the time, thinking the pair deserved each other.

The contradiction between her appearance and her past was indeed confusing.

She was pushing at a piece of the meat on her plate with her fork, and Vaughn wondered if she did so to avoid looking up and seeing him watching her. Was she aware of him? By her sweet looks, he would have judged her an innocent, but her reputation told him she probably knew and understood every hot thought running through his mind.

Vaughn sipped at his brandy thoughtfully, alternately watching Rufus eat and Elisa toy with her food. She really was a lovely creature, he realized. He was not at all surprised two men had fought to the death over her.

She touched her mouth with her napkin, then lifted a fingertip to slide it across her lips a second time, without the linen. It was unconsciously graceful and sensuous. Vaughn's body tightened with an old familiar ache, intensified beyond reason like a taut bow string stretched to the limits of endurance, vibrating with tension and packed with potential power to explode...

The realization slammed into Vaughn with the shock of ice water.

He wanted her.

And the wanting was not a casual, passing impulse. It was burning in him, pushing aside thought, reason, caution.

Vaughn stared at her, feeling his heart thump erratically, and the beat echo in his temple. What was happening to him? Had he lost all good sense?

His thoughts were scattered when Rufus' hand thumped into his upper arm.

"You're silent, boy," Rufus said, not bothering to hide his loathing tone. "One would wonder why you're still sitting at the table if you've got nothing left to say."

"I'm finishing my brandy, thank you." The calm tone Vaughn produced took enormous willpower.

He saw Rufus' eyes swivel to glance at Elisa before glaring at him again. "That'd better be all, boy."

"I am hardly a boy, Father. You may call me 'son' if you would prefer, but as you've called me nothing at all these past twenty years, either in person or by mail, I won't insist upon it."

"If I am such a horrible father, then why are you here?" Rufus asked, one corner of his mouth turned upward in a mocking smile.

Vaughn's heart gave a little jump. This was it. This was the moment of confrontation he had been anticipating for three days. The anger that had been building for those three days renewed itself, washing over him in waves as he met Rufus' intent stare.

Elisa abruptly cleared her throat, and the tiny sound reminded Vaughn of her presence. Suddenly, he was reluctant to discuss the matter in front of her, despite three days of mentally rehearsing the cutting speech he had intended to bestow upon his father regardless of who was there to see it. In truth, his imagination of the confrontation had always included the harlot Elisa on hand to hear all he had to say of his father's base qualities. Now, it seemed the height of rudeness to let his fury spill out unheeded while she watched.

"What brings you to Fairleigh Hall, boy?" his father asked again.

"I thought it was time to pay a visit before I settled in at Kirkaldy." The mention of his estate was intentional, and he didn't blink as he waited for his father's response.

Rufus shifted in his chair. "So…will you be leaving at first light?"

Vaughn's indirect challenge had completely misfired.

"Surely it has not been twenty years since last you were here," Elisa remarked, and Vaughn was grateful for the interruption, although irritated it was she who supplied it. He didn't want to be grateful to the whore. He didn't want any association with her at all. Now he must play out the little social by-play.

"Indeed, it has been twenty years. Fairleigh Hall has not changed in all that time. Tell me, how do you find Fairleigh?"

She lightly touched the napkin to those pink lips. "It's very nice."

Her words completely lacked conviction, as well they should. The manor sat in rocky countryside and had little to offer anyone under the age of fifty. He could only imagine how lonely it would be for a young woman to live in such a cold, desolate place.

"How long have you been here?"

"I arrived a little over a month ago…along with my maid, Marianne."

So, her maid was with her. How very proper. "Do you ride?" he asked. He already knew she did. Rumors of her shocking skill in the saddle had reached every men's club in London and beyond. Vaughn's friends had taken great pleasure in telling him about his soon-to-be stepmother's shortcomings. She wasn't content to keep to a decorous trot upon a sidesaddle. In her teens she had ridden astride like any man, her dress hoisted up to her thighs to give her the freedom to ride recklessly.

It was well known she had beaten many men on horseback.

"I fear I have little time for riding these days."

He watched her intently. "Why not?"

His father slammed his drink down, bringing Vaughn's attention back to him. "Vaughn, you're making Elisa uncomfortable."

"He's not making me uncomfortable, Rufus," Elisa told him. She smiled soothingly at Rufus before glancing at Vaughn again. "I've missed riding."

"I'm certain Father has a vast array of mares to choose from."

"I've asked Rufus to go with me, but his back pain prevents him from doing so."

"Certainly a short ride wouldn't tax you too much, Father?"

Again, he received one of his father's icy glares. Rufus took a long drink of his claret, keeping his eye upon Vaughn. "I'm too old."

The response came from him unbidden, unplanned. "Very well. I'll ride with her, then."

His father's face turned purple with anger, but Vaughn barely heard what Rufus was trying to say, for he had seen Elisa's surprised expression. Then, briefly, a flare of joy followed by a soft, warm smile lifted her lovely full lips. The smile was for him and her eyes sparkled. Vaughn felt his heart give a painful leap in response.

Then abruptly, all expression was removed and her gaze dropped to her plate, as if she had suddenly remembered her place. But the afterglow bathed Vaughn in a heady warmth that threatened to make his hands tremble.

Rufus finally found his voice. "You'll not be here long enough to have idle time on your hands."

How like Rufus to dictate how and when he should come and go. Some of the earlier fury leapt a little in Vaughn's chest. "Father, long ago you gave up any right to tell me what I can and cannot do." His voice echoed his anger, emerging low and strained.

Rufus' eyes narrowed a little. The moment of silence between them grew and Vaughn knew his father was studying him anew, reassessing. Vaughn did not look away. He had no intention of backing down in this petty game of willpower.

Finally Rufus cleared his throat with a harsh hack and reached for the wine.

Vaughn drained his own brandy, needing the small sustenance, knowing he had won but a small victory that would make Rufus all the more determined to bring him down in the very near future. Rufus bent on vengeance was a dangerous man indeed.

While Rufus called for another decanter, swearing at the lack of foresight of the footman, Vaughn dared to glance at Elisa once more and he recognized fear in her eyes. She shook her head a little, her lips opening as if she breathed a warning. She understood what was happening then.

Vaughn smiled at her reassuringly, pretending a confidence he did not wholly feel.

Her hand came to her mouth, as if she was distressed, and she looked away. After a moment she looked back as if drawn, perhaps reluctantly.

Vaughn struggled to hide the shock her glance sent through him, for he had understood that searing gaze with perfect clarity.

Elisa wanted him, too.

This was a complication he dared not play with. Rufus was already set on defeating him, and Vaughn had no illusions about Rufus' power to hurt his enemies. If Vaughn gave in to the temptation presented by her desire, then Rufus would have moral and legal grounds to utterly destroy them both.

Chapter Two

Elisa's heart ached as if she had run too hard, too far. An invisible hand was squeezing at her insides, making her feel wretchedly ill, but at the same time there was a heady, intoxicating bubbling in her blood and her mind.

Her entire attention was focused on the man sitting across from her. It was her inability to dismiss him from her mind that made her fearful. She stood to lose far too much if she gave this little attraction any freedom to grow.

Vaughn Wardell. She let the name roll through her mind. As much as his appearance surprised her, so did his actual existence. Rufus had never mentioned having a son. There was not a single portrait of the heir to the Fairleigh dynasty to be found anywhere in the manor, and she had been in every public room since her arrival a week ago.

One servant had told Marianne that all portraits of the previous marchioness had been burned. Apparently Rufus wanted no reminder of the woman who had betrayed him — or that woman's son.

Elisa had been a little shocked at the barely disguised venom emanating from Rufus. Vaughn's welcome home had been grim at best. Why did families feel it was permissible to treat each other that way? Against her will, it drew upon her own memories — the hatred Roger's family had done little to hide from her once he was dead. While Roger had been alive she'd had no idea of the extraordinary depth of that vile emotion buried inside them. Its emergence had been twice as shocking because it had been hidden so completely.

She studied Vaughn discreetly, wondering if he was reeling from the same sense of shock she had once suffered. Her sympathy rose a little higher. He was hiding it well, for he must surely be suffering some sort of reaction after Rufus' less-than-endearing display.

Standing well over six feet in height, dressed in a dark gray suit, Vaughn dominated the room. His wide shoulders were emphasized by the way the fabric of his coat fit snug against them. Elisa glanced at Rufus' diminutive height then back at Vaughn. Where had he acquired such stature, and such power? His height could only have come from his mother. The power? Men had a unique ability to build power from nothing; they were naturally endowed with more strength than women to begin with. Yes, men had power, certainly. But Vaughn's whole body radiated strength of both muscle and mind, working in concert, which gave him a potential far greater than those who used only physical force to get their way…

When Vaughn had looked at her over the top of her hand, his eyes had casually swept across her face, drawing her breath from her. His eyes were astonishing; emerald green, framed by long lashes as dark as his hair. Then he'd lifted the square chin, which spoke of a determination that belonged to a much older man and smiled a little, the white teeth revealed behind unexpectedly full lips. *Lips made for passion*, her treacherous mind had whispered.

Such abundant good health and sleekness was to be found in any young male, but there was an added quality about Vaughn—a sensuality, an animal magnetism that reminded her of her womanhood in a way she had not truly experienced it for many years. Her heart would not stop pounding and her breath grew quick. There was a tension, low in the pit of her stomach, that stirred and throbbed. How many hearts had this man broken? How many women had sought his arms, enjoyed his virility?

A surge of envy raced through her as she remembered what life had been like as a married woman—before it had all come to a shocking end. There had been privileges of the marriage bed she had secretly enjoyed while women in her social circles had whispered of the disgusting lewdness and depravity their husbands demanded of them. Roger had been a willing and excellent teacher in that regard, and it had never occurred to her to ask who had taught him.

Of course it was different for men before they were married — they were expected to sow their wild seeds. Because of that leniency, she had been slow to realize Roger's philandering was systemic and had gone completely unchecked despite their engagement, wedding, or the birth of their son. His conscience had not appeared to hinder him, either. His endless parade of mistresses made it virtually impossible for her to leave her London townhouse or show her face at any social gathering.

Roger's death, which should have been the end of her exile, had instead turned society's pity of her into an unyielding condemnation. Their disapproval had been unanimous and unrelenting. Then she had met Rufus who had, astonishingly, believed her. It seemed he was the only one in the world who did.

Rufus, who was barely tolerated by polite society himself, was the one man who would help her find her son and get him back. Of course, Rufus, being a man, could afford to disdain society's approval, and thrive despite it. She, on the other hand, had no help or offers of security, making his friendship impossible to refuse.

She bit into her bottom lip, harried by doubts she wished would cease plaguing her. Marrying Rufus was the only door open to her now. For her son's sake, she would do anything.

Elisa let her mind run through the litany of her past, deliberately recalling her reasons for accepting Rufus' marriage proposal. The repetition of reasons for her decision usually calmed her emotions and helped her accept the distress her new role created.

It should have calmed her now, but it did not.

She looked at Vaughn, taking in his features like a woman starved for the sight of her lover. A warmth spread through her veins, down low into her belly.

This will soon be your stepson, she reminded herself, but it didn't matter, because her body was responding to an attraction that was ageless, wordless and far beyond logic or sense.

For her son's sake, she had to resist her own betraying body.

Then Vaughn's gaze met hers. Her thoughts scattered under the direct, challenging stare. There was a sensuality in that look, an implied promise that made her heart jump. The dizziness imparted from his first appearance leapt high and make her senses swirl until all she could do was stare into his eyes, which had reached out wordlessly across the table and stroked her soul.

Flustered, she reached for the barely touched wineglass by her plate, only to topple it to the cloth. Blood red liquid flowed across the spotless linen, as the overturned crystal clattered against unused cutlery.

Rufus shook his head. "Oh, for heaven's sake!" he raged, throwing his napkin on top of the mess.

She breathed deeply, trying to gather her scattered wits, to bring herself back to normal. She must keep her mind upon mundane realities!

Vaughn rose to his feet. "It was a simple accident. Linen will wash." His voice was a lazy drawl.

"And you, you unwelcome upstart...If you've finished your brandy you can get the hell out of my dining room. You're spoiling the mood."

Elisa couldn't help but look up at Vaughn, then. Rufus' snarled obscenities would have been enough to send her running for her room. But Vaughn merely smiled and gave a graceful nod of his head. "If your claret is of the same inferior quality as the glass of brandy I just drank, you'd best look to your victuals for the source of the sour mood. Since I've depleted my tolerance for both mood and brandy, I'll bid you goodnight."

"Don't you mean goodbye?" Rufus shot back.

"Hardly. I've decided to make an extended visit, Father. After nearly twenty years of silence, we have so much to discuss."Rufus' cheeks turned a deep red. "You'll be out of here before dawn!"

Vaughn turned abruptly, and his back was facing Elisa, so she could not see his expression. "And throwing me out is certainly your right as master of the house," he said coolly to Rufus. "But if you try to have me ejected from this house one moment earlier than I intend to leave, I will immediately seek a hearing with a solicitor in London, to discuss with him certain irregularities in the stewardship of my mother's estate and the execution of her will."

Rufus stared at Vaughn, his eyes narrowed in disdain.

"Do we understand each other?" Vaughn added after a moment.

The corner of Rufus' mouth curled. "Yes," he snapped.

"Then I'll bid you goodnight."

Vaughn turned toward Elisa. She rose from her chair, staring at him, trying to fathom the cryptic exchange she'd just witnessed. How had Vaughn managed to bring his father to heel so easily?

Vaughn reached for her hand. She allowed him to lift it to his lips. For another small moment time halted, as his lips touched her skin, igniting it with a delightful heat that spread up her arm.

As he straightened she dared risk another quick look into his eyes and was astonished to see a sad shadow there, a hint of hurt behind the bland, cavalier pose.

"Oh, Vaughn," she said impulsively. "I'm glad you are to stay a while."

He smiled and when he spoke his cynicism was more than apparent. "You stand alone in that gladness, madam, but thank you."

Without another word he turned and left the room, not bothering to shut the door behind him.

"Insolent brat! How dare he threaten me!" Rufus pulled himself up to the table again. He motioned for the footman to pour him yet another drink. Already he'd been through one bottle and was now working on another.

The ugly consequences of excessive drinking were more than familiar to her. Rufus' drinking was a trait her husband had shared. Elisa reminded herself yet again of the reasons she had agreed to this marriage. Her son Raymond was worth any discomfort.

"Come, play a song for me," Rufus firmly suggested, standing up.

Elisa willingly followed him through the archway into the adjoining drawing room where she took her seat at the piano. The grandly formal room was as proper and soulless as the rest of the house, but while she sat at the keyboard she could forget her surroundings.

Perhaps she could forget Vaughn, too.

She began to play, letting her mind drift. It was a struggle at first, for her mind would return to the puzzling questions and danger Vaughn's arrival at Fairleigh Hall created. But moment-by-moment the music wove its spell and her heart calmed. The well-worn daydreams she had spun of a rosy future filled her mind—gentle summer days spent caring and raising Raymond, loving him, watching him grow...

Soon the sounds of snoring filled the room. Unwilling to risk waking Rufus, she played for another half-hour. Only when she was certain he was soundly asleep did she rise silently from the piano and leave the room.

With her mind and body quiet, she felt the true depths of her fatigue. She had gone for long months now holding the tension inside her, for when hopelessness, despair and frustration took away her courage, the tight coil of tension was all that kept her on the path towards her dream.

Wearily, she climbed the cold stone stairs to the first floor and turned right toward the west wing where the guest quarters were located. The west wing was smaller, older, but Elisa had been drawn to the charming rooms from the first. Warming southern sunlight lit them for most of the day, and the prevailing breezes would cool the rooms on hot summers' nights.

Rufus, thank goodness, occupied a much grander and larger suite in the east wing. Apart from two guest bedrooms—

Vaughn was using one of those rooms.

—apart from the two guest bedrooms, Rufus' suite took up the rest of the wing on that floor.

Elisa locked the door against all and any unexpected entries. Her maid, Marianne, was already waiting. She helped her undress and slip into a cool silk nightdress and peignoir. Elisa had learned to appreciate the sensuous, hedonistic feel of silk against her bare skin when married to Roger. In the security of her own private rooms, where there wasn't the remotest risk of anyone being able to raise the accusation of impropriety against her, she continued the indulgence. Then she sat in front of the mirror.

"I hear his lordship's son is quite handsome," Marianne said, while pulling the pins from Elisa's hair.

"Indeed, he is."

"All the maids are aflutter over his appearance. They say he hasn't been home since he was but a child. Most of them had no idea he even existed."

Usually Elisa had no interest in such gossip, as she knew firsthand how hurtful it could be. But her interest had been piqued this time, so she did not try to change topics as she would normally have done.

"I actually overheard one of the scullery maids say that she would slip into his bedroom tonight." Marianne shook her head. "Can you imagine?"

Yes, she could easily imagine stealing into Vaughn's bed, but she wouldn't dare admit it to anyone, even Marianne whom she trusted completely. That other women might be similarly tempted was an unpleasant fact she had overlooked until then.

Her mood abruptly slid from calm peacefulness to a fermented sourness, and Elisa dismissed Marianne with a firm goodnight as soon as the woman had put away the dinner gown. Finally alone, she methodically began brushing her hair, barely glancing at her reflection. Then she caught a glimpse of herself, and became still, staring at her reflection in shock.

Her blue eyes were dull, as though the very life had been squeezed from them. Her face was pale, her cheekbones stark from the weight she had lost since Raymond had been taken from her. Her spirits had been low since then, but she did not think her melancholy would be so plain for the world to see.

She ran a trembling hand down her face. The last thing in this whole world she wanted was to be dependent upon a man. Her solitary life at Greenwood Manor in Perthshire, the only estate Roger's family hadn't taken from her, had been one of contentment. Raymond had also loved the little hunting lodge that at one time had served as a playground for Scotland's aristocracy. It was her solace, but she had no money with which to maintain it.

Now she had the chance to live in the country again and though it was not the small manor in Perthshire, it was shelter away from people and the society that had banished her.

And she would get Raymond back. Rufus' reassurances were enough to keep the hope and excitement alive in her. Oh, how she missed Raymond! He would be ten years old next month, and this would be the sixth birthday they had not celebrated together.

With a quick motion, she wiped at the tears that stung her eyes, and sent a plea to God that he might assist Rufus and deliver her son to her soon.

She knew sleep would not come easily tonight. Vaughn's arrival had upset her predictable world and now her thoughts were chasing each other endlessly in her mind.

A book might pass the time until sleep arrived, however. One of the untouched old volumes in Rufus' pristine library would allow her to escape to other fantastic worlds, living adventures vicariously through the characters.

She rose to her feet and slipped silently from her room. There was no danger of meeting anyone. At this time of night everyone else would be tucked into their beds in the servants' quarters, or else asleep on the other side of the house. She could slip down to the library and back without being seen, if she was cautious and quick.

The house was silent, the stone stairs cold under her bare feet. There was a lingering heat from the day in the still air which brushed against the silk of her peignoir like a breeze as she hurried across the foyer to the gallery. The wide gallery gave access to a number of rooms, including the library at the far end of the house, on the same wing as her bedroom. She slipped into the room and stood still for a moment, blinking, until her eyes adjusted to the darkness.

There were tall, stately windows on three sides of the room and from most of them poured milky, glowing moonlight. It spilled on the floral patterned carpet and across the high-backed reading chairs and side tables. Typically, there was not a single book out of place anywhere in the room. Rufus was not an avid reader.

She moved towards the bookcases, but the ghostly light beckoned her and she drifted over to the window instead, drawn by the alien landscape the full moon painted beyond the glass. She rested her hand against the pane, staring out.

"My god, look at you!" The low curse was uttered from close by.

Elisa whirled, startled, her heart leaping hard and hot, her hand at her mouth to smother the shriek she gave.

Vaughn was rising from the depths of one of the chairs, his eyes riveted on her, sweeping her from head to toe.

She tried to calm her heart by taking a deep, steady breath, but it continued to patter on restlessly. Vaughn in the moonlight was a dreamlike being that might have stepped straight from the pages of the books she favored.

He had obviously been sitting in the dark, staring out the window. His tie had been removed and lay over the back of a nearby chair. He'd taken off his jacket and waistcoat and the shirt was loosened. Even the top two or three buttons had been undone, revealing the powerful muscles and tendons of his upper chest, which she could see flex as he lifted himself to his feet. His skin in the moonlight was smooth, tanned and looked like it would be velvety to touch. The pants were form fitting, revealing strong thigh muscles that bunched as he stepped towards her.

She swallowed. No, her heart was not about to slow down.

"So this is what the real Elisa looks like," he added softly, as he came closer.

She realized how he would see her—her silky nightdress stopped short of her ankles, revealing her bare feet. Her peignoir was made of the sheerest pink chiffon, and would hide nothing of what she wore beneath, despite the ruffles and bows at wrist and neck. And her hair was down, brushed out and bereft of any ornament or cap.

She hastily gathered the peignoir's collar in her fist, trying to draw it closer together.

"Vaughn! Why are you…I thought…I did not think anyone would be in here."

He stopped barely a pace from her, and she was forced to tilt her head to look up at him.

"Neither did I," he admitted, his voice low. He studied her face, his expression giving nothing away. "By heaven, you are beautiful!"

Her heart gave a funny little jerk. "Don't," she said breathlessly.

"I don't say that merely to flatter you with meaningless compliments." His voice was low.

Alarm shot through her. A casual flirtation she could quash, but the thread of sincerity in his voice—that was something she did not have the skill to combat.

"I should leave…" she murmured, turning to go.

"Don't. Not yet."

"I must, and you know it," she insisted, looking over her shoulder.

He didn't respond. He was simply looking at her. As he stood there wreathed in moonlight, his dark hair crowned with luminous highlights and his eyes shadowed and hiding his thoughts, she saw his chest lift as he drew a deep breath.

"You know there is something between us, then," he said, moving towards her. "You felt it tonight, just as I did."

Fear rushed through her, more powerful than the squeak of momentary alarm she'd just felt. Instinct told her that what might happen next would threaten everything for which she had worked and waited. She faced him properly. "Vaughn, please, I beg you not to pursue this…" She wished he would take a step or two backwards.

"I have sat here debating that decision myself," he said. His voice was low, resonant. "I had decided prudence was wiser and despite tweaking my father's nose tonight, I would have left for London on the morrow, but then you floated in here like a goddess in a dream. Elisa…" And his jaw flexed as if he clenched it briefly. "You are driving away my better sense."

Held to the spot despite her mind whispering she should run from the room this instant, Elisa looked into his eyes. Green eyes…in the dark they appeared to be lit from within. They glowed with a radiance of their own, as if the power of his soul shone from them. Her body seemed to tighten up, the coil of tension settling low in her belly.

She found the words she needed. "Don't do this, Vaughn. Please."

"Then turn around and walk away," he said.

He was so close she fancied she could feel the heat of his big body against her, warming the silk of her nightgown, caressing the skin beneath with a featherweight touch. Her breasts ached to be touched, and she was aware of them thrusting against the silk. She could feel her tight nipples pushing at the delicate fabric, and with each minute movement it stroked them with a exquisite delicacy. Vaughn was so close he merely had to lift his big hands a few inches and he could touch them...

Elisa looked up at him again. "God help me, I cannot," she breathed.

And she heard his answering sigh.

His hands did lift then and very gently slid beneath the open front of the peignoir, lifting away the gauzy fabric. He cupped his hands around her waist, gathering the silk in against her.

She tightened her throat to prevent a gasp escaping her.

His hands were of a size that she could feel the tips of his fingers almost touching each other. They lay a sizzling imprint against her flesh there. The strong thumbs moved in a restless arc against her midriff, pulling the silk tight over her breasts. The taut fabric transmitted the sweeping motion of his thumbs to her aching, sensitive nipples, and it was as if he had caressed the breasts themselves.

She couldn't help it. She drew in an audible, shuddering breath.

"Your waist really *is* that small," he said. His voice was hoarse. "I wasn't sure, what with tight lacing..." He frowned.

"Why do you bother wearing a corset at all? You certainly have no need of one."

"A proper lady wears one." Her own voice was thick with wanting, with demon desires. "Vaughn, the danger in this...if your father were to—"

"You're in no danger with me, Elisa," he murmured. "I just want a sample of you, a taste. To remember..."

He pulled up at her waist a little, as if he was about to lift her off her feet and bring her closer to him, and she felt herself bowing backwards instinctively. Her head fell back a little. The power behind his controlled, slow lift told her of the untapped potential of his body, and she knew her own response was the equivalent of offering herself to him, but she was helpless to prevent it. She was mortally aware of his restless thumbs, barely a fingertip away from her breasts which longed for his touch.

"Oh, but the pleasure I could give you..." His voice was so low she barely heard it, but she saw his lips mouth the words as he lowered his head towards her.

"No, Vaughn, you cannot. Please, I beg you."

His mouth hovered over hers.

She added hastily, "I am to be your stepmother."

Vaughn hesitated, and she felt her feet touch the floor once more as he lowered her a little. She put her hand against his shoulder, intending to push him away, but the hot flesh beneath the shirt sent a weakening wave of longing through her. Such strength and size, poised above her, with the potential to explode with energy and drive...

He lifted his chin. "You truly intend to marry him, Elisa?"

"Yes," she said, as steadily as she could, thinking of Raymond, and the reason she was willing to live her life out in this place. "Yes, I do," she said levelly, looking him in the eye. "Let me go, Vaughn. You and I both know you could force this issue—you are much stronger than I. But I will do nothing to stop you except to ask that you do not."

"And at the same time raise that odious pending marriage as a shield." His tone was dry.

"Thank you," she said quietly, trying to calm herself and ignore the sizzle of unfulfilled desire in her nerves.

He had not moved, but his eyes had narrowed again. It was not lust that hooded their gleam, but quick thought. "Come riding with me tomorrow."

"What? No, no…that would not be respectable."

He shook his head, silencing her. "A simple ride, Elisa. I am offering you what no one else in this echoing mausoleum has bothered to think of offering you since you arrived here. A day of doing what *you* like. A day of riding."

"No, I don't think so."

"By the morrow you'll have your hair up and your boots on, and there will be no moonlight and silence to beguile me. I will be completely trustworthy…like a proper soon-to-be stepson." The last was added with a sour note she could not fail to miss.

She swallowed. A whole day of riding. And Vaughn had given her the key for keeping him at arms length. Any mention of her marriage to Rufus soured any yearnings he might have.

It was a simple matter. She agreed to a day of innocent pleasure and he would let her go, and she could run back to the safety of her room.

"Say yes, Elisa," he growled, bringing his mouth towards hers.

"Yes!" she said breathlessly.

She was released with such alacrity that she staggered a little, and reached out to the window frame for support.

He straightened. "If you know anything of men at all, Elisa, and I know you do, then you will go back to bed now."

She did know about men. Regardless, a response came readily to her lips, but she bit it back and turned without a word.

She hurried towards the door, her heart trip-hammering at the closeness of her escape.

"Elisa?"

A single, soft hail and she found herself halted halfway across the room as effectively as if he had physically anchored her to the spot. She didn't want to risk looking back at him, but she did anyway.

He was standing by the window, his arms crossed over his chest. With his back to the light, his eyes were shadowed and all she could see were the sharp planes of his cheeks, the strong jaw, and the powerful neck. Her heart hammered within her chest.

"Don't wear your corset tomorrow," he instructed.

The low words raised the hairs on her skin. Wordlessly, she turned and hurried from the library, back down the wide gallery to the cold marble floor of the foyer. By the time she reached the spiral stairway, she was running, and gasping with the release of belated fear and relief at her close escape.

She reached her bed, and burrowed beneath the covers, trembling.

She would not go riding on the morrow. *I will not go riding with Vaughn tomorrow. It is unthinkable,* she repeated the phrases over and over until she fell asleep.

Chapter Three

Vaughn had been up for hours when Elisa finally made her way downstairs.

He spent the time brooding and kicking himself over his behavior in the library last night. What on earth had possessed him? He'd been sitting there, having decided that the sane thing would be to go back to London and fight with his father over Kirkaldy via lawyers...until she had walked in—and it was as if he'd made no such decision at all. He'd acted without thought, without sense.

Even this horse ride was madness. A moth did not hover around the flame once he'd discovered it had the power to pull him in and burn him. So why was he, Vaughn, hovering around Elisa?

He did know the answer to that one. Last night, in the moment he had offered to take her riding, there had been a softening in her face that had stopped his heart. He would not depart for London now and take that pleasure from her.

One short ride, and then he should go. Leave, and never come back. The forbidden flame was far too perilous. Rufus was extraordinarily skilled at exacting retribution. He was a fool to even consider staying here and risk being overtaken by the madness that had possessed him last night.

As he wandered about the shining marble floor, Maud, the oldest maid in the hall, came through from the kitchen carrying a heavy silver tray laid with breakfast dishes, her old, deformed fingers clenched around the handles as she hunched over the load. She had not changed from what Vaughn remembered of her. It seemed she had always been old. He took the tray from her despite her protests, and carried it to the door of his father's suite after asking her who it was intended for. At the door he paused and waited for her to catch up with him, and open the door. Before she took the tray back she reached up to pat his cheek. She smiled fondly.

"You used to open doors for me, too, young master."

"I did?"

"Whenever your father couldn't see you do it. It's good to have you home, Master Vaughn."

He descended the stairs back down to the ground floor, thoughtful. Who else in the hall thought he was here to stay? That this was home for him? He rested against the newel post at the bottom of the stairs, frowning. He was here to retrieve Kirkaldy, and that was all.

Then Elisa came down the stairs and he straightened, abruptly and foolishly glad to see her. Dressed in a demure riding habit of dark blue velvet that made her eyes sparkle, she was not quite the temptation she had been last night when her golden curls had swung loose and brushed her waist.

Personally, he preferred women in riding habits. They couldn't wear so many petticoats and disguise the true line of their legs. He had noticed last night that Elisa had long legs, and today he enjoyed their length yet again, as they were not disguised by flounces.

Obviously she was not going to make excuses as to why she could not ride, as he'd expected her to do. Unwillingly, he felt a touch of admiration for her courage. She was going to abide by their agreement, regardless of the duress she'd been under when she'd made it.

However, she managed to avoid looking at him as she slid on her leather gloves and put on a wide-brimmed bonnet.

"Good morning, Elisa," he bid her. "Have you eaten?"

"I ate in my room, thank you," she said softly.

"Then there's no reason not to start out immediately," he said. "I'll have the horses brought around."

"I'd rather go to the stables," Elisa returned, a touch too quickly.

Vaughn studied her anew. Did she want to be away from the house? He noticed the hint of dark circles beneath her eyes, the high color in her cheeks. Then he understood; she wanted to get this over and done with as swiftly as possible. She wasn't about to wait idly with him for the horses to be brought to her. She wanted to go to the horses instead.

He suppressed a smile. Did she really think she was safer walking through a garden than standing here in the foyer?

"Very well," he agreed, and offered his arm. When she did not take it, but instead stepped around him and marched to the tall French doors at the back of the foyer, he let himself smile fully. Oh yes, indeed, she was avoiding him.

The doors led out onto the large formal garden at the rear of the manor. It was a tamed, regimented and manicured area filled with straight paths and symmetrical borders of flowers and plants.

Elisa walked swiftly down the path. It led directly to the stables at the foot of the garden. Vaughn quickened his pace a little and easily caught up with her.

"Are you wearing your corset?" he asked.

"A lady always wears a corset. That is not a question you have a right to ask me, either."

"That's not an answer."

"It is all the answer you will get from me."

He grinned. He would see about that. Deliberately, he stepped a little sideways, and brought his foot down upon her train. Immediately, Elisa was jerked backwards. Immediately, Vaughn took his foot off the train, and she was thrown forward by the sudden cessation of force from behind.

Swiftly, Vaughn stepped around to catch her before she could measure her length on the path, and she fell neatly into his arms, her own outstretched to save her.

He gripped her by the waist again, and put her neatly back on her feet. And he kept his hands around her incredibly small waist, feeling the warmth of her beneath the soft velvet.

He could also feel the unyielding wall of corsetry.

"Elisa, you disappoint me," he murmured, although he was not at all unhappy. He may have been a little dissatisfied if she *had* given in so easily.

Her chin jerked up. "Vaughn, *you* expect far too much of *me*. I am your father's fiancée, and propriety demands—"

"Sod propriety!" He tightened his grip on her waist. "Propriety, morals...they're just words, Elisa. You know the difference—I know you do. Just as I do."

She was studying him. Listening. Weighing. It was a trait he'd never seen in a woman before—to have his words considered with such care, to be so taken to heart.

"What do you want, Vaughn?"

Yes, what did he want? What was he doing, standing here in the middle of the rose garden, holding her by the waist for all to see? To what end? He'd already decided to go back to London. He shrugged. "To go riding."

"No, Vaughn. What is it you *really* want?"

"What I want I cannot have," he answered truthfully.

"You must take your hands from my waist. People might see us from the house." She was staring at him steadily with her intense blue eyes, made brilliant by the color of her gown, and there was not an inch of retreat in them.

Let go of this delicate, gorgeous creature? Suddenly, he found it almost impossible to lift his hands away, even though he knew she was right—there might well be servants observing them from the windows. There was no danger Rufus would see them. The old sot was most likely still snoring off last evening's claret.

"Vaughn, please...whatever you think of me personally, you do me an injustice by risking my public reputation in this way."

Never had he expected to find anything innocent about her—not a woman of her sordid past—but there she stood, wisps of golden hair escaping her bonnet, framing her delicate features. Her big blue eyes were entreating him to do the gentlemanly thing and turn her loose.

And then there had been the moment of pure joy in her eyes when he'd offered to take her riding last night. Its appearance made him wonder how mournful the rest of her life was, if such a simple offer could bring such delight.

Elisa, he realized, was a complicated woman. The simple assumptions he'd made about her were not an exact fit. It intrigued him.

He let go of her waist and stepped back a little. "If I can't have what I want, then I would accept friendship, instead," he said, and was mildly astonished to realize he was sincere.

"Friendship?" she repeated, her voice tinged with disbelief.

"Yes, friendship. Or is that too much to ask?"

She watched him for a few moments, as though she expected him to say he wasn't serious. Then a slight smile came to her lips. "Of course it is not too much to ask. I would like your friendship very much. Yes, very much indeed."

The way she said the words made him think that perhaps she was trying to convince herself.

"Then let's not waste this beautiful day."

She nodded and walked beside him toward the stables, her shoulders erect, her chin high, her cheeks flushed a flattering shade of pink.

As the stable master readied their mounts, Vaughn watched her fidget with her gloves. She was going out of her way to look at anything but him. He took a step closer and she glanced up, her breath leaving her in a rush.

"I make you uneasy," he said, not bothering to state it as a question.

"No," she said, shaking her head. "You don't."

"Then why are you so on edge?"

Her gaze shifted to something beyond his shoulder. Then relief flooded her face. "Look, our horses are ready."

She brushed past him and hurried over to the gray the stable master was holding for her. It had been readied with a sidesaddle. As she settled herself into the saddle and arranged her skirts properly, he smiled a little, forming an image of what she must have looked like in those years when she rode astride like a man, defying society, convention and death all at once. This properly stiff-backed lady who controlled her horse with a gentle, deft touch was nothing like that image.

Impressed with her skill already, he mounted his horse and with a challenging smile, he was off like a shot, sending up grass and dirt in his wake.

He heard the thunder of pursuit. His blood raced, excitement flaring through him, pushing him to go faster. He told himself he should be careful for she might be hurt, but he knew she needed to feel the wind whipping her hair and feel the excitement race along her spine…just as he did.

They were far from the hall already, racing across ripe fields and fallow green meadows, through copses of trees and fens.

Her laughter rang out from behind him, and he glanced over his shoulder to find her leaning over the horse's neck, pushing it harder and faster. She had removed the cumbersome bonnet, and her golden hair gleamed. She laughed. Her smile was devastating — all white teeth and dimples.

Such a strong response to such a simple stimulation as a horse ride was a measure of Elisa's potential sensuality. What would she be like in a man's arms? In his arms? The possibilities made his gut clench with a raw excitement completely unrelated to the swift clean joy of riding a galloping horse.

Then he heard her laugh again, and the pretty silvery sound was much closer.

She was gaining on him!

He spurred the horse onwards, entirely caught up in the spirit of the chase. What a delight it was competing against such a carefree and challenging rider. And his mind was busy with an illicit dilemma: Should he let her win and claim compensation, or should he win and claim the victor's spoils?

Elisa's heart pounded, matching the rhythm of the horse's hooves hitting the hard-packed ground. It was a glorious day, the sun shining down on her and Vaughn as they raced across the meadow.

She had lost her bonnet long ago—they would have to retrieve it on the way back. And her hair was threatening to break free of the careful braid. There was hot blood flowing through her veins and she felt absurdly excited, skittish like a colt. And determined to beat Vaughn despite the severe limitations of a corset and sidesaddle.

It had been so long since she'd felt this free, this alive. And she had Vaughn to thank for it.

If only she could look at him without remembering his hands about her waist, and the color of his eyes as they stared into hers. If only she could look at him without thinking of making love to him. She wanted to erase the memory of last night completely, to rid her mind of the sensation of his thumbs smoothing their way across her flesh. Just the memory of it brought her nipples taut and alive, and caused her body to tighten and throb.

She was truly evil. What kind of a woman would desire her fiancé's son? She must purge this longing.

At least Vaughn seemed to have settled for only her friendship. She should be happy he had made the compromise.

Or was she beyond wickedness—was it that she really wanted him to tell her he had to have her, that he felt a desire for her so intense he could think of nothing else? What else could last night have been but an outward hint of such an obsession?

But she knew with a hard-earned wisdom she was hoping for something that wasn't there. He was a striking man, used to flirtations and casual affairs. No doubt many women had fallen victim to his charm, for that charm was clearly potent enough for any woman.

Vaughn brought his mount to a halt a good ten yards in front of her. Following his lead, she reined in. Before she stopped, he was at her side, helping her down.

"Come, I want to show you something." He took her hand in his own and headed towards a copse of trees.

She had never ventured from Fairleigh Hall before. She had no idea what to expect. But in Vaughn's company, she felt safe from the world at large. He had the authoritative size and power to protect her from anything and now he had declared he would settle for friendship, she felt she could trust him.

"When I was a boy I used to come here to fish. There's a stream that runs from the northwestern corner of Fairleigh land to the southwestern corner. Only here is it deep enough to swim."

Stopping abruptly, she let go of his hand. "You don't intend to swim today, do you?"

He shrugged. "Who knows? It is rather warm."

It suddenly seemed warmer than it had been moments before.

He took her hand again, sliding his own warm one around hers. "Come on."

The trail ended at a swimming hole larger than she'd anticipated. Clean, sparkling water rippled over smooth rocks. The water was so clear she could see rounded rocks and pebbles at the bottom. It was difficult to judge how deep it was. Further out, it shone invitingly in the hot sun.

I am not remotely tempted to swim, she told herself.

However, it appeared Vaughn was, for he was already stripping off his jacket and shirt.

Her heart missed a beat as the items landed on the grass by her feet. Naked to the waist, he was a sight unlike any other she had seen in her life. A broad, well-defined chest tapered down to an abdomen that was rock-hard, the sinew flexing beneath the tight olive skin as he removed his boots. He was watching her.

Elisa swallowed hard and quickly looked away. "It isn't *too* warm," she said, her cheeks turning hot.

"Really? I feel like I'm on fire."

The tone of his voice made her turn quickly, only to find he had divested himself of his breeches as well, giving her a full view of his firm backside. She gasped aloud. Her stomach clenched at the sight, and her breath stopped. A heartbeat later he dove in, disappearing beneath the surface.

"I do not want him...I do not want him..." she chanted under her breath, but even as she said the words, she found herself taking a step closer to the edge of the pond.

Just then he broke the surface, whipping his hair out of his face, his smile wide and inviting.

"Sweet Jesus," she blurted before she could stop herself.

It was hopeless. There was no way she could not want him. He was everything she had been denied for far too long—a friend, a person she could laugh with, a man close to her own age...a lover. How many years had it been? Too many.

"Come in, Elisa," he said, his eyes smoldering.

She took a quick step back, tripped and fell onto her bottom.

He swam toward her, but she scrambled to her feet and held a hand up. "No, stay there. Do *not* get out!"

His dark brows furrowed into a frown, but he remained still.

The water lapped at his narrow waist, scarcely hiding that part of him she yearned for. She knew *that* part of him would be as impressive as the rest. A warning voice whispered in her head.

"Why don't you want me to get out?" he asked, his voice soft.

"I...just do not want you to."

"But what if I want to?"

"Then...I will leave."

"No, you won't." His smile fled. "I will not get out. Sit down and relax, Elisa." He motioned to a large rock five feet to her left.

She nodded, grateful to be looking somewhere else and to get off her feet. Smoothing her skirts around her, she sat down and glanced up to find him swimming across the pond, away from her, his strong arms gliding through the water with an ease she'd seldom seen.

He was entirely too handsome, and much too unsuitable, she told herself. Worse, since he would be her stepson, he was also forbidden to her. She should be looking at him in a maternal way. He had grown to manhood without a mother. Perhaps he lacked a matronly guiding hand...

He stood up at the far side of the pool, water streaming from him, and she was again given a view of his back and buttocks. He was turned a little, and she could see the start of the highly pronounced ridge of muscle that ran in a V down to his pelvis. She followed it with her eyes. If he was to turn only a little more—

Quickly, she shut her eyes. It was no use. She could not possibly view him in a purely maternal manner.

"Elisa, are you sure you won't join me?"

She opened her eyes to find him closer, treading water again, watching her with an intensity that made her nervous.

"I cannot."

"Cannot or will not?"

"Both."

He smiled devilishly, and she jumped to her feet. "I'll meet you in the clearing." She didn't wait for his response. She only knew she could not sit there a moment longer with him so close, and so…naked.

She couldn't stand another moment of staring at his hard body without wanting him to take her to the ground and have his way with her.

In a similar way she had once been taken by her husband — before drink and lust had driven him far beyond her reach. On that occasion, she had conceived Raymond.

An intense ache ripped through her at the thought of the son she'd been denied. The son who had been hidden away and was being raised by a family who despised her and who had no doubt turned her son against her. And here she was, responding with the wanton desires she had been accused of — those that had taken her son from her in the first place.

Emotions she had buried came rising to the surface and with them a hurt so devastating she felt she could die from it. She started running, ignoring Vaughn as he called out to her, and she knew she ran not from him, but from herself.

* * * * *

Vaughn dressed quickly. He didn't know if Elisa would be there when he reached the clearing. What had made her run off like that?

He'd seen the play of emotions on her face as she'd watched him swim. She wanted him — in that regard, her face was unmistakable. But something else had driven her from the clearing.

What was it that haunted her?

As he emerged from the trees he was relieved to find her standing with her back to him, looking off into the distance.

"I think you should leave."

That was not what he had expected her to say. He pretended to misunderstand, to draw her out. "And we shall, if you are ready."

"I mean, leave Fairleigh Hall."

"Elisa, look at me."

She made no move to turn, so he put his hand on her shoulder. She whirled around, her eyes wide. "Stop it!"

"What?" he asked. Shockingly, there were tears brimming in her eyes. His heart gave a jerk. "What is it?"

"You must leave here."

"Why?"

"Because I can't bear to have you under the same roof."

Her words brought a rush of desire to his already heated blood. As though they possessed a will of their own, his fingers reached out to caress her cheek. It was damp, and soft to touch. "If leaving here will bring you happiness, then I'll go."

Her face was filled with so much pain he instinctively pulled her into his arms. She remained stiff, but as he smoothed his hand up and down her back, she started to relax and finally leaned into him, her cheek pressing against his chest.

"If you left I would be miserable, but I couldn't live with myself if we became...more than friends."

"I would not force such an issue on you, Elisa."

"Yet I see something else in your eyes. You forget I am not a young girl fresh out of the convent. I know how these things work, Vaughn, just as much as you do."

Of course she was right, and they both knew it. She was not naïve. "I won't lie. I desire you, yet I know you're not willing to give yourself to me. I understand. But I cannot simply leave. Therefore, in order to be close to you, I will be your friend."

"Then you must act as a friend, and not as a lover would."

How ironic it was they talked of friendship as he held her tight within his arms, her breasts pushed against him, her heart beating so strongly it pounded against his own. It was as if the devil entered him whenever she was near—he forgot everything of prudence and discretion, and could only think of the need to have her. The goading words he spoke, the actions he took that inflamed the passion...none of it occurred because of any choice he made. He was being driven by a power he did not fully understand, and therefore had no control over. That in itself should be reason to obey both her wishes and his own dictates: he should leave Fairleigh Hall.

If only she had found him undesirable, he might have been able to ride out the temptation and divert it. But Elisa was clearly as caught up in the spell as he was. Knowing his advances were wanted goaded him to play out this madness.

And yet...for all her desire, something was holding Elisa back. It could only be something or someone other than her, to hold such power over her. He only hoped it was strong enough to hold them apart because he was very much afraid his own will was not enough.

Chapter Four

When they returned from their ride Elisa went straight to the safety of her room for a nap, although sleep did not come easily.

When she did at last slip into slumber, she dreamed of Raymond as she had last seen him—a small, sweet boy with big blue eyes—and woke with her resolve firm; she would be a friend to Vaughn and nothing more. If Vaughn wanted to stay at Fairleigh Hall indefinitely, then so be it. She would cope with it. The price was too great to give in to the madness of her desires.

Yet as she opened the door to the dining room, that resolve was shaken. The dinner table was better occupied than usual. They had guests, and Natasha Winridge, daughter of Baron Munroe, neighbor of Fairleigh Hall, was sitting to Vaughn's left, clinging to his every word.

Hot acid surged through Elisa, making her stomach churn. Her heart sank. She had dismissed Marianne's comment about the maids' whispered desires for Vaughn as petty gossip. Vaughn didn't seem to be the sort who would dally with maids. She had not considered the possibility of another woman taking up Vaughn's attention. Or worse, becoming his new obsession.

What irritated her even more was how handsome Vaughn looked tonight, dressed in a black suit and snowy white shirt and cravat that complimented his dark, exotic looks.

"There you are, my dear. I was getting ready to send Marianne up your way." Rufus came to his feet, an uncustomary smile on his face. He appeared to be good at pretending when in the presence of titled friends.

She took her seat at Rufus' side and looked up to find Vaughn still engaged in conversation with Natasha. The girl was pretty, with dark hair and a fresh complexion. Her prettiness was supported by an unstinting application of money and attention to her wardrobe. And Elisa had to admit the debutante had youth on her side. Her unsullied, just-budded perfection made Elisa feel used and discarded.

She laid her napkin across her lap, waved the wine decanter away and asked for water, puzzling over her jealous reaction to Vaughn talking to Natasha. She was forced to acknowledge another horrid fact about herself: she had enjoyed Vaughn's attentions. Even though she had no intention of allowing him to press more than ardent words upon her, she had taken a secret delight in being the object of his powerful desire. It had been much, much too long since someone had flattered her by showing more than polite, superficial interest in her.

And she very much did not like that center of focus shifting from her!

It was pure folly, she knew, to be upset about such a natural occurrence. She had made it clear she would never respond to his advances, so she could not be angry when his attention roved elsewhere. She could not expect him to maintain a devotion that was unrequited, no matter how much she enjoyed the attention.

She glanced at the two young people, their heads together, whispering.

No, she did not like it!

Elisa turned her attention to the baron on her right, Natasha's father. "Sir William, where is Lady Munroe this evening?"

Sir William patted her hand. "I'm sorry to disappoint you, but Caroline is a little under the weather—a headache—but she bid me tell you hello and assure you she would come calling as soon as she was feeling better."

"Please be sure to tell her I'm hoping for her quick recovery."

"Indeed, I shall."

"William, what ever did you decide to do with the extra acreage I gave you?" Rufus asked, his chest puffing out with self-importance.

Elisa suppressed a sigh. In her short time here she had already learned that Rufus used favors like currency. Once he had done something for another, he considered that person to be indebted to him for life. In those moments when her guilt and worry over Raymond's absence were quieter than usual, she could see her situation with more clarity and it had occurred to her more than once that perhaps Rufus was using the same yardstick with her, that the impending marriage was another of his bargains. But then Rufus would show her a moment of tenderness or kindness, and she would become confused yet again about the reasons for Rufus's rough courtship and proposal. He was a more complex person than he appeared to be.

Elisa gave up pretending to eat. She took a deep breath and sat back in her seat, doing everything she could to keep from staring at Vaughn, sitting across from her. It was torturous. Natasha's laughter, as light as a bell, accompanied every one of Vaughn's sentences, humorous or not. It grated on Elisa's nerves.

She twisted her hands in her lap, feeling tension growing in her. She wanted to run from the room but could not for it would later require explanations she could not give. She was forced to behave like the decorous lady of the manor, beaming approval upon the flirtation across the table from her as Baron Munroe was, when she really wanted to grab Vaughn's lapels and shake him violently and take back his attention that way.

With each peal of Natasha's carefully cultivated laugh, the tension in her twisted a little tighter.

Time passed. Slowly. Elisa picked at her food enough to prevent further questions regarding her behavior, and tried to not eavesdrop on the low conversation across the table.

"Madam, Vaughn tells me you are an accomplished rider. How is it you never told us of this?"

Elisa glanced up at Natasha, who waited with a polite smile for her answer, her dark eyes glimmering, her flawless skin radiant under the light of the chandelier. She looked a little flushed and flustered. As well she might, if Vaughn was practicing the same intense, blunt conversational sallies on her as he had on Elisa the previous evening.

Elisa sought to turn the dangerous subject, and the focus of the conversation, away from her. "Do you ride, dear?"

Natasha shrugged. "A little, though Mother tells me it is not proper to enjoy it too much."

Proper. That was not something she had ever been accused of being. Well, perhaps at one time, when she was a young girl of Natasha's age, desperately in love with a fiancé whose reputation had been deplorable. Her only sin had been loving a husband who had but one use for her—to get himself an heir. After Raymond's birth, the only time he had slept with her had been when he'd had no one else at his disposal.

Her throat tightened. For a short time she had forgotten society felt she was not a proper woman, regardless of the truth. Now she found herself here, desperate for the attention of a man she could not have. She was, indeed, the improper woman society had painted her to be.

She focused her gaze fiercely on the ivory damask of the tablecloth, fighting the need to look at him once more. Then she felt a soft pressure on the toe of her right slipper, which quickly moved to her ankle, then up the inside of her calf. Warm flesh was smoothing its away up her leg.

She looked up abruptly to find Vaughn watching her, the picture of complete innocence. His stockinged foot inched higher under her petticoats, against her pantalets. He was stroking the flesh of her inner thigh through the fine linen, and her legs fell open without resistance.

He coughed, and in so doing sank into his chair, while turning his complete attention to the young woman at his side.

Elisa couldn't move. It was as though she were made of stone. She dared not move unless she destroy the moment. His toes crept ever closer to that part of her that had begun throbbing the second she'd realized it was his foot that slid against her leg.

She reached for the water glass, trying to disguise her sudden inattention to the conversation. She took a sip, nearly choking on it when Vaughn grew ever bolder. Her breath left her in a rush as his toe slipped between the edges of the opening of her pantalets and actually pushed inside her.

The sides of his mouth curved into a devilish smile as he glanced in her direction, a dark brow lifted in silent challenge.

"Madam, will you be attending the ball?"

Elisa forced a smile. "Ball?" Her voice came out a squeak, and Vaughn's grin broadened.

"Yes, Mama is throwing a ball for my coming out, just shortly before I leave for London. Please say you'll come."

"Certainly, I'll come."

She heard Vaughn laugh under his breath. "I knew Elisa would not disappoint."

Elisa realized with a cold shock she was allowing Vaughn the liberties that just a short while ago in her room she had promised herself she would not give him. So much for her resolve—she had been undone by the simple threat of Vaughn's favors wandering elsewhere.

Remember Raymond.

"So…you will be spending the season in London?" Elisa asked, pulling her chair back the slightest bit, causing Vaughn's foot to fall from between her thighs. He would have to literally slip beneath the table to touch her now.

He sat up abruptly, releasing a heavy sigh, not even looking at Natasha, who was watching him intently, her lashes fluttering.

"I will be spending a season with my aunt." Natasha barely glanced at Elisa as she answered her question. She looked back at Vaughn. "She lives near Hyde Park. I so hope that you can visit." Then the girl turned her attention back to Elisa, though it was obvious the statement was directed at Vaughn.

Vaughn smiled softly at Natasha, his finger tracing the rim of his glass, which had been replenished only once during dinner. Elisa stared at his strong hand. His long, tapered finger as it lazily stroked the glass. God, what would it feel like to have those hands on her body!

She was shocked at the direction her thoughts had taken yet again. And he was watching her with a smile so wicked there was no misinterpreting it—right in front of his father and guests, no less.

She must stop this, here and now. She must!

Feeling Rufus' stare all the way to her bones, she glanced over at him. His customary frown was in place as he looked from her, to his son, then to her once again.

Oh God. He knew!

Vaughn's foot rubbed against hers, and she jumped as though bitten.

"What's wrong with you?" Rufus snapped.

Elisa cleared her throat, her mind spinning. "Marianne tightened my corset too much. It's pinching me," she said quietly.

"Perhaps you should loosen it," Vaughn suggested, his voice lazy.

"Do you feel light-headed?" Natasha asked, her eyes filled with genuine concern.

"Actually—"

"Marianne should be scolded for having been so careless," Rufus said, completely cutting her off. He took a deep, exasperated breath and stood. "Well, I'm about ready for my cigar. What do you say, Sir William, shall we all adjourn to the parlor?"

Elisa took a deep breath, stifling her resentment, as everyone around her stood up, her faintness instantly forgotten. Rufus was staring at her impatiently, and she rose to her feet and took his arm. Natasha was on Vaughn's arm, she noted, not her father's.

In the parlor they arranged themselves on the settees and couches as Natasha sat at the harp. Her light voice filled the room as her proud father watched with a wide smile on his face.

Vaughn paced behind them, as though he was too nervous to sit idly by, and it unnerved her. She couldn't see him, yet she could feel him. Wherever his foot had touched her, she burned still. Such a knowing touch…there was little doubt he would be a sensational lover —

Realizing her thoughts, she flinched as though she'd been pinched. She was truly sick.

Natasha finished her song. The Baron turned to Elisa and asked, "Madam, would you do me the honor of playing?"

Elisa glanced in Rufus' direction and saw his head sat on his chest. Quiet snoring emanated from him.

"Of course, Sir William." She stood and went to the piano. She noticed Vaughn stopped his pacing as she took a seat. She was uncertain about what to play. Yet, as though they had a life their own, her fingers moved over the keys, and the music that came to her was a simple, poignant melody of unrequited love she remembered from years before and had once loved. She had memorized the notes, and now they came to her without hesitation, giving her heavy, aching heart momentary release.

She poured herself into the playing. Not once did she look at anyone, especially not the tall, dark man in the far corner, who watched her intently. She didn't want to look at him, for she knew her feelings would be too easily read.

Tonight had been the longest night of her life. Tonight she learned that desire and the forbidden went hand in hand. She must have control over her feelings and actions. She must not, as Vaughn's future stepmother, behave like a jealous lover, for she was not his lover, nor would she ever be.

In time he would marry someone like Natasha. A young woman who would give him lots of children. A woman who was not jaded from all she'd seen. A woman whose reputation was as pure as the driven snow. A woman who would have no idea what to do with a virile man like Vaughn.

An image come to her—of Vaughn walking up behind her, and stilling her hands on the keys with a soft touch. His lips would sear their imprint on the nape of her neck, making her shiver and sigh. Then he would pick her up and lay her across the piano. He would make love to her, with his hands and mouth playing upon her, making her ache for more…

But that would never be.

She sighed, and pressed out the last, throbbing chord of the tune, and grew still.

Silence surrounded her.

Finally, there was the patter of soft, solitary applause.

She turned to find Vaughn coming toward her, clapping gently. Then William and Natasha belatedly joined in the applause.

Rufus continued to snore.

Vaughn took her hands in his own. His touch was hot. His smile and the look in his eyes was for her alone. Had he understood what she had outpoured with each poignant note?

She sensed movement behind him, and refocused to see Natasha was on her feet and quickly coming towards them. She was staring at Elisa's hands enfolded in Vaughn's.

"Madam, that was…astonishing."

No doubt the girl found it lacking, but Elisa didn't care. She'd played it for herself, and no one else. Well…perhaps for one other person.

"It was a very eloquent rendering, indeed." Vaughn's voice was low. He did not seem to care that the Baron and his daughter were watching them. "Simply beautiful," he added.

Then he *had* understood.

Elisa pulled her hands from his. "Thank you." She felt heat race to her cheeks. She must get away from him before indiscretion was their undoing.

She turned to her fiancé, who was slumbering peacefully. "It has been a splendid evening, but it looks as though Rufus is ready to retire. Vaughn, could you please see Sir William and Natasha to their carriage?"

Vaughn bowed, a soft smile on his lips. "As you wish."

Natasha frowned. "But it is early still!"

"Natasha!" William scolded.

Elisa pulled her mouth into a sympathetic smile. "Ah, the energy of irresponsible youth."

Her slur went unheeded. Natasha turned to Vaughn, and touched his arm. "Vaughn, I want to stay longer. Can you not entertain us?" There was a distinct and very unattractive whine to her voice.

"Perhaps I can interest you and your father in a game of chess," he suggested.

"I don't play chess." She all but pouted.

"I believe your father does." Vaughn turned to the other man. "Isn't that right, Sir William?"

Sir William nodded eagerly. "Indeed, I do."

"Well, good night, then," Elisa said.

"Why don't you put him to bed and join us?" Vaughn's voice held a challenge.

Elisa did not turn to look at him—she didn't trust herself. Instead, she shook her head, and went to Rufus. "Another night, perhaps. It has been a long day."

With Joshua's help, Elisa got Rufus to his room and then retired herself.

* * * * *

Marianne helped her undress and prepare for sleep, and Elisa kept her chatter to a bearable minimum by refusing to respond. She was keen to climb beneath the covers and seek an escape from the day, but when she finally did so, sleep would not come.

Instead she remembered the feel of Vaughn's toes upon her thigh, and found her hand tracing the path he had taken, her heart quickening. What if she had followed the debauched habits of her youth and worn no drawers beneath her gown? How would Vaughn have reacted when his foot had found not linen, but warm, willing flesh?

Lying in her lonely bed, she drew in a ragged breath and rolled over on her side, curling up tight against the wanton surges shaking her body.

Near midnight she heard the sound of a carriage pulling away from the portico. Their guests had left, and Vaughn would probably be going to bed himself.

Her heart thudded as she strained to hear sounds of him. Would he go to his room? Or would he come to hers?

* * * * *

Vaughn closed the door behind him and leaned heavily against the ornate wood.

God, what a night!

Being the only son of a wealthy marquis, as well as possessing the title of viscount, Vaughn was a natural target for matchmakers and debutantes with an eye for golden opportunity. He had become practiced at foiling these attempts.

He just hadn't anticipated his father's neighbor and good friend to be one of those matchmakers. He had no intention of marrying for some years yet. There were far too many adventures and pleasures to sample before settling down to dull duty.

Sighing, he pushed away from the door, and started for the steps. A smile formed as he remembered Elisa's piano playing tonight. She had been in her own world, a place far away from the rest of them. A place she no doubt went to often to escape reality.

He took the stairs two a time. At the top, he stopped and looked down to the floor below. Finding no one about, he turned right and went straight to Elisa's room.

Elisa heard the turn of the door handle, and was out of the bed and moving across the room before the handle fell back into place. She tiptoed to the door and leaned against the frame, her heart thudding.

"Elisa." The call was low. Vaughn's voice.

She held her breath.

"Elisa, you lock the door against me?" He sounded aggrieved.

The temptation to turn the key and unlock the door was powerful. There was no one about to see or care that she invited a man into her room…

"Elisa. I know you're there. I wanted to talk to you. To tell you I know what you were feeling at the piano tonight."

"How could you know?" she murmured.

There was a little silence.

"I know." The sensual tone slipped through the door and wrapped itself around her.

She found herself pressing against the door, but she did not unlock it.

"You have no need to resent Natasha," he added quietly. "Her youth and vapid ways hold far less charm for me than the deep, hidden waters that move in you. I want to drown myself in them. In you."

Her pulse jumped alarmingly. "You promised friendship."

"A friend can still desire."

"But not pursue."

"I said I would not."

"But tonight — at the table…"

"That was the only way I had of assuring you I had not abandoned you."

She sighed. He spoke aloud her own private thoughts.

"This is a dangerous game we play. Do you understand just how dangerous it is, Vaughn? Don't pursue me anymore. Do not…touch me."

Silence was his answer.

"Go to bed," she told him.

"I will. But first I would bid you goodnight."

"Good night," she responded, relieved he had conceded to her wishes.

"Just one more thing," he added.

"What?"

"When you lay off your corset for me, Elisa, leave off your pantalets, too."

Her breath caught, and her heart thudded hard. "What…?" she breathed. After having just told him… "I said do not touch me," she whispered back, terrified he would force this issue against her wishes.

"I will not," he returned swiftly. "But I want you to be bare for me. So that only you and I know, and when you see me looking at you, you can imagine what it would feel like if my hands were to follow the same path my foot took tonight…or my mouth. Against your bare flesh."

And the whore in her moved and rippled at the thought.

She laid her head against the door. God give her the strength to deny this part of herself that stirred so stridently.

"Good night, Elisa," he murmured.

She heard him walk away.

It was a long while before she moved away from the door and returned to her cold bed.

Chapter Five

Elisa pricked her finger with the needle for the tenth time in as many minutes. She looked away from her embroidery to the wide window that gave such a magnificent view of the couple walking in the garden.

Vaughn and Natasha.

Baroness Winridge had wasted no time in bringing her daughter over for a second visit. It had only been last evening the Baron and Natasha had been here for supper. Suddenly, here was Caroline, with Natasha in tow, the very morning after the Baron had pronounced her prostrate with a painful headache. The headache had remarkably disappeared.

Such alacrity could only mean one thing. Vaughn was the attraction.

Usually Elisa would enjoy another woman's company as they embroidered, took tea and chatted, but today she found Lady Munroe's presence irritating.

"He is incredibly handsome, Elisa. I remember him as a small boy. He was quite lanky. Very tall for his age. Little did I know he would grow up to be so striking."

Elisa managed a smile. "Indeed, he is handsome."

"Natasha could not stop talking about him all morning. I found it impossible to keep her at home. I hope you don't find us too rude, by calling on you unannounced?"

"Of course not."

"Will you look at that?" Caroline said, nodding toward the window.

Vaughn was handing Natasha one of the blood-red roses Elisa had been carefully tending since her arrival. Elisa secretly hoped the young brunette was pricked by one of its thorns.

"Perhaps at the ball we'll be announcing another engagement beside yours," Caroline murmured.

She was entirely too hopeful, Elisa thought resentfully. "Vaughn is still a young man. I'm certain he has plans to see the world before he settles down."

These were obviously not the words Caroline was expecting, for she sat forward in her seat and frowned as she watched Elisa closely. "I'd have thought you would find it a suitable match, given how close you are to Natasha. And just think…we would be family. We could share grandchildren."

Elisa felt her heart start to patter unhappily. She had never lied to Caroline, beyond the single exception of keeping her supposed unbefitting past a secret. If she was not to reveal the most unsuitable feelings she had for Vaughn, she must put on the act of a lifetime.

She shifted uneasily in the chair, and put her embroidery hoop down. Elisa turned away from her friend's burning gaze and looked out at the couple in the garden.

The two were sitting on a stone bench, talking amicably. Vaughn laughed at something Natasha said. His smile—full, joyous and touched with a devilment that caused an ache deep within Elisa's chest. She wanted that smile to be for her, and for her only.

"Elisa…"

Elisa glanced at her friend, her cheeks warming as the woman watched her quizzically.

"I do not want Natasha to get hurt," Elisa replied. "She is so young, and Vaughn…well, perhaps in a few years after he's seen more of the world."

Caroline ignored her completely and instead continued to outline an ambitious plan for the pair in the garden, including the engagement ball, the wedding itself—a full state occasion befitting a prince of the realm—the obligatory Grand Tour of Europe, a honeymoon in Paris, where Natasha could stock up on the latest styles by Worth, a season in London.

Elisa heard none of the details of what her friend said. She was too conscious of the couple in the garden, watching them from the corner of her eye and with carefully casual turns of the head, as they stood and walked toward the house. Her heart skittered as she heard the garden door open and close.

She had to get firm control of her emotions.

The door to the parlor opened.

Elisa looked up and saw the pair standing side by side, with small smiles on their faces as they looked at each other. There was a sense of mutual enjoyment, perhaps even secrets they shared. Her heart sank to her toes.

"What a lovely day it is," Natasha said, her voice breathless. Her cheeks were flushed a flattering shade of pink that matched her dress to perfection.

Elisa forced a smile. "Indeed, it is. Did you enjoy your walk in the garden?"

She considered Vaughn. How dare he play with the girl this way? How could he spend time in her company, flattering her and flustering her with what could only be frank innuendos? Had he lied last night when he professed Natasha meant nothing to him?

But he had not said she meant nothing to him at all. He'd said Elisa meant more to him than Natasha...but he had *not* said the girl held no charm for him.

Elisa felt the anger pulse in her. It was ridiculous but very real. Vaughn saw it, for the side of his mouth lifted the slightest bit. Amusement? "Yes. Natasha is delightful," he drawled.

She dropped her gaze, unwilling for him to see the hurt that surely showed in her eye. The pain stabbed through the rest of her body, and smothered her anger completely.

"Your roses are beautiful, Madam," Natasha said abruptly. She seemed to be completely unaware of the tide of feeling flowing between Vaughn and her. "Vaughn picked one for me. I hope you do not mind?" Natasha looked up at Vaughn with complete adoration while she stroked a petal of the rose with her thumb.

"Perhaps you should show your mother the beauty of the rose beds," Vaughn suggested, looking down at Natasha with a boyish grin.

Natasha hesitated only a moment. "Mother, would you like to see the garden?"

"I should certainly like to see Elisa's roses. I understand you have toiled over them since your arrival. Elisa, come, show me your pride and joy, dear," Caroline answered.

"I cannot. The sun is much too strong for me at this time of day," Elisa lied desperately. "But please do go and inspect them. They won't last much longer, I believe." She wanted merely to be away from Natasha and her mother—so she might shore up her defenses and recover her composure.

"Well, of course, if you insist," Caroline replied in a strained voice.

Elisa did not dare look at the other woman as she stood and left the room with her daughter, but she felt their absence all the same. More than that, she felt Vaughn's presence. It seemed to fill every crevice of the room.

He was studying her. "You've made a mess of your embroidery," he observed. "You've injured your finger. Look, there are blood stains." He took a few steps toward her, sending her heart racing.

When he stood before her, he took her trembling hand in his and brought it to his lips. "I saw you watching us through the window," he said, kissing each fingertip. "What did you feel seeing me with her?" His lips were hot and moist on her sensitive skin. Shivers of delight rippled down her arm.

"Don't do that," she replied, the words little more than a whisper.

He slowly drew the injured fingertip into his mouth and suckled it, his tongue velvety and hot. For a fraction of a moment she almost pulled away, but found she could not as his smoldering green eyes held her pinned. Her heart pounded in her ears, and she heard herself draw in a ragged breath.

"Vaughn, someone will see," she said, pulling her finger away. She stood and quickly stepped around him, but it wasn't far enough. He surrounded her, invaded all her senses to the point she couldn't think straight.

"They're out in the garden, and the servants will not bother us."

She turned back to face him. "Rufus—"

"Is no doubt taking his daily nap."

"This is insanity."

A dark brow lifted. "Is it?"

As he approached her, she stepped back, away from the window and from prying eyes. "Yes, it is insanity. Every day I feel like I'm coming undone, and now with Natasha—"

"Why, what do you feel about Natasha?"

She turned from him, unwilling to look at him. She did not want him to be able to read all her feelings from her face and eyes as he would surely do—her emotions were too volatile.

She straightened a picture on the wall and took a deep breath before blurting, "I hate it. I hate the way she looks at you. I hate the way Caroline desires to have you as a son-in-law."

"Ah…" There was a wealth of knowledge in his voice. Then he added, his voice low, "It is no different than what I feel when I think of you marrying my father."

She turned abruptly, surprised into it. He was watching her intently. "You cannot be serious?"

The corner of his mouth lifted the slightest bit. The expression seemed to be a sour one. "The only difference is that you're already committed to become his wife."

His words stirred her anger back to life. This time the anger was aimed at her own wretched circumstances. Her impending marriage to Rufus was a prison sentence. She was trapped, where Vaughn was free. His whole life lay before him, uncharted. Hers was cast in stone. Tears stung her eyes.

He touched her cheek, gently, sending another tiny burst of pleasure through her.

"I wanted to know how you felt when you saw me with someone else. I wanted to know I wasn't the only one who desired." His hand cupped her face. "And I can see I am not alone." His thumb slid across her lips. "Am I, my sweet Elisa?" he murmured, his voice caressing her.

Her heart was fluttering painfully. If she were to acknowledge she felt as he did, where would he take it next? The excitement, the absolute danger that could come of speaking the truth! The possibilities made her tremble anew, helped by the sensual brush of his fingers across her lips, light and maddeningly erotic.

Natasha's laughter in the hallway was a douse of cold water. Elisa jumped. Vaughn's hand fell away just as the girl entered the room with her mother close on her heels.

"Your flowers are divine," Caroline said, her smile in place as she walked in the room, her cheeks flushed with laughter.

Vaughn had moved away from her, with the silence and sleekness of a cat.

Elisa struggled to keep her voice normal as she replied, "Thank you. I work very hard at tending them. Sometimes the climate here makes it difficult."

"Indeed, Lord Munroe tells me I need to find more interest in gardening, yet I find it sparks nothing within me. Now my watercolors, those are entirely—"

Elisa's nerves tensed as Caroline stopped in mid-sentence and studied her intently. "My dear, you look so pale. Do you not feel well?"

"I...have a headache. The heat..."

"I am so sorry, my dear. Perhaps you should lie down?"

Elisa wanted nothing more than to escape Natasha and Caroline. She nodded. "Perhaps you're right."

"Here, I will escort you," Vaughn said, coming up beside her and extending his elbow. He glanced over his shoulder at the other women. "You'll be staying for dinner?" he asked, voicing the polite question.

"Yes!" the ecstatic reply came, in unison from mother and daughter.

* * * * *

Elisa remained silent as Vaughn walked her to her room. Her hand was stiff and unmoving on his arm. She was jealous. He had seen it on her face, had read it in her eyes.

He deliberately let the silence stretch.

"Why did you invite them to stay?" she asked at last, without looking at him.

"Actually Rufus invited them."

"Rufus?"

Vaughn understood her incredulity. Rufus did not invite anyone over. Usually the neighbors arrived and he "rested" while Elisa entertained.

"Is it not the polite thing to do when a neighbor comes calling?"

"They have been here all afternoon."

He shrugged. "I thought you would enjoy their company."

This was met by more silence.

Vaughn suppressed a smile. The air of injured pride in her upturned nose and down-turned mouth must surely mean he was beginning to break down the impervious barrier she had erected against his advances.

When they arrived at her room they both reached for the handle at the same time, their hands brushing against each other. He heard her quick intake of breath but she didn't remove her hand, or pull away.

He wove his fingers through hers. They were such small hands, so dainty and feminine. Everything about her was fragile.

"Thank you for walking me to my room," she said stiffly, opening the door.

He let his hand fall away. "My pleasure."

She stared straight ahead. But there was a fine gold ringlet brushing the nape of her neck he longed to brush aside. "Rest. Recover," he told her. Then he gave into temptation, and slid his hand beneath the curl. His fingertips grazed her skin, and she quivered. His body tightened up at that minute sign of responsiveness. He leaned down, bringing his lips close to her ear. "I'll see you at dinner tonight," he breathed, and kissed the tender flesh just below her ear. He was rewarded when he felt a deep, bone-jarring tremble through her. But she kept her head averted. She remained silent, and her silence was a challenge.

He slid his hand around her tiny waist, and pressed gently. "Ah, Elisa, you deny me still," he said with mock despair, as he felt the corset beneath.

"Let me go," she breathed.

"Certainly," he agreed, dropping his hand.

"Thank you." She stepped into the room, and turned to grasp the door handle. Her gaze at last met his, and those big blue eyes seemed almost luminous. Vaughn felt his heart give a little skip.

Slowly she closed the door, and still he didn't move.

"Sweet dreams, my lady," he whispered, and then it finally closed.

He smiled at the door, knowing she still stood there on the other side. Was her hand on the wood as his was now? Did her heart pound like his with the anticipation of what was to come?

Hearing footsteps behind him, he dropped his hand and turned to find Marianne watching him. The maid's mouth was in a grim line as she walked toward him. He read a number of warnings in that stare.

He knew the Frenchwoman cared deeply for Elisa and it was patent she didn't like him.

"Good afternoon, Marianne," he said, reinforcing the greeting with a smile.

The maid did not smile back.

* * * * *

Elisa woke late. Marianne stood over her, a cup of tea in her hand.

"My lady, dinner has already begun. I thought you were awake when last I came in or I would have never left."

"Oh, goodness," Elisa said, sitting up quickly.

"His lordship is asking for your presence. Quickly, get up and I will help you dress."

Rufus would be furious.

Her heart thumping erratically, Elisa climbed from the bed. She glanced at the Ormulu clock on the mantle, and groaned under her breath. Though she had slept for three hours, it felt like only minutes. And now she was late and Rufus would not let her forget it.

Elisa took the teacup and drained the lukewarm tea with a grimace while Marianne scurried about, pulling out underclothes, a fresh corset, choosing a gown. Then she put the cup and saucer down, and stripped off the bed gown as Marianne held out the clean chemise.

Within quarter of an hour she was dressed. There had been no time for any decisions, and she realized the gown Marianne had picked was more daring than Elisa was used to wearing. It was a deep vibrant blue water-washed satin creation she'd had made just before Roger's death—when she'd hoped an alluring gown would help their relationship ease a little, when all her hopes for a happy marriage had not been completely dead. The bodice and waist were tight, and Marianne had laced her accordingly, lifting her breasts high. As a consequence, the low neckline showed much more of her breasts than usual. The gown barely skimmed the edges of her shoulders, and the big bell sleeves seemed to threaten to pull the gown from them altogether, although her corset and the tight bodice in fact assured the gown would not slip to reveal more than it should.

The layers of petticoats beneath let the wonderful material fall in ruffles and ripples that showed off the moiré effect, and when she walked the very slight train pulled the skirts back, fanning them and displaying the fabric to best effect.

While Elisa stared at herself in the mirror, wondering how she dared appear in such a gown and knowing she had no time to change, Marianne piled her curls on top of her head and pinned them with artistic facility, leaving her neck and shoulders completely bare. She slid diamond drop pendant earrings onto her ears and stood back, her head tilted, waiting for Elisa's approval.

"Thank you for your help," Elisa murmured.

"They'll be just starting the soup, ma'am. You had better be on your way."

"Yes," Elisa agreed distantly. Her heart was starting to thump. What would Vaughn think of this daring ensemble?

Together, they walked down to the marbled entrance hall, as Marianne would be going to the back of the house for her own meal.

At the bottom of the stairs, as Elisa turned to the dining room, Marianne touched her wrist. "My lady…"

"What is it?"

Marianne licked her lips nervously. "My lady, I would warn you of master Vaughn. I see what is happening. I see what is in his eyes, in his mind. And I am afraid."

"Afraid?" Elisa was a little surprised. She could understand someone fearing Rufus, but Vaughn? "He would not hurt me," she responded.

"Perhaps not physically, my lady. But there are other ways of hurting a person. Forgive me, my lady, but I thought I should warn you."

The maid's eyes were pleading, and though Elisa felt warmed by Marianne's concern, she also resented it. Granted, she did not use her head when in Vaughn's presence, but she was a woman of nearly thirty years and she could do what she wanted, with whom she wanted. Elisa patted her maid's hand. "Thank you for the warning, but I do realize my own folly. He is better suited to someone younger. Someone who has not been jaded by all she has seen and heard. Someone like Natasha. I believe I was merely lonely for companionship, and he is my friend."

Marianne looked relieved. She gave a slight nod and moved off down the corridor that eventually led to the kitchen.

Elisa walked the few steps to the dining room doors and stopped. Inside she could hear both feminine and masculine laughter. She straightened her spine. Tonight would be difficult, but she would get through it. After all, there were only five of them. A small gathering, and at least Caroline was here to keep her occupied. She could not—she would not—start looking at Caroline as the enemy.

As for Vaughn…

Her heart thumped again, and she could feel the weakening waves of longing already beginning to wash through her. Excitement burrowed deep into her belly. Would he like her gown? Would his eyes narrow when he saw her for the first time, and his attention be pulled away from the woman-child next to him?

Her courage buoyed by a wicked anticipation, Elisa turned the handle and stepped inside, her head high.

Chapter Six

As soon as she stepped into the dining room, she looked for Rufus. Anger darkened his face immediately, and she found herself coming to an unsure halt just inside the door. Fear rippled through her.

Then she saw Vaughn and realized her unplanned halt afforded him a long moment in which to study her fully. And he was, indeed, studying her from top to toe. She found her shoulders were straightening and her heart picking up speed.

Then she realized everyone was watching her, including Natasha, who sat with a forkful of food halfway between plate and mouth, her eyes wide with astonishment.

Was her appearance so dramatically different it deserved such silent consideration. She brushed at the satin with a hand suddenly damp, smoothing the skirt down unnecessarily and swallowed on a throat gone dry. "Forgive my lateness, please," she murmured. "I fell asleep."

Vaughn got to his feet and came toward her, a slow, appreciative smile on his face that only she could see. He picked up her hand and bowed low over it. "My lady, allow me," he said, offering his arm to take her to her place at the table.

Rufus' wine glass hit the tabletop with a loud, wet thud, and he cleared his throat with a harsh, vicious sound. Elisa's heart jumped once again, fear squeezing her throat.

Vaughn laid his hand over hers on his arm. It looked like a perfectly normal, natural action, but the slight pressure on her fingers relayed a message just for her, a reassurance in the face of Rufus' choler. He was wordlessly telling her everything would be fine.

He seated her without another word and went back to his side of the table, next to Natasha.

Caroline was on her right. Elisa looked at her friend, avoiding Rufus' furious face. Caroline smiled warmly. "You look beautiful, Elisa. Is that a new dress?"

"Yes, I had it made not long ago," Elisa lied with only a small hesitation, then turned to Rufus with a purposeful smile. This seemed to bring relief for he nodded, looking pleased that she'd had the dress made for him.

Elisa's cheeks grew warm, and she reached for her glass and took a drink of the cool lemon water. She could feel Vaughn's stare on her from the opposite side of the table. No doubt Rufus had seated him beside Natasha and across from Caroline to keep him away from her. It would be difficult to keep her gaze averted. His very presence seemed to draw her attention to him. She could feel him. She could feel him staring at her.

"Yes, now I remember that dress." Rufus said, his tone insinuating something sensual between the two of them.

"I'm delighted you chose to wear it again," Vaughn drawled.

"Thank you," Elisa replied.

His white shirt was daringly open at the collar, covered by a navy waistcoat with shards of silver running throughout. His hair was slightly mussed. Elisa wondered if he had been riding while she slept. He seemed to crackle with energy and life, just as he had when they had gone riding yesterday.

The reminder of what had happened at the pond made her breasts ache and she grew moist, almost instantly ready.

Had Natasha gone riding with him?

Pain lanced through her at the thought.

A loaded plate was placed in front of her, and everyone's attention was drawn back to the meal. The conversation gradually picked up again, leaving Elisa to her own thoughts. Vaughn was once again a captive audience, attentive to every vacant word Natasha uttered. The dinner dragged on relentlessly.

Caroline began a conversation with Vaughn, drilling him for information about his future plans. Natasha, meanwhile, hung on every word.

Which left Elisa to Rufus' dubious company.

"Why are you wearing such a lavish gown tonight?" he asked, his words little above a whisper.

Elisa dropped her hands to her lap and dug her fingernails into her palms. She said nothing.

"I wonder…do you seek the attention of someone here?"

Elisa looked directly at Rufus. "Marianne laid it out for me. As I mentioned before, I slept and when I awoke there was little time to do anything but don a gown that had already been pressed." She sighed heavily. "I thought the gown would please you," she lied. "If it doesn't, then I'll go and change at once."

He watched her intently and she forced herself to keep eye contact. She could hear nothing over the beating of her heart as he stared.

Ever so slowly his expression changed, no longer hard and quizzing, but instead full of fondness.

She would never understand his moods. Ever. At times, when he offered her nothing but curses and accusations, she despaired that the impending wedding would be called off and she would be cast aside once more. Then, unexpectedly, he would display a small sign of some gentler emotion, and she would again wonder why he had sought her hand in marriage. He had professed a need for companionship, nothing more, when he had proposed.

Finally, his attention shifted back to his plate, and he attacked the large helping of gravy-covered ham upon it.

Her appetite was nonexistent, but she ate anyway, knowing if she didn't Rufus would comment on it.

For the remainder of the meal Caroline spoke of the new Limoges china set her husband had arranged to be shipped from France for her. William had commissioned the pattern to be designed especially for her, and stamped with the family crest.

Elisa envied her friend for her happy marriage. Caroline and William apparently deeply loved each other and went to great effort to show it.

On the contrary, Elisa had found in her experience that the fantasy of marriage was far better than the reality.

Natasha's laughter sounded often. It was an irritating, light trill that filled the room. Natasha and Vaughn were again whispering to each other. Natasha leaned a little closer, and rudely whispered behind her hand. Vaughn's brows raised a little, and he threw his head back and laughed loudly, plainly delighted.

Elisa abruptly stood, the back legs of her chair scraping across the floor beyond the rug.

Vaughn looked up from his conversation, and Caroline lifted her eyebrows.

"Elisa?" she asked. "Are you alright?"

"Please excuse me for a moment." The words were all she could manage.

Rufus merely nodded, too preoccupied with his dessert to speak.

Elisa glanced at Vaughn as she turned from the table. His eyes were narrowed, his expression a reflective one. Natasha was already reaching for his forearm to gain back his attention.

Elisa gritted her teeth and hurried from the room. She was barely to the stairs when she called for Marianne. One of the footmen from the dining room went scurrying for the kitchen — perhaps he could read her impatience, her fury, in the imperious ring of her voice, for he went to fetch Marianne without waiting to be sent.

Elisa strode to her room, pounding out her frustration with every step. She burst into the room, and came to a halt, looking around wildly.

She would show Vaughn the shallowness and predictability of the company he had chosen to keep tonight. She would show him the unexpected depths he had foregone for the sake of Natasha's off-key nasal twittering. Elisa reached for the closures at the back of her dress.

Marianne hurried into the room, breathless, her eyes wide. "Madame?"

"Get this off me. Hurry," Elisa said, tugging at the hooks.

"*Off?*"

"Yes, off, damn it! I can't take off my corset without first removing the dress!"

"But...your corset, madam?" Marianne appeared truly bewildered.

"It is pinching me and I can scarcely draw breath," Elisa said without hesitation. "Hurry!"

"At once," Marianne said, her fingers reaching for the hooks and nimbly releasing them, one after another. Together they lowered the dress, and released the ties on the petticoats enough to undo the corset and pull it away from her body. Elisa plucked at the chemise she wore beneath. "It is soaked through," she declared and took it off.

"Madam!" Marianne breathed, deeply shocked.

"Who will know?" Elisa said, retying the petticoats around her waist, her bare breasts free of restrictions. "Hurry, please, Marianne. Rufus is already furious at my delayed arrival. This interlude will anger him all the more."

The implied threat was enough to get Marianne moving again. She re-fastened the petticoats, and pulled the satin gown back up onto Elisa's shoulders. With deft fingers she began re-hooking the back closed.

The touch of satin against her breasts was shocking and...delicious. Without the confining structure of her corset, the plunging décolletage felt dangerously wicked and insecure. A sweet ache began in her cleft at the thought of Vaughn's expression when he realized she had taken her corset off.

Marianne stepped back, and waited.

"Thank you, you may go," Elisa told her, running her hands down the sensuous satin bodice, feeling her bare skin beneath.

"Madam?"

"I said go!"

"At once," Marianne replied, and hurried from the room.

Elisa waited until she heard the maid's footsteps pattering down the hallway, then reached beneath her skirts and took off her drawers, too.

With a deep breath, she turned and headed back downstairs, feeling the freedom and sinful bareness of her body beneath the gown with every step.

The double doors loomed before her. She swallowed. Dare she go through with this?

Suddenly, a hand snaked out from behind one of the pairs of pillars in the foyer and snagged her wrist.

She stifled her gasp when she saw it was Vaughn, standing behind the pillar. He put a finger to his lips and pulled her towards him, closer and closer, until she was pressed up against his hard body. In the dim light his eyes glittered with an intense light.

She swallowed hard and looked up into his handsome face.

"I was beginning to worry," he said, his breath warm against her cheek. His hands came up around her waist, and pressed against the material.

Suddenly, he became very still. His breath was expelled gustily.

Elisa glanced over her shoulder. Her fear was great. If they were caught in such a compromising situation… "Vaughn, we cannot…not here."

Vaughn stepped backwards, pulling her between the white columns, so they would be hidden from all…but it was still far too public a place. He turned her around so his back was to the entrance, which hid her a little.

"And I cannot walk away when I know that beneath this magnificent gown you are completely bare." His hands swept up her bodice, and she could feel their heat through the fabric, burning her. They stopped short of her breasts, and a little sigh of frustration escaped her.

She had his attention now, she realized.

"Is it a complete bareness, Elisa?" he asked, and his voice was low and rough.

"Yes," she whispered.

He groaned, and the sound seemed to be ripped from deep inside him.

Her heart raced with an intense excitement. She was mortally aware of how many people wandered the public rooms of the hall at this moment—staff, guests…perhaps even Rufus. The danger of being seen was so great…

Her back was flush against the cold marble, her hands at her sides as he leaned into her, his long hair brushing her bare shoulder. "Kiss me before we go back."

"Vaughn…"

"Just a single kiss." His arms were on either side of her, trapping her against the pillar.

He would not walk away without some sort of prize, she realized. She lifted her face to his. "Just one and that—"

His mouth captured hers.

Elisa drew in a gasping breath, surprised. For a moment her heart and body seemed to freeze. Then she registered the heat of his lips, and the closeness of his big, powerful body. This was

Vaughn kissing her. Vaughn! Her body leapt with a victorious, primordial excitement.

The kiss was at first light, then swiftly grew more intense. He parted her lips with his tongue, which swept past her teeth and teased her mouth.

Elisa found herself leaning into him, her arms of their own accord wrapping around his broad shoulders, holding him tighter, pulling him closer.

Then his lips left hers, and traveled along her jaw. They were hot and moist, and left a trail of sizzling flesh in their wake. Her eyes were closing, as waves of pleasure drained her strength. His teeth caught at her earlobe, and then his tongue traced her ear, before plunging hotly into it. Thrilling bolts of excitement thrummed through her. Desperate for more, she arched her back, making her breasts thrust against the satin. His mouth was traveling down her neck, while his hand held her steady. His lips and tongue were swirling across her flesh, and his hair brushed it in a light, maddeningly erotic sweep.

Elisa bit down on the gasping groan that tried to emerge from her as his mouth moved further down, to the tops of her breasts, where his hot tongue traced a pattern on her skin, searing it.

Then, suddenly, she grew aware of the shocking looseness of the top of her gown. He had unhooked the first handful of fastenings, and it sagged around her shoulders, sliding down her breasts and threatening to fully reveal them. She clutched at the bodice, trying to hold it up, her breath leaving her in a rush.

"Vaughn, no…"

His hands rested against her bare shoulders, and he looked deep into her eyes. There was an implacable will shining in his eyes that silenced her weak protest. While watching her face, he swept his hands down her arms, pushing the offending sleeves down, and bringing the bodice with it.

Her breasts were completely bared.

Elisa caught her breath. How did he dare…?

But the hazy, incoherent thought scattered as his hands cupped her breasts, and the two thumbs brushed her upright, painfully tight nipples.

She gasped and saw him smile a little.

She tried to raise her hands, to push him away, but her arms were caught in the lowered sleeves, effectively trapped at her sides. Then even that weak defensive motion ceased as he lowered his head and placed a hot kiss on her upper breasts, where his fingers had last been.

One of his hands fell to her waist, while his mouth slid with agonizing slowness further down her breast. The other hand played with the nipple of the other, sending shooting sparks of delight up and down her body. When, at last, his mouth closed hotly around her nipple, a deep groan of pleasure was pulled from her.

His teeth played with her nipple, tugging it, and his tongue laved it with velvet moisture.

Elisa looked down at his head against her breasts, then up at the foyer and their very public position. While he suckled her, the door to the dining room opened, spilling light out into the foyer. Vaughn either did not hear, or did not care, for he continued his sensual assault on her breasts. She could not see the door from behind the pillar, but she heard someone emerge. The door shut behind the intruder, and he or she walked across the foyer.

Elisa held her breath.

Whoever it was moved into the passage that ran the length of the west wing, and suddenly they were alone again, still undiscovered.

Vaughn's mouth moved to her other breast, and his other hand captured the one he had abandoned.

Her pulse skittered as his mouth covered the taut nipple.

At the sight of him suckling her, warmth raced through her, settling low into her belly and lower, to her cleft and pulsating pearl.

Helpless to protest, her arms still trapped, she let her head fall back against the wall and closed her eyes, fully immersing herself in the sea of pleasure and need swelling in her.

It was as if he had sensed her capitulation, for his mouth left her breast, and his hand fell away. She opened her eyes, deprived.

He slowly pulled her gown back up over her shoulders, and refastened the hooks, while remaining silent. When she was decent again, he ran his fingernails lightly over the fabric that covered her breasts, sparking a white hot current through her nipples and taking her breath.

He smiled a little and stepped back away from her.

He gave a short bow. "And good evening to you, my lady," he said, his voice low.

He turned and walked back to the dining room, leaving her to follow him on weak legs. Her whole body was trembling with unfulfilled need—a hot, sweet-sour ache that caught her mind. She could think of nothing but carnal thoughts of how she might appease that ache.

She waited a few minutes, trying to still her heart before entering. But it was useless. And she had been gone too long. She must return. Now.

She entered the room.

The entire table was laughing at something Vaughn had said. All but Rufus, that was. The look he gave her was sharp.

Was he wondering why she and Vaughn had both dismissed themselves from the dinner table? Elisa had never done that before, for fear others would see it as rude.

Vaughn did not even glance her way. He was leaning back in his seat, as if he had been there all night, and had not, just moments before, been recklessly seducing her right out in the open foyer where anyone might have seen them.

He seemed to be completely without nerves. The boldness of his actions took her breath away.

Her heart still pounding, she took her seat and smiled at Rufus. He sat back in his chair, his smile tight as he looked from her to Vaughn. His eyes narrowed, and anger reddened his face, except for two whitish rings around his nostrils and the lines running from his mouth to his nose. His fury was even more frightening for he kept the stiff polite smile in place, a rictus that held no genuine emotion in it at all.

Elisa's heart began to hurt, her stomach clamped tight.

Rufus had become an enemy.

Chapter Seven

Elisa's breath fogged the window as she stared out over the land she'd grown to dislike immensely. Though it wasn't raining, thick, dark clouds in the distance threatened to ruin what had started out as a sunny day.

Last night sleep had been all but impossible. Every time she closed her eyes she saw Vaughn's face, remembered the feel of his hands on her, the taste of his lips and the way he'd taken her nipples into his mouth, so expertly, bringing her to a feverish pitch that threatened to consume her.

He'd been able to walk away as cool as could be.

Throughout the remainder of the meal he hadn't looked at her once.

Perhaps he'd overheard Rufus mention that he seemed to be paying Elisa far too much attention of late. If that were so, it would explain why Vaughn paid so much attention to Natasha.

So she had remained silent, her every movement being scrutinized by her future husband. Rufus had sat with the tense stillness of a cat ready to pounce on a mouse.

And now another day at Fairleigh Hall. She sighed heavily.

No doubt Natasha and Caroline would be visiting again. Last night Caroline had mentioned something about bringing over a tea her husband had bought while in the Orient—a special blend that thrilled the senses.

The only thing that would thrill Elisa would be for Natasha and Caroline to stay home.

The door opened and closed behind her. "My lady, perhaps you should reconsider going for a ride. The weather looks like it is about to take a turn for the worse," Marianne told her.

Elisa pointed to the blue velvet riding habit on the bed. "I'll be amply covered. The gown goes from neck to ankle."

"Your fiancé would not approve," she replied, helping Elisa slip into the gown.

How Elisa was beginning to hate the word fiancé. "And who will see me in this godforsaken land?"

Marianne shrugged. "That means very little. We both know he'll be furious you've been riding alone."

Elisa ignored the awkward fact. She put her boots, gloves and hat on, and without a backward glance headed for the stables.

It was early enough that there were only the servants about. The grandfather clock chimed seven. Elisa quickened her pace. She had no desire to face Rufus on the off chance that he was awake already.

In fact, she wasn't in the mood to face Vaughn either.

At the stables, she requested the gray again, and walked in restless little circles until the horse was brought to her. She gripped the saddle, ready to hoist herself up, and paused. Then she stepped back. No, today was not the day for delicate mincing about.

"Please take the saddle off," she told the stable master, who was hovering anxiously, waiting to assist her mount.

His eyes widened, but that was all. With a quick word to a stable hand, the pair of them stripped the gray of its saddle and girth and stood back. Elisa could see the stable boy's puzzled expression, and stifled a smile. He was wondering how a lady could possibly mount and ride a horse, wearing what she was wearing.

She took the bridle from the stable master. "Thank you. That will be all."

He touched his forelock and hurried away, pulling the boy with him.

Elisa led the horse out into the yard and around the back of the stable to where the sweet grasses began. A wooden fence ran from the stable wall off into the distance, and there was a conveniently placed stile just there. She walked the horse over to the stile, and checked quickly around her for observers. She was completely alone.

Swiftly, she took off her bonnet, her gloves, and — her heart thumping erratically — her boots and stockings. She tucked them beneath the stile. She scrunched her bare toes up in the grass, feeling it tickle. Swiftly, she pulled all the pins out of her hair and shook it out, and rubbed at her scalp as the weight dropped away.

With another quick check over her shoulder, she gathered her skirt and petticoats up in one arm. The gentle breeze swept past her bared calves and knees. Quickly, she grabbed the horse's reins, clambered up onto the top step of the stile, and slipped onto the back of the horse.

The skirts, of course, rode up high around her thighs. She re-arranged them as well as she could, but the long green field ahead of her, with its rolling slopes, beckoned her. She wanted to start as quickly as possible.

Her excitement caught her breath in a little hitch, and she kicked the horse into a full gallop, her blood thrilling.

It wasn't until she had ridden a good mile at breakneck speed that she finally began to relax. The last few days had been entirely too tense. And now with Rufus' growing suspicion it could only get worse.

Why had she put herself into this position...and how could she get out of it?

Every day she yearned for escape from this hellish life. Whenever she thought of reconsidering, her son's face would appear in her mind, reminding her that if she left Rufus all the old rumors would resurface. And, she knew society well enough to know that trying to get Raymond back would be futile.

Vaughn should leave. It was the only solution.

But the very thought of him walking out the door and never coming back to Fairleigh Hall was more than she could bear. Perhaps if he were to marry Natasha it would not be so agonizing. At least then he would consider moving in and living at least part of the year at Fairleigh Hall.

In her mind came an image of Vaughn and Natasha making love. He would be resting over the girl, his broad bare shoulders gleaming in moonlight streaming through a window above them. His hand would tenderly reach to caress her face…

Elisa groaned as her heart squeezed painfully at the emotion-filled scenario she had conjured up. She knew she would not be able to bear having him living in Fairleigh Hall, either, if she would be forced to witness his tenderness and endearments for Natasha.

She willed the images away and pushed her mount harder and faster. Faster. To the point where she knew she was barely in control of the horse. The touch of fear kept her mind focused and away from the dilemmas that awaited her back at the hall.

When the horse showed signs of flagging, she brought him to a halt beneath a stand of old oak trees. She dismounted and walked the horse, giving herself time to relax before returning to the manor. As she walked, she unbuttoned her bodice and sleeves, and flapped them, letting the cool air circulate her heated body. She was strongly tempted to remove the few petticoats beneath her skirt. It was much too warm to be wearing so many layers, after all.

Finally, with a hurried look around her, she reached beneath her skirt and removed the stiff linen undergarments. She rolled them up and tucked them behind a tree. This far away from any manor or farm cot, they might stay there and rot for years before they were discovered.

She smoothed the velvet out over her hips and thighs, feeling both wicked and comfortable for the first time that day.

Thunder rumbled across the fields, pulling her attention to the sky. She looked up at the billowing, angry clouds overhead.

Until this moment she had taken little notice of the impending weather. At any time the sky would open up and pour.

She looked around, trying to establish exactly where she was. She knew she'd traveled a great distance from the manor and had been gone for at least an hour.

She should return to the manor, or risk a soaking, and quite possibly be caught out in the open when the lightning began.

She turned the horse back toward Fairleigh Hall and began to ride as hard as she had before. If the rain settled in for days, as it was wont to do this time of year, this would be her last moment of freedom for some time.

She had traveled a long arc on her outward leg of the ride, and now she found herself approaching the hall from the front. It stopped raining just as she topped the last crest before the manor, and cantered down the long, gently sloping field before her. Half way up the next hill, the hall was spread before her.

Elisa saw two people walking the wide, luxurious lawn spread before the building. They were hand in hand. And there was no mistaking Vaughn's wide shoulders and height.

Natasha and Vaughn. Hand in hand.

Elisa's stomach turned. She would not get jealous, she told herself. It didn't matter that he'd kissed her senseless, or that he'd taken liberties with her she had never granted to any other man. She could not afford to have Vaughn in her life in any other capacity than that of a stepson.

Her gaze shifted from the couple to the high drystone wall at the end of the field. It had been at least four years since she'd last taken a jump on horseback. Back then she'd ridden every day and it hadn't intimidated her. Yet it loomed before her now.

Taunting her.

Thunder rumbled ominously.

With a glance at the couple, she put her knees to the horse's flanks and flew toward the wall. Her heart hammered with every gallop. Even as she felt the thrill of the challenge, she questioned her wisdom. She had never jumped this gray before.

What if he was a poor jumper? He was a big horse, and just like humans, the bigger animals were often clumsy...

Fear touched her. But it was too late. She was committed to the jump.

Vaughn heard the galloping horse and turned to look towards the sound. Just beyond the drystone wall that marked off the field from the formal gardens of the hall was Elisa — astride a horse and racing towards them.

An invisible hand gripped his throat and chest and squeezed as he realized she intended to jump the wall.

Insanity.

"Good lord!" Natasha murmured, her gloved hand at her mouth. "What *is* she wearing? And her hair!"

Irritation flashed through him, and he let her hand go. "For god's sake, she's going to jump!" he told her, starting towards the wall.

"Well, I don't see why that excuses..."

But he didn't hear any more of Natasha's indignant words, for he was racing forward, his heart hammering in his chest, echoing in his throat and temple. Fear was a live snake in his belly.

"No, Elisa! Don't!" he cried. But it was too late.

The horse tried valiantly to take the wall. He watched the big beast gather himself, the powerful hind legs bunching and pushing off, the woman in blue clinging to his back like a burr. He saw Elisa's white face and big eyes as the horse lifted. Fear and exaltation were fighting for expression.

The gray almost made it. Almost.

His forelegs smashed through the capstones of the wall. If it had been a mortared wall, the animal would have been brought to a solid, crashing halt, but the loose stones pushed away, and the horse was reaching for solid ground on the other side, whinnying.

He landed hard, and Vaughn heard the wet crack of breaking bone. The horse and Elisa both screamed. As the horse went down Elisa was thrown over his head.

Vaughn watched with sick horror as she curled herself into a protective ball. She hit the ground with her shoulder and rolled for several yards before coming to a halt.

He didn't remember covering the ground between him and her still figure. He was just suddenly there, gathering her into his arms, too scared to even breathe.

She was conscious, and as he lifted her she opened her eyes and gasped. "I am unhurt," she told him as he brushed at the dirt on her cheek.

"How could you not be hurt?" he whispered, his voice strangled by the tension in his throat—in his whole body.

She gave another gusty sigh. "I learned how to take a fall before I turned seven." She reached up and caressed his jaw. "Truly, I am fine."

Relief swept through him, and the release of tension was so great he was dizzy with it. He swallowed. "For my sake, Elisa, please don't do that again."

She was gazing at him, a gentle, knowing smile on her perfectly formed lips. "I won't," she assured him. She looked past his shoulder.

"Vaughn, is Madame Elisa hurt?"

Natasha.

"She's fine," he told her shortly, keeping his face averted from her.

He grew aware of the horse, then. It was grunting and squealing, over by the wall. And it was lying on its side, in writhing agony.

Sad pity touched him. "Natasha, you must go back to the house. Quickly now."

Elisa caught at his sleeve, and turned her face into his chest with a little moan. She knew what must be done.

"Why?" Natasha asked, puzzled.

"Get Joshua. Tell him to fetch my father's hunting gun. Please hurry."

"I don't understand."

"Oh my goodness—I saw her fall! Elisa, my dear!" It was Caroline, hurrying as fast as her skirts would allow.

The noises the horse was making were distressing. Vaughn couldn't spare time to explain unpleasant facts to Natasha. He looked at the older woman, instead. "Caroline. Please, most quickly, you must take your daughter inside. Fetch Joshua, or the first manservant you find out here with my father's rifle."

"But…Elisa?" Caroline asked.

"She's fine. Please, hurry."

Caroline grasped her daughter's arm. "Come, dear," she coaxed as Natasha stood staring at Vaughn, and the woman in his arms.

Movement behind Caroline caught his eye. Vaughn shifted a little to see behind her.

It was Rufus, stalking towards them as fast as his short legs would carry him. His face was a deep, angry red, and his eyes…

Vaughn shivered. Rufus had the eyes of a man going mad. His gaze was locked unwaveringly on Elisa and him.

Alarm gripped him. What was Rufus about to do? Almost instinctively, Vaughn shifted Elisa's weight to one arm, freeing his right arm.

Rufus strode straight past Caroline, who was still coaxing the reluctant Natasha inside. As he brushed past them, he reached into his jacket. He pulled out a silver pistol, and cocked it.

Vaughn's mind tried to deal with the shocking possibility that Rufus would simply shoot him where he knelt and Elisa, too. His left arm tightened around her, as he scrambled to think of a way out of this. But Rufus was moving too fast, and his wild expression said he would not be reasoned with. Not now.

Vaughn took a deep breath as Rufus reached them, ready to spring up and stand between Elisa and the little man, but instead of raising the pistol and aiming at him, Rufus kept walking straight past them.

Vaughn turned his head to follow Rufus as the man walked straight up to the kicking, screaming horse, pointed the gun at the horse's head. He did not wait to aim, or brace himself. He simply fired, his set expression and wild eyes not changing one iota.

The horse went still.

Natasha screamed, and Vaughn heard the rustle of skirts and a soft thump behind him. She'd fainted.

"Oh my…" Caroline said, her voice weak.

Elisa's hand on his arm tightened its grip. "Oh god, Vaughn…what have I done?" she whispered. "He will kill us both."

Before he could form an answer, Rufus swung back to face them. He walked towards them, the smoking gun hanging from his hand. He came right up to them, staring down at Elisa. The legs of his fawn pants were splattered in blood.

"I told you I didn't want you riding," he said, his voice very calm. His mouth pulled back in a smile. "I always get my way, do you see?" He stared at Vaughn as he placed the pistol back in his jacket.

Elisa trembled against him as he stared up at his father.

Rufus grinned again, the expression one of wolfish pleasure. Then he turned and walked back to the house with the same direct gait as before, straight past Caroline where she was bent over her daughter's prostrate body.

Caroline quailed as he passed her.

Vaughn took a deep breath, and tried to let the knot in his stomach unravel. Elisa was right. With only a little more provocation, Rufus might very well shoot them both. He had not foreseen that death could be the price for his obsession with Elisa.

Thoughtfully, he got to his feet and lifted Elisa into his arms, intending to carry her back to the house. "I'll send some people to help you with Natasha," he told Caroline as he passed her.

"Thank you, Vaughn," she said quietly, with the full dignity of the lady she was.

Vaughn kept on towards the house, and looked down at Elisa. Tears were streaking her smeared face, and making the blue eyes sparkle. Her hair was a halo of unruly golden locks about her face. It was then he noticed the unfastened bodice, and the glimpse of soft white skin between the gaping closure. His lips had been there.

He remembered the scent of her, and his body tightened in response. His hand under her legs identified flesh guarded by only the thin layer of velvet. Elisa had been out riding bereft of every accoutrement of a proper lady.

"Why, Elisa?" he asked her.

"Because of you." Her answer, like her expression, lacked shield or disguise.

He looked away from her face, from the naked emotion there, and concentrated on the front steps of the hall where servants were spilling down onto the grass, coming to help, their faces shocked.

He must cease this mad, forbidden game. Now and at once, before events spiraled far out of his control.

* * * * *

Elisa sat in her room for hours, staring at the mundane landscape that had been on the bedroom wall since she had moved into it. It had been a present from Rufus to mark their engagement.

She'd always hated the picture.

She was certain Rufus would be paying a visit upon the morrow to express his dissatisfaction with her actions. No doubt, he would not content himself with expressing it verbally.

The thought of Rufus beating her held a certain grim, stark comfort. She deserved whatever he chose to mete out to her. She had earned every stroke, lash or blow he laid upon her.

And once it was done, she could retreat to the mundane safety of her life as Rufus' future wife, and wait and work for her life's ambition: to get back her little boy. The appalling blandness of that life would take her away from temptation, from wickedness.

But then, oh then, she would never again feel the thrill of being in Vaughn's arms, or experience the weakening rush of hot pleasure as he touched or tasted her with his knowing hands and lips. She would be forced to send him from her and never again see his broad shoulders, the lithe cat-like way he prowled about a room, watching her, *wanting her*, scheming his sensual schemes…

Elisa had reached this aching impasse a dozen times in the hours she sat in the chair looking at the drab landscape, her body throbbing with need, and her mind dizzy with the erotic recall of Vaughn's mouth on her breasts. She would remember the touch of his hands on her waist, and the gentle caress of a fingertip across her cheek. With her eyes closed, she would conjure up a memory of the scent of him, the sound of his voice against her ear when she had rested her head against his chest. Finally, when she truly knew she must die if she did not have him, then she would deliberately look up at the picture and remind herself that she was Rufus' fiancée.

A knock at the door made Elisa start. Wiping away the tears with the back of her hand, she walked toward the door, suddenly cold and trembling.

Was it Rufus, come so soon for his pound of flesh?

It occurred to her that she was completely without defense here, lacking even the small pocket knife that women who traveled widely regularly carried with them. But then, if Rufus had decided to beat her, he was perhaps entitled. Why did thoughts of weapons spring so quickly to mind? But she knew the answer to that: Rufus always carried at least one small

Derringer on his person, and today had seen fit to use it. He had proved he was capable of violence.

Taking a deep breath, she opened the door.

Vaughn stood before her. He wore no jacket, and his neckwear was missing. His shirt was askew, as though he'd gone to undress, then reconsidered. His eyes were smoky with emotion.

Her heart lurched and she took a quick step back.

"May I come in?"

It was highly improper and risky considering Rufus' current state of mind. Despite that knowledge, she motioned him in, his very presence corroding her judgment.

He walked past her, his masculine scent lingering behind him. As she shut the door, she closed her eyes for a moment and inhaled deeply. She wanted him.

By the time she turned to face him, he was sitting on her bed. Her pulse jumped. How virile he was! So tempting...especially to a woman who hadn't made love in over five years.

"Come here," he said, his voice low and seductive as he motioned to the space beside him.

His long-fingered hand lay on her coverlet invitingly.

"I won't bite."

She slowly walked toward him. He moved his hand and she sat down, making sure to leave a respectable distance between them. The corner of his mouth lifted in a grin that only added to his striking looks.

"Where have you been?" she asked, her voice cracking.

He reached out and took a lock of her hair between his fingers. "I needed to get away from here for a little while. I took a walk." His fingers brushed against her neck, causing her stomach to tighten.

"We must stop this, Vaughn," she said desperately. "Now, before it is too late. We are not guilty yet—"

"In my heart, I have been guilty since the moment I saw you," Vaughn replied. "The guilt of the flesh is a minor transgression in comparison to what you and I have done together in my mind."

She swallowed hard as his eyes settled on her lips.

"I don't know what Rufus will do if we do not stop this," she told him.

"How will you be able to stand it, alone in this mausoleum with *him* as a husband?" He cocked his head slightly, studying her. "You're so young...so very desirable."

"I'm too old for you," she blurted, dropping her gaze to his chest. It was a mistake, for she caught a glimpse of smooth, well-defined muscle where his shirt opened. Strong, sculptured, firm...how she wanted to feel and taste every inch of him!

"You're a beautiful, desirable woman, Elisa. Have you forgotten that in your time here?"

"I am to be your stepmother."

He shrugged. "We're not related by blood. And in truth, I care not what Rufus might do. Not when you are here next to me. When I look at you I forget everything but the fact that I desire you." His eyes were smoldering with need.

"We must not—"

His arm wrapped around her waist and lifted her. She was slipped onto his lap, trailing blue velvet across his knees. The strong muscles of his thighs flexed beneath the back of hers, and as he shifted, she felt the evidence of his desire, hard, long, and thick against her hip. "I want you," he whispered against her neck, his hot breath fanning her ear a moment before he kissed her there. A shiver went through her.

She turned, ready to deny him, when he kissed her. Swiftly, his soft lips grew more demanding. His tongue was like velvet against her own, sweeping the recesses of her mouth, stealing the very breath from her lungs.

She felt his other hand on her bare ankle, sweeping up beneath the fabric. It was hot against her flesh, cupping her calf, caressing her and sending heated spikes of pleasure coursing through her. She moaned as his hand slid higher, over her knees, to stroke the sensitive flesh of her inner thigh. Delicious surges wracked her body.

His lips and tongue were hotly plundering her mouth, searing her lips. She melted against him, pliant and utterly biddable to his every desire.

A knock sounded at the door.

Reality slapped Elisa in the face. Dear God, she was sitting on Vaughn's lap, kissing him, her arms twined tightly around his broad shoulders as though she were drowning.

She jumped up.

"Yes, who is it?"

"Marianne, madam. I have a tray of tea and biscuits for you."

"I don't want it. Take it away, please," Elisa called out.

There was a hesitant silence.

"Yes, madam," Marianne finally replied.

Elisa turned to face Vaughn where he sprawled on the bed, with lazy half-shut eyes.

"You should go before he comes looking for you," she said in a strangled voice.

He lifted a dark brow as he took her hand in his and slowly brought it to his lips. Elisa's heart beat in triple time when his lips touched her burning skin.

"Do not do this to me," she said under her breath. "We cannot be lovers. You know that as much as I do. Rufus knows something is going on between us. He only requires proof, and we are at his mercy."

He shrugged. "Let him call me out. I shoot straighter than he does."

If only she could be so unconcerned!

"Why would you deny yourself something you've been wanting for far too long?" he added, sitting up. "We are good together, Elisa."

She wondered how he could read her so clearly. Slowly, she felt her will slip away under that smoldering stare. "I have my reasons," she whispered.

He stood up, which put him too close to her. But before she could step away he grasped her shoulders, and turned her around.

She found she was facing her cheval mirror. The image she beheld was fascinating. She stood in front of Vaughn, in her blue riding habit, her bodice unfastened, and the shape of her legs clearly outlined beneath the fabric.

Vaughn was sweeping her hair up into one hand, gathering it. He twisted it into a coil and rested it on her head. "Look," he said, gazing at her eyes in the mirror. "This is what the world sees of you."

With her hair up, she looked as she normally did. Proper. A lady.

He let her hair fall, and it swung about her shoulders and face, a tangled mess.

"This is what I see when I look at you," he added, his voice low, sounding right next to her ear. His hands settled on her hips, cupping them. Then they slid down, at an angle, to rest over the junction of her thighs, and she drew in a startled breath. "I see everything," he added.

"Don't," she pleaded, fighting the renewal of need in her.

His eyes, in the mirror, were dark as they stared into hers.

"Look at me, at us," he told her. His left hand slid up across her abdomen, lifting higher to cup her breast through the fabric. "Tell me we are not supposed to be together."

She could not deny it. In the mirror she did not see a wicked woman. She saw two young people who went well together, who looked like a couple.

She watched with her breath stilled as his hand slid through the opening of her bodice, and cupped her other breast beneath the velvet. As his fingers slid over her aching nipple she was unable to stop her head from falling back with abandoned sensuality, or her hips from thrusting. His hand, splayed across her abdomen, applied a gentle, wonderful pressure, and she felt him against her buttocks, hot and hard, contained still, but throbbing powerfully.

His hand emerged from her bodice, and lifted to her mouth. His fingertip touched her mouth. "Suck them," he ordered, and his voice was hoarse.

She obediently opened her mouth, and watched as his fingers slipped inside. She sucked, bathing them with her tongue. Then he reached back inside her bodice and anointed her nipples with her own juices. The slight chill of the moisture crinkled the aching tips into hard tight nubs, and sent a bolt of pure white excitement to her aching, slippery cleft.

Her head fell to rest on his chest, and she could feel herself thrusting her breast into his hand, encouraging him, just as her hips were pushing against him.

The knocking at the door was startlingly loud.

Vaughn's hand grew still beneath her gown, and his eyes met hers in the mirror.

"Yes?" Elisa called, her voice weak and husky.

"My lady, is everything all right?"

"My maid. Marianne," she told Vaughn in a whisper. She lifted her voice. "What now, Marianne?"

"I am worried for you, madam. You have had a fall, and you have been locked up in your room for ages and ages. I would speak to you, ma'am, and reassure myself you are all right."

Elisa sighed heavily. "She will not leave until she sees that I'm fine."

He smiled slowly. "Which means I must leave?"

Elisa nodded, and pulled his hand from her gown.

"My lady!" Marianne's voice was taking on a shrill-like quality that would soon wake the dead.

"Marianne, I'll be right there," Elisa called out, her voice cracking with unrestrained emotion. "You have to go," she said, turning to face Vaughn.

He moved to the window.

"Sweet dreams, Elisa," he said softly, then without another word he slipped out the window and was gone.

With a steadying breath Elisa smoothed out the coverlet that still held the imprint of Vaughn's body. Running her fingers through her hair, she walked slowly to the door, her heart racing with an excitement that, after Roger's death, she thought never to feel again.

How could she possibly consider sending Vaughn from Farleigh Hall when he made her feel this way?

Chapter Eight

"Elisa!"

Opening her eyes, Elisa squinted against the early morning sun that spilled through the lace at the window, casting her room in a golden, dappled light.

"Elisa!" Her name was bellowed once again, causing her to jump and sit upright, and bring the covers to her chin.

It was Rufus and she could hear his clumping footsteps in the hall outside her room. A heartbeat later the door swung open and thudded against the wall.

Rufus stood with his hands fisted at his sides, his face red from either temper or the effort of climbing the stairs and traversing the long west wing of the house—no doubt a rare occurrence.

"Good God, don't tell me you couldn't hear me," he roared.

Swallowing the lump that had formed in her throat, Elisa sat up against the headboard. "I did not hear you until just this moment," she lied, knowing full well he expected her to come running.

He shut the door and walked towards the bed, his eyes never leaving hers.

A shiver ran down her spine when the mattress dipped beneath his weight and he sat down beside her.

She could smell whiskey on his breath. Had he brooded all day yesterday and this morning, building his temper?

He smiled a little and lifted a hand to her chin. The small gesture surprised her, and made her heart skip a beat as she realized the existence of another awful possibility. *Please God, no,* she said in silent prayer. Surely he did not want to consummate their relationship before the wedding? Now was not the time, so soon before the marriage, and particularly in the light of day.

"You've dark smudges beneath your eyes again. You didn't sleep well?" His expression was the picture of concern, yet she knew better. He was quizzing her.

"Actually I slept very well. I suppose my age is beginning to show."

This statement seemed to please him for he smiled. "Well, it's time for you to wake. I have plans for us today."

Awkwardly, she cleared her throat. She'd hoped to stay home…to spend time with Vaughn.

"What kind of plans?" she asked warily. Was he not going to chastise her for yesterday?

He merely shook his head. "It is a surprise, my dear." And he remained steadfastly silent on the subject as he ordered her to get dressed in clothing appropriate for market day.

Accordingly, she called for Marianne and had her select a worsted wool traveling gown in dull brown, for the rain still fell in silent drips. She started to strip her bed gown off, then stopped, realizing Rufus was still there watching her intently.

She nodded toward the door, and with a slight smile, he left the room with a comment about seeing to the carriage.

When she was dressed, she made her way slowly downstairs, wrapping a shawl about her shoulders. She hoped that Vaughn might appear, but only Rufus stood impatiently in the foyer, awaiting her.

Reluctantly, she let him lead her to the carriage waiting in the drive.

The surprise was an extravagant shopping expedition in the nearby town of Gillian. The cobblestone streets were filled with men and women marketing their wares, and lined on both sides were stores with quaint storefronts that beckoned one to come inside. Elisa found it ironic that Rufus chose the most elaborate carriage he owned to visit such a township whose clientele most likely boasted farmers, smithies, and other artisans.

Rufus told the footman to stop at one such store, with a big window displaying bolts of cloth, draped artistically. "I've decided you need some new gowns," Rufus said in explanation as he motioned her into the store.

They were immediately greeted by the proprietress, a buxom woman with dark hair streaked with gray and an adoring smile. Although Elisa had never met her before, the woman seemed to know exactly who they were. Rufus introduced her to Elisa as Miss Johnson.

She was puzzled. Rufus told her if she was in need of gowns, he would simply call in Mrs. Roland Gadfrey, an elderly woman who worked only for a few select clients in the district. What were they doing in this retail establishment? Why had Rufus not sent for the proprietress to come to them?

She was ready to question Rufus, but decided not to. He was already sitting in a chair, his hands propped over his cane, waiting for Miss Johnson to begin.

Miss Johnson went into raptures over Elisa's tiny waist and perfect hourglass figure. "It is a pleasure working with such a perfect model," she assured her. She took a step back, her lips pursed together. "I have a gown that would suit Madam perfectly. The gracious lady who ordered it changed her mind regarding the color, which is understandable, as the lady in question is a brunette, and such a color would have been less than flattering." Miss Johnson smiled widely. "But for Madam, it is just the thing…"

As she chattered, Miss Johnson pulled away tissue paper from a box, and held up a deep purple day-dress, with white lace at the collar and sleeves, and shining gilt metal buttons on the bodice. The dress was spread across the counter for her inspection. The skirt was very full, obviously designed for many petticoats, and the hem was a rich, box-pleated ruffle with a tiny row of lace at the top and small ribbon roses at every six inches, in a pretty pale green.

Elisa felt her breath catch. It had been so long since she had seen any new fashions. She studied the details, tallying what had changed, what was new…and, oh, the dress was so pretty!

"It pleases, madam?"

"It pleases," Elisa murmured, reaching out to touch the dully, glowing fabric.

With a satisfied smile, Miss Johnson shepherded her off to a private room where she could try the dress on.

Two hours later Elisa walked out the door on the arm of her fiancée, wearing the purple gown. They had only had to take the waist in by two inches.

Elisa had chosen bolts of cloth and accessories to match, and discussed styling details for five more gowns, which Miss Johnson had promised delivery of by the end of the month.

Taking her seat opposite Rufus, Elisa smiled at him. "Thank you. The dresses are lovely."

"Nothing is too good for my princess," he replied, his smile warm, yet it did not seem to reach his eyes.

Uncomfortable with his stare, she turned toward the window. "It is a lovely little town. Why is it we have never visited before today?"

"I thought it was time to get away from the manor. Vaughn is putting me on edge. I only hope that he bores easily and will soon be gone." The words were sharp, and he watched her intently, as though gauging her reaction.

"What has he done to make you so uneasy?" she asked.

Rufus lifted a brow. "He seems to have taken a liking to you."

Elisa's stomach tightened and she managed what she hoped appeared to be an amused smile. "And you do not wish for your son to like me?"

"The boy can go to hell as far as I am concerned." There was no misinterpreting the violent hatred he felt toward Vaughn.

"Why do you dislike him so?" The question was pushed out of her in reaction to the naked hatred on his face. She realized it was the first time she had ever asked him such an intimate question.

Rufus' mouth turned down as if he had tasted sour milk. "His mother pampered the boy. I told her she would spoil him, and she did. Though he is full grown, I can still see her damned influence."

The words held so much venom, Elisa wondered if it was directed more at Vaughn or his mother.

"Perhaps you could try to get along?" she suggested.

"Perhaps he can leave." Rufus turned his head to look out the window, as if the conversation was of no interest to him.

Elisa shifted in her seat. "What if you were to mend your relationship?"

"There is nothing to mend. We've never had a relationship, and I have no intention of beginning one. I grow tired of this conversation, Elisa. I have indulged you enough on the subject." And he turned back to staring out the window, a tick jumping at the corner of his eye.

Elisa's heart ached for Vaughn. As a child, he must have yearned for this man's love and been utterly rejected. Without a mother, he would have been completely alone. Elisa understood what that sort of loneliness was like.

No wonder Vaughn's hatred for Rufus was so immense.

* * * * *

Vaughn stood at the parlor window, watching as the carriage carrying his father and Elisa rolled up the long drive. They had been gone for the majority of the day, and now with evening upon them, he would have only a few hours with Elisa.

The house had been like a tomb without her presence. Everything about it felt different, smelled different.

What would his father do if she were to go from this place forever?

Vaughn smiled to himself, envisioning the old man going slowly insane.

He let the curtain fall back into place and took a seat at the piano. His fingers lightly touched the keys in a lullaby his mother had taught him when he was three. He'd sat on her lap, watching her long, delicate fingers as they pressed the ebony and ivory. Her laughter had been light and airy, filling the vast room, making it feel smaller, warmer and comfortable.

The front door opened, then closed. Vaughn's fingers froze on the keys.

"Marianne," Rufus' voice vibrated through the thick door. "Your mistress has some items she wishes to be put away at once."

"Yes, my lord. Right away," Marianne said, the patter of her feet on the marble echoing as she ran to do his bidding.

Vaughn saw the fear in her eyes as she turned away, the same fear that was there whenever Rufus dealt with her directly. Because she was Elisa's maid, her contact with the man was minimal. However, in his short stay here Vaughn had noticed the majority of the servants lived in fear of the old man, all but scrambling to get out of his way. He had been too young to recognize it when he had lived here as a child.

Why would anyone in their right mind work for Rufus Wardell? Certainly there were other positions available in the district—even with a prominent family, one that would not abuse their servants.

"Joshua, get me a port," Rufus yelled. A moment later Vaughn heard his father begin his creaking ascent up the staircase. "I'll see you at dinner."

"Yes, of course," Elisa replied politely, from right outside the parlor door.

Vaughn smiled as he went to the door. He counted to ten, then opened the door to find Elisa standing five feet away, watching Rufus as he took the final step. Though he knew she saw him, she didn't look in his direction.

Until Rufus had rounded the corner.

"Come here," Vaughn said, holding his hand out to her.

She looked glorious, in a dark purple gown that in contrast made her eyes the dazzling blue of a hot summer sky. She looked at his outstretched hand as though he were a leper.

"What are you afraid of?"

The sides of her mouth lifted in a soft smile. "You."

He took a step forward, grabbed her wrist, and pulled her into the room. Closing the door behind them, he pressed her up against the hard wood. "I've thought of you all day. I wanted to spend the entire day at your side, but instead I've stood here looking out the window, watching and waiting for your return."

Her eyes searched his face, and he wished he knew exactly what she was thinking.

"Rufus believes that you like me."

"Then he would be right."

She took a deep breath and released it. "Vaughn, I can't keep doing this. He knows that something is happening between us. It's entirely wrong. We both know it."

He laughed under his breath, and she looked up, her brows furrowed into a frown. "What is so funny?"

"You are." He reached his hand behind her, and cupped her bottom through the layers of skirt and petticoat. He pulled her forward until her hips were against him. "I remember this being pressed against me, and the look in your eyes as you did it. I remember the delicious sound that emerged from you when I took your breast in my mouth."

He heard the tiny sigh she gave as his words prompted her own memory.

"You want more than that. You know it. So do I. Say it, Elisa. You want more."

She shook her head. "No."

He smiled, amused. "Yes, you do. Let me show you." He leaned down, more than happy for an excuse to kiss her. He put his hands on either side of her head, preventing her escape, and took her mouth with his.

Her lips were hot, moist, and sweet against his own. The full lips parted a little, and he took the tiny offering, plunging his tongue into her mouth. She was pliant against him, and as always, soft, delicate and womanly with a sweet scent and skin that seemed to melt at his touch.

How could Rufus ignore such a delectable pleasure sitting at his right elbow every night? If she were his wife he would never leave her alone. He would spend all his spare time exploring her delicate beauty.

He could feel the taut thrumming in his loins that bespoke a powerful need. He had deliberately held himself away from other sensual activities while pursuing Elisa. In fact, solitary and commercial acts paled to insignificance when he considered what he might be doing with Elisa. The desire throbbing within him combined with his deliberate abstinence made him all the more anxious to secure her surrender.

The need burned in him.

He pulled her away from the door, and into his arms, smothering her face with heavy kisses. "Tell me you want more," he said into her ear, watching the frantic beat of her heart echo in the pulse just below his lips.

She shook her head, mute.

Damn, but he would have her agreement on this! He reached down to flip up the hem of her dress, and slide a hand beneath all the petticoats. He ran his palm over silk stocking, then higher, to the edges of pantalets. He could feel the curve of her thigh underneath, then her round buttock. Experience guiding his hand, he reached around to the front of her waist, and tugged the drawstring loose.

"Vaughn," she whispered. "No…" But the protest was a sigh breathed into the air as his hand loosened the drawers and slid inside. He felt the flat plane of her stomach, and the rounded angle of her hipbone. He slid further down, feeling the light tangle of body hair beneath his palm and pressed against her mons, the fingers probing at her cleft.

She gasped hard. But she did not try to pull away from him.

He looked into her nearly closed eyes and saw hungry torment there. Slowly, he slipped his hand further down, around the delicate mound, and inside the folds of flesh. He worked his fingers deep into her cleft, feeling heated slickness. His heart was racing at this blatant sign of Elisa's responsiveness. He probed deeper, and muscles clenched around his fingers. Her flesh pulsed.

Eliza groaned, and her hand, gripping his shirt, clenched in a tight spasm. Her eyes shut.

He withdrew his hand enough to stroke her pearl and was rewarded with the parting of her mouth, and a trembling that wracked her entire body.

Vaughn heard harsh breathing, and realized it was he making that barely controlled sound. He was excited almost beyond endurance by simply pleasuring her.

Regretfully, he drew still.

Her eyes fluttered open a little.

"Tell me you want more," he murmured, his voice as rough as his breathing.

She swallowed, and a furrow appeared between her brows. "I want more," she said, her voice low. And she turned her head away, as if she was shamed for saying so.

The turning of her head took the glow from his victory.

Gently, he withdrew his hand, righted her garments, and stepped away.

She kept her head averted.

He spoke, his voice still betraying his own exorbitant response. "You cannot tell me 'more' one day, then tell me it is wrong the next, Elisa."

She lifted her chin a notch. Her eyes sparkled beneath dark lashes. "I am flattered that you find me…desirable, yet it is folly to keep doing this. Your father suspects something going on and he would be right. I have not behaved like a married woman should."

"You're not married, yet."

She frowned at him.

"He buys you a pretty dress, so now you're happy?"

She gasped, and a second later her palm hit his cheek.

The shock of it was more of a jolt than the actual strike.

"*How dare you,*" she said, her voice a bodiless, intense hiss.

She quickly left the room, not bothering to shut the door behind her.

* * * * *

As the clock struck quarter past eight, Elisa looked across the table at the empty chair. Vaughn was late, and of course Rufus had made no move to delay the meal and wait for him.

Since she and Rufus had spent the afternoon together, they had very little to talk about. Instead she made comments on the flower arrangement, and complimented the chef on his superb turtle soup. Thankfully, Rufus seemed to be more interested in his meal and claret than conversation. He tackled his plate with gusto when the main course was served, while she pushed the ham, potato, and carrots about on her plate.

She wondered where Vaughn was. Surely he had not left the manor? Her heart lurched at the thought. What if he'd returned to London?

Her fears were laid to rest a moment later when the double doors opened and Vaughn strode into the room, running his hand through his hair, and tousling it agreeably. "Sorry I am late. I received correspondence from London and found myself entranced with the gossip."

Elisa wondered if any of the correspondence had been from a female. She pushed back the jealousy that quickly rose to the surface. There was a whole other side to Vaughn she had almost forgotten. His life in London must be an exciting one, full of gossip, parties and glittering people.

What did he see in her that made him pursue her so ardently?

Or was it that she was at hand, while other genuine beauties were far away in old London town?

Vaughn sat down, just as the butler slid a full meal in front of him. "Oh, and I also received this invitation today." He pulled a cream-colored envelope with a broken seal out of his inner pocket and offered it to Elisa. "It was addressed to me, but the invitation is extended to you and father as well."

Rufus plucked the invitation from Elisa's hand. He read it, frowning over the script. Rufus' intellectual skills were not the strongest, but no one dared point out that weakness by offering to read his correspondence for him.

Elisa looked at Vaughn to see if he was offended by Rufus taking the invitation away from her, but Vaughn was eating, apparently unconcerned.

"Lady Munroe has invited us to a soiree," Rufus told her. "You'll have to write an acceptance on our behalf."

"I thought you disliked such events," Elisa replied. She forced a smile to remove any offense. "Surely she invited us because that is the polite thing to do. I am sure she only expects Vaughn to be there."

Rufus placed the invitation in his waistcoat pocket, as though it had been addressed to him and not Vaughn. He lifted a challenging brow. "Do I need to make the acceptance card out myself?"

It was obvious he had every intention of attending the soiree. Why was he suddenly so keen to go to a social event when he had previously told her he abhorred them? Suddenly, the explanation for their trip to the dressmakers today became clear. Rufus had known about the ball all along.

"Are you determined to go, Rufus?" she asked, fear biting at her belly. It had been so long since she had been to a dance or even something as simple as a card evening. And this was a ball.

"Have you not been listening to me?" His voice was low, soft, yet resolute.

She nodded, her throat to tight to respond.

He grasped his glass and gulped noisily.

A ball! One of the dresses she had ordered this morning could do as a ball gown. She frowned as she recalled that Rufus had encouraged her to choose the fabric, and dropped suggestions about using this or that accessory — always picking the more formal designs.

Yes, Rufus *had* known.

Elisa wet her lips, and glanced at Vaughn. He was frowning, staring at his plate. Then he could not guess what Rufus was scheming, either.

Elisa put her knife and fork down, her appetite so completely fled she could not even pretend an interest in the meal. She sipped her water, her mind racing.

What was Rufus planning?

Chapter Nine

The library was almost silent.

Elisa sat at the correspondence desk, struggling over a note of acceptance for Caroline. She hadn't accepted an invitation in years, and the formal phrasing did not come to her as easily as the words of regret and refusal to which she had grown accustomed.

Beside her, the fireplace crackled cheerily. She had asked it to be laid and lit for the evening had grown sharply chill—a reminder of the coming winter. Over the pop and crackle of the fire, Rufus' discordant snores sounded. He was sitting in the wing chair facing the fire, so Elisa could only see his profile, with the bulbous nose and the loose skin beneath his chin sagging as his mouth hung open.

They were alone. At dinner, Vaughn had produced a superior bottle of port he'd had imported at great cost from the Continent and newly arrived today—along with his correspondence, Elisa reminded herself. He had opened the bottle on the spot and insisted Rufus sample it. Rufus had indeed sampled it thoroughly. In fact, Elisa rather suspected he'd drunk most of the bottle, while Vaughn had merely sipped at his glassful.

Now Rufus sprawled in the wingchair, completely soused and mindless of the unmusical notes he was playing. Vaughn had gone about his own business.

Elisa returned her attention to the note, frowning over it. What was Rufus planning with this ball? He had forced her to accept for a reason, and despite endless speculation, she could find no suggestion of an answer.

She should ask Vaughn. He had a head for such intrigues.

Her frown deepened, as she recalled their last meeting. He had behaved unforgivably. To suggest her loyalty was bought with a pretty gown...

Suddenly, Elisa crumpled up the sheet of paper and threw it in the fire. Damn. Yet another mistake! Her hand did not want to write the words, and it showed in her unsteady penmanship.

Hands with long hot fingers touched her bare forearms, making her jump. It was Vaughn, leaning over her, his arms laying over hers. She could feel the heat of his body against her shoulders.

"Forgive me," he breathed into her ear. "I was a cad today."

"Vaughn, you startled me," she began. At the sound of her voice, Rufus stirred, his snores breaking rhythm. His lips smacked together.

"Shhhh..." Vaughn breathed again. "You'll wake him."

She licked her lips. "Vaughn, take your hands from me," she said, her voice low.

Rufus stirred again, snuffling, and for a horrible moment she thought his eyes opened. But he settled back again.

Elisa's heart was racing. Of course, she could turn and breathe her words into Vaughn's ear as he did with her, but she was not willing to encourage such intimacy.

She tried to pull her arms out from beneath Vaughn's hot hands, but dislodging them made them fall across her breasts. His hands molded themselves around her, and she drew in her breath sharply.

His mouth, hot and soft, kissed the nape of her neck, and she could hear his own hurried breath. He was laying a trail of moist kisses down the side of her throat onto her shoulders, bared by the evening gown. His hands lifted away from her breasts to her shoulders, and the edges of the gown slid to the ends of her shoulders.

"No chemise, no corset...I believe you are teasing me, Elisa."

She let the pen fall from her nerveless fingers, ceasing her attempt to write. Her eyes closed in delight as his hands pushed her sleeves down her arms. He did not bare her altogether as he had last time, but the gown sagged about her. She watched as Vaughn's hand slipped beneath the edges of the gown, and captured her breasts. Her eyes closed. His thumbs rubbed the already taut nipples, and the jolt of excitement that coursed through her and made her groan aloud.

Alarmed, she scrambled to her feet. She could not allow this! In the same room as her fiancé, for goodness sake. It was depraved. She was a whore for enjoying it.

"Vaughn, stop!" she told him, trying to turn to face him.

Rufus stopped snoring with a startled snort. He sat up a little, turning his head, questing. "What?" he asked, his voice slurred.

Elisa froze. If he turned his head much further, he would see his son and future wife standing together, his son's hands holding his fiancée's bare breasts.

She swallowed, fear looming large in her chest, squeezing her heart.

Rufus' head slowly sank back onto his chest, and his deep breathing told her he had returned to sleep.

"You mustn't speak," Vaughn whispered in her ear. "Not at all."

She began to tremble.

He removed his hands, and she felt him step away from her. From the corner of her eyes, she saw her chair being moved away from the desk.

He returned to her, pressing his long warm body against her. His hands were at the fastenings of her dress, and she felt the gown loosen even more, the sleeves sinking further down her arms.

Vaughn pushed them almost to her elbows. Her heart was scudding along frantically, driven by enormous fear...and excitement. She almost moaned aloud, for the danger was adding its own spice to what Vaughn was doing to her.

His hands caught at her breasts, toying with them, kneading the nipples, stroking them with long sweeping caresses until she was afire with the need for more.

His mouth bathed her ear with kisses, the tongue probing with a shocking, delightful thrust inside. His teeth bit gently at the lobe.

Elisa was almost panting, and she desperately clamped her jaws together lest a sound emerge that would alert Rufus. She was unable to protest, to tell Vaughn he must stop, but even the notion was melting away like snow under sun. His knowing assault was devastating.

He put her hands on the desk, silently coaxing her to prop herself on the desk top as his support was removed. She obeyed, her arms trembling.

His hands dropped to her ankle, bare above the ties of her slippers. With a slow sweeping movement, his hands smoothed their way along her calves, her thighs, her hips, gathering up the dress and petticoats as they climbed, baring her completely.

Her trembling intensified. She could feel cool air about her cleft, fanned by his movements.

His hands on her hips moved restlessly. He was but inches from her moist, throbbing sex. His fingers had stroked her there just that afternoon, and she ached for them to return to that place. Her hips thrust in anticipation, and she heard Vaughn's deep, almost silent groan in response.

His fingers slipped into her, and she bucked again, violently, and clamped her teeth against the cry that threatened to rip from her. Her up-thrusting breast was caught by his other hand. She could hear his breath in her ear, ragged, harsh with excitement as it had been this afternoon, and rejoiced in the ability she had to bring him to such a point.

His questing hands were withdrawn, and she almost whimpered at the deprivation, but he was pushing at her shoulders, bending her over the desk.

His hands ran over her hips and buttocks. She felt his mouth taste the flesh over the back of her hip, then move on to her buttocks, licking, sucking, and once, a gentle nip of the flesh. Endlessly fizzy waves of pleasure were circling through her, building the tension in her, making her throb and ache for fulfillment. Her whole body trembled.

His hands found that throbbing pearl of her sex, and stroked it, and she quivered with each knowing stroke.

She heard the whisper of cloth, the sound of releasing buttons, then the brush of a blunt, questing probe against her. Alarm threaded through her suddenly unbearable excitement. Surely, he did not intend to take her here? Now?

She could not protest if he did, and her body ached for him, in truth. As his hands caught at her hips, she closed her eyes, helpless to do anything but accept him into her, coherent thought sundered and beyond her.

But his hands on her hips were turning her, lifting her up, and turning her to face him. She went willingly, and found herself lying on the desk, her feet barely touching the ground.

As he gripped her thigh, lifting her leg aside to make room for him, she looked at him.

This was not the Vaughn she knew. There was nothing of the knowing, experienced seducer in his eyes. They were the wild eyes of a man pushed beyond endurance. The lids were half-closed, drugged with sensuality. His full lips were parted to allow his panting breath to emerge. And his hands trembled against her skin.

He was more driven than she.

He stepped between her thighs, and she could feel his rigid shaft against her, hot, thick and throbbing, twitching, and his hips were thrusting in little spurts and spasms.

He could be inside her in one simple thrust, yet he did not. Did he do it to torture them both?

He leaned over her, and his mouth took her breast, suckling, as his hand caressed the swollen flesh around the nipple he tortured. His hair brushed across her face and chest, and Elisa let her head fall back off the edge of the desk in exquisite agony.

Her surrender was complete, she knew. But he did not take it. He was toying with her, teasing her, driving her to a wild abandon she had never felt before. His lips and teeth and tongue were goading her. And his hand slipped into her hot, throbbing cleft and stroked and caressed the nub.

She could not help it—her legs wound around his waist, and pulled him to her. The invitation was explicit. She saw him close his eyes, and expel a harsh breath. He became still.

His hand fell away from her breast, and formed a tight, convulsive fist, which he pummeled gently against the desktop. Then he straightened, pulling away from her. His trembling hands gripped her thighs, and encouraged her to release him. He refastened his clothing with unsteady movements, his chest rising and falling rapidly, as she watched with a growing sense of disappointment. Even though she had not wanted him to take her here and now, he had been so close to that first delightful thrust inside her that she ached from the lack of it

He leaned over her one last time, and lifted her to her feet. She stood, shaking, as he refastened her dress. He lowered his head to whisper to her. "Soon, Elisa. Soon. But I would have us find our own moment—not steal it from someone else."

And he straightened and nodded towards Rufus. Then, he lifted his hand, brushed a curl from her face, and smiled a little. It was an attempt to show that devil-may-care attitude was in control, but she knew it was a lie.

He left her the same way he had found her. In silence.

Elisa pulled her chair back to the desk with arms that had no strength, and lowered herself into it, to stare at the scattered paper.

She had no wits left with which to write a dry formal acceptance letter.

She looked over at Rufus, soundly asleep, then buried her face in her hands. She had completely given herself to Vaughn, and had been rejected.

She could still save herself. It wasn't too late. Not yet.

But, oh, it had been so very, very close!

* * * * *

Outside the library, Vaughn propped himself up against the wall, letting his body recover and the trembling subside. He ran a hand through his hair, and was sourly amused to realize it still shook as badly as it did moments before, when she had lain open to him, willing, driving him beyond sense.

He tried to grasp what had taken place in there.

What was happening to him? He had intended only to kiss her, to keep her on her toes, to let her know he desired her. Instead it had escalated to a point where he had nearly lost all control.

No, the truth was, he *had* lost control. He had bent her over the desk, and nearly...*very nearly* taken her right there and then. He had been driven beyond sense, to a point where all he could focus on was the desperate need to have her. Now. This moment.

Somehow he had clawed himself back from that abyss. And that was the strange part. He wanted her when he was in full control, not when he was this mad creature driven by sense alone.

So he had turned her to face him, and still could not let her go. He had been compelled to pleasure her, to watch her body tighten and thrill to his touch, and her limbs and eyes melt in response. Her sweet, sweet flesh had driven him on.

And what of Kirkaldy? While the needs of flesh had tormented him, he had not spared a thought for his inheritance. When had Kirkaldy slipped from his mind? When had he lost sight of his reason for being here?

He had to hold it together.

But how could he when even now his body was tight and pulsing with the need to have her? She was in there, behind the wall he leaned against, and the door was three steps away.

He could walk back in there, and she would be his.

He had to have her.

He held his arm out, palm flat against the wall, reaching towards the door, feeling his control slip a little more.

Dear god, but she was casting a spell over him he'd never felt the like of before.

He closed his eyes and let his head fall back against the wall. Women he'd known aplenty. Their ways were no longer mysterious, but Elisa...

His body ached to plunge into her, to taste her, to have her whole and complete, to watch her pleasure build and know it was him giving her that pleasure.

He gritted his teeth together and growled, trying to drive out the frustration.

He should stay away. Go away. Go back to London, to the parties, the women, the gambling...

He pushed himself from the wall with a compulsive shove and strode down the passageway, intending to find the brandy decanter in the dining room. As he walked he smashed his fist into his other hand, because he knew he would not be able to stay away from her at all.

Chapter Ten

Having spent the majority of the morning pacing the confines of her room, Elisa knew she could no longer keep from going downstairs. If she did not emerge from her room in the next little while, questions would be asked.

With a hand on the doorknob she took a steadying breath. She told herself she could face Vaughn and act as though nothing had happened last night. She could forget the way his hard body had pressed against her, the feel of his lips against her flesh, the promise in his touch. How close they'd come to making love...and in the same room as Rufus...

What would have happened had Rufus woken? An image of him shooting the horse point-blank flashed before her. She knew he would not hesitate to do the same to her — and Vaughn. The certainty had driven her to acquire a hunting knife from the head stableman, lying about the need for adequate protection when out riding. The knife now rested under her pillows, where it would be close at hand should she ever need it.

Nodding at the servants she passed, Elisa made her way down the stairs.

"Elisa, is that you?"

She jumped as Rufus' voice reached her from the drawing room. He was up early for once, and now she must face him. Folding her trembling hands before her, she walked into the room and forced a smile.

Rufus sat in the Queen Anne chair he always favored when he took time for a libation. A tall glass was filled with his favorite port. He brought it to his lips, all the while watching her over the rim.

It was not yet noon and already he was drinking. It was not a good sign.

He motioned to a nearby chair with his free hand. "Come and sit with me."

Taking a seat on the settee, she folded her hands in her lap and forced a smile.

His gaze shifted to the low bodice of her gown. It was one of the styles he had picked out, and a triumphant gleam came into his eye. "I apologize for falling asleep so early last evening," he said. "I wanted us to spend the night together."

Elisa sat up straighter, wondering if she'd heard right. She had no wish to become intimate with him now. "I was tired as well last night. I haven't been feeling well lately," she remarked, while brushing imaginary lint from her skirts.

"Not feeling well? You were well enough to go riding the other day."

She heard the accusation in his voice and shifted in her seat.

His brows furrowed into a frown. "Well…what ails you?"

An insane urge to giggle came upon her. What ailed her? If only she could answer truthfully — *your son!*

Last night, she had surrendered utterly and completely. Only some whim of Vaughn's had saved her from physically betraying her future husband. In her heart she was already guilty, but if she could somehow retreat from this position, then she might still save herself.

In the tiny moment while Rufus sipped his port, awaiting her answer, she recalled the reason why she must not give in to Vaughn: her son Raymond. This man sitting in front of her had given her the only hope of ever having Raymond back in her life. He'd been paying independent investigators to search for her son.

If she were to cuckold him then Raymond would be utterly lost to her. She could not give in. It was as simple as that.

On the odd occasion where he was agreeable enough to share details on the progress the agents were making, he would explain they were working tirelessly, but the family who originally received the caring of the boy had passed him on, and the trail was quite cold and difficult to follow. However, he would assure her with a pat to her knee, the agents he employed had excellent reputations, and he would say, "Be patient, dear."

And so she had continued to be patient.

She studied Rufus now. Was he in the frame of mind to indulge her yet again on the subject? His mention of sharing the night with her and the marketing expedition yesterday boded well, for they hinted that some of his good humor might be returning. When Rufus had first come into her life she had thought he held a genuine fondness for her, hidden deep where no one could spot his weakness. Since Vaughn had arrived, that doting manner had completely disappeared.

...since Vaughn had arrived.

Elisa felt her chest tighten with a rush of fear mixed with astonishment, as she considered this aspect of matters at Farleigh Hall. The shooting of the horse, the snarling belligerence; it was almost like a dog barring its teeth. Scaring off competitors.

Guarding its bone.

Had she underestimated the degree of feeling Rufus held for her? His courtship had been as rough as his manners, but even though he had not arrived bearing baubles and flowers, he had brought with him a greater gift that won him her hand: the promise to find Raymond.

She cleared her throat. "What ails me is the absence of my son. I...miss Raymond. I desperately want to see my little boy again."

He looked surprised, and put his drink down on a nearby table and sat back in the chair, his paunch stressing the buttons on his waistcoat. "I have men working on it as we speak. You know that if I heard anything, I would tell you."

Tears welled in Elisa's eyes. Her whole world seemed hopeless at the moment. The only thing that would set it right would be Raymond. His presence would save her from depravity, she knew.

"If you could only give me a little more encouragement," she murmured, looking down at her lap. "I would feel better…stronger, if only I knew it would not be much longer to wait."

It was as close as she dared come to speaking the truth aloud. If he could show her a possible end to the waiting, then she would find the strength to hold out against Vaughn's enticing ways.

Rufus' eyes narrowed, and a shrewd gleam came into them. "Is that so?" he remarked casually.

Her heart beat a little harder. Had he guessed her thoughts?

"If it will make you happy, I will visit with my London solicitor. The agents report to him, and in truth, it has been a week or so since I inquired as to their progress. I will get a new report for you. How would that be?"

It was said with the casualness of a man discussing a report on fatted calves for market. But he had made the offer. It was a victory of sorts.

"I appreciate anything you can do," she told him truthfully. "I feel such a void without him."

Rufus flinched as though struck. "Do you doubt I could give you a good life?"

"That was not my meaning," she replied, digging her nails into her palms. "I am his mother, and I need him, just as I'm certain he needs me."

"We will see what we can do." Rufus lifted the bell and rang it, signaling the end of the discussion.

Joshua stepped inside the room a moment later. "The carriage is ready, my lord."

"You are going somewhere?" Elisa asked, keeping the hope from her voice.

Rufus stood and with a smile, replied, "We're going to the Munroe's soiree." His tone indicated that he was stating the obvious.

Elisa's heart pounded. "But...that isn't until tomorrow evening."

"We were invited to stay the night, remember?"

Elisa flinched at the tone of his voice. Of course she could not remember. She'd not had a chance to read the invitation before Rufus had all but snatched it out of her hand.

Rufus extended his arm. "Come, my dear. We don't want to keep them waiting."

It was too soon. She wasn't prepared.

"My clothes...a gown..."

"All packed, my dear. I had Marianne see to it yesterday. The ball gown was delivered early this morning, just in time."

Her heart began to beat hard, and fear touched her. She had felt all along that Rufus was planning something. Now her guess was confirmed, but she still did not know *what* he planned.

She touched the low bodice of her gown. "I must change first," she began. Although the gown was not particularly revealing, for her first public appearance in many years, she knew she must be the absolute model of propriety.

"No, there is no time," Rufus told her. "What is it, woman? Do you seek to make us arrive late? I won't have you make a fool of me, you know."

She swallowed. "Yes, Rufus." She took his offered arm, and let him lead her out to the carriage.

Where was Vaughn? She could not help but wish he was here in the carriage with her, for she knew he would stand between her and whatever the consequences of Rufus' scheming.

* * * * *

That night was torturous.

To begin her woes, she and Rufus were placed in connecting chambers, as though they were already husband and wife. She wished he were not so close.

One other couple had arrived that night beside themselves, and it appeared no more were expected. Elisa hid her dismay when this fact was made clear to her by the number of places at the dining table. It meant Vaughn would not be nearby — she would have to deal with Rufus and his schemes all by herself.

In addition, the couple who had arrived just that afternoon were the Duke and Duchess of Wessex. The Duchess was Lady Cynthia Crowley, and until her marriage she had lived in the same county as Elisa's family.

Elisa recognized the redheaded woman with a sinking heart. There was little chance Cynthia did not know about Elisa's tarnished past. Elisa's own family had disowned her after her husband's death and would have taken great pains to let the district know they had no association with her erring ways.

Cynthia Crowley nodded her head when the introductions were made, her face neutral. But then she started and stared at Elisa with a measuring eye.

The Duke had been delightful. He had obviously married late in life, for he was much older than his wife, quite silver-haired and with a dashing monocle. He treated Elisa with an old-fashioned courtliness that took the edge off Cynthia's disdain.

But partway through the pre-dinner drinks, Elisa saw the duchess lean towards her husband and whisper behind her fan. The Duke's monocle dropped and he fumbled to return it to his eye as he tried to examine Elisa without appearing to stare.

Elisa's heart sank slowly lower and lower as throughout the meal the Duke and duchess snubbed her repeatedly — failing to hear her requests for condiments to be passed to her, and when their gaze wandered around the room, they would pass over her like she was not there.

Elisa sat wringing her napkin under the table, fighting tears. Because their station in life was higher than Elisa's, it was her place to leave the room and the party, as they had made it clear she was not welcome there. But she could not leave unless Rufus made their excuses, and he seemed to be completely oblivious to the unspoken disapproval settling around the table.

Caroline appeared to feel the tension, but as she had no idea about Elisa's past, she could not possibly understand its source. She tried to lighten the atmosphere with gay chatter, with her husband William supporting her.

Rufus was not a conversationalist at all. He ate hungrily and steadily, with a positively cheerful air. If Elisa had been calmer, she would have said he was enjoying her discomfort. But that notion was a product of her upset.

She was never more grateful for a meal to come to an end as she was when William stood, proposing brandy and cigars in the library for the gentlemen, and the Duke agreed with alacrity.

That was the moment Elisa had excused herself and went immediately to her room.

She lay tossing and turning in her strange and uncomfortable bed, reacquainting herself over and over again with the fact of her blighted past. It was not going to go away. Time would not obliterate her reputation, however false it was. She could only hope upon the morrow that she could find the company of guests who were ignorant of the rumors—people who saw beyond the whispers and the falsehoods.

Abruptly, she yearned for Vaughn's company.

She curled up in the bed, hugging herself, wishing mightily he would appear suddenly, and take her in his arms. He would provide the comfort she longed for...

She must remember Raymond. The comfort she wished to convince herself she would find in Vaughn was a momentary one only. The consequences of giving in to him were not worth the price, no matter how much she craved the luxury.

She had to go through this alone.

A solitary, bitter tear splattered her starched pillow.

* * * * *

Her wish that she could meld into a number of guests and effectively disappear from general notice was a fool's hope, as she quickly discovered the next day.

Elisa sat at a table with five other women of varying ages, sipping tea, playing cards, and trying to pretend they were not snubbing her. Caroline was too caught up playing hostess to give her any mind, and Natasha kept watching the door, no doubt hoping to catch Vaughn the moment he walked into the manor.

How Elisa wished she could allow herself the same distraction!

As Natasha's attention was called back to her hand yet again, Caroline smiled indulgently.

"Natasha can hardly wait to visit her aunt in London. We're hoping Lord Vaughn will be gracious enough to escort her."

All eyes turned to Elisa. Obviously they waited for her to express her enthusiasm at the idea.

She swallowed.

Natasha was watching her without blinking, her expression hopeful.

"Vaughn is his own man, I am afraid. He does not share his agenda with me."

Natasha's shoulders slumped and Caroline's smile tightened.

Elisa couldn't imagine Caroline being so desperate as to hand her unmarried daughter over to a young man for a five-hour ride to London without a chaperone. Obviously Natasha's father planned on being in London to meet them...with a shotgun.

"Speak of the devil," Lady Frederickson said in an undertone, motioning toward the door.

"Vaughn, come in, my dear." Caroline all but purred.

Elisa's pulse jumped and she sat up straighter, resisting the need to turn toward the door. She was morbidly aware of being monitored by the woman — were they watching her for any signs of a breakout of her rumored whorish ways? Perhaps they were afraid her evil influence would rub off on them. She had to appear totally disinterested in Vaughn.

She was mildly amused at the way most of the other women preened at his arrival.

"Good morning, ladies," Vaughn said from the door. "Lady Winridge, you must surely have arranged this collection of beauties to satisfy my eye."

There was subtle straightening of shoulders, unconscious patting at hair. The more timid of the women grew rosy cheeked and flustered. The card game came to a complete halt.

Vaughn stepped into Elisa's range of vision. Her heart fluttered at his appearance. His dark morning suit outlined the broad shoulders and emphasized his trim hips. His hair was pulled back in a queue, and his green eyes danced with devilment. He commanded attention — his stature, and his attitude, the way he seemed to prowl about the room, intent on mischief.

All of the woman, married or not, were responding to his overtly sensual smile, brooding eyes and experienced air. It took effort to remember how young he really was, for he seemed to ooze confident charm befitting a far older man.

A cat amongst pigeons, indeed.

And it is me he wants. The sinfully proud thought made her heart race, and something low in her belly turn slowly over, sending a warm wave of longing through her. For a brief moment, the women's snubs and the exclusion she had experienced that morning mattered not a damn.

Until Natasha stood and went to him, a radiant smile on her face.

Elisa's warm feelings congealed, and she looked at her lap, heedless of what they might think of such a telling action.

"I would not want to interrupt your card game, Natasha. Ladies, please forgive me the intrusion," he said.

The ladies in the group laughed and smiled, instantly forgiving him. He came closer, his footsteps sounding heavy to Elisa. Reaching for her cup with a trembling hand, she took a sip and set it back down before turning her attention to the only man in the room.

Vaughn looked right at her, his smile wide and inviting. "I am pleased to see you and Father made it, Elisa. Did you sleep well?"

He took the seat beside her, not breaking eye contact for a second.

Elisa could feel the women avidly soaking up this spectacle, storing away the details to bring out and discuss at length at a later time—perhaps to live again the thrill of observing a scandalous woman in action.

She swallowed and forced a polite, completely emotionless smile. She knew Vaughn was careless about his own reputation, but he had less to prove than she.

"Yes, I slept well. And you?" Her voice broke and she shifted in her seat, ignoring how the side of his mouth lifted just the slightest bit.

"Very well, thank you," he replied. He turned to Caroline. "Your home is very comfortable, Lady Munroe."

Elisa's heart turned to ice. Vaughn had been here last evening? Where? Why had she not seen him? And...Natasha had not been at the dinner table.

She recalled the radiant smile on Natasha's face a moment ago, when she had approached Vaughn.

A hot sickness washed through her, making her head spin and flood with a coppery taste she thought might be the flavor of disgust. She almost moaned with it. Had Vaughn been with Natasha last night? Had he found Elisa's unwillingness to accommodate his desire finally too much for his impetuousness and moved on?

"I'm glad you're pleased with your room," Caroline was rattling on. "Natasha made sure everything was perfect in your quarters." She beamed as she squeezed her daughter's hand. "Natasha wanted you to have a view of the hillside."

The woman were gobbling up this intimate little setting. A romance in their midst. They would dine on the details for a month.

"The heather is in bloom and ever so fragrant," Natasha blurted, her hands folded together. The picture of complete innocence.

Vaughn finally shifted his attention to the young woman who sat on the very edge of her seat. "Thank you, sweet Natasha, for seeing to my needs so thoughtfully."

Sighs filled the room.

Vaughn sat forward, poured himself a cup of tea and sat back.

Elisa was more than aware of the bare inches that separated them. Every eye was on him, and she wondered if they thought his behavior odd. Did they wonder why he sat by her, his soon-to-be stepmother, when there was a spot beside Natasha, and another across the room by Lady Farrow? Or was she just being paranoid?

He finished the drink in a few swallows, set the cup down and turned to Elisa. "Would you like to take a stroll in the gardens with me?"

Horror swept through her. Surely he would not insist she make such a spectacle of herself…?

He didn't give her time to respond. Instead, he stood, then pulled her to her feet. He turned and bowed to the other ladies.

"Elisa has the most beautiful garden, does she not, Lady Munroe?" He turned to Caroline, who merely nodded, her disappointment obvious as she sat her cup down noisily.

"Lady Munroe has some roses the most wonderful shade of purple that I really must show Elisa. Please excuse us, ladies."

Elisa could have melted into the ground right there and then, for rather than offering her his arm as a proper gentleman would, he kept her hand captive in his big, warm one. She did not dare look to confirm the women were all watching and remembering the shocking fact.

Elisa waited until they were outside the manor to pull her hand from his.

"Vaughn, for goodness sake…have you no decency, no sense of discrimination? Are you trying to ruin me?"

He looked completely innocent. "What do you mean?"

"You interrupt our game, then you proceed to sit by me amongst those women who scarce acknowledge me, then ask me to take a walk. Holding my hand! Do you know that mere moments before you arrived they were talking about you escorting Natasha to London? I have little doubt what they must be thinking now."

His air of innocence fell away. She saw his jaw ripple, as if he had clenched his teeth, and his brow furrowed. "And what are they thinking, Elisa? That I wanted to take time to be with my future stepmother. They would object to such a simple entertainment as inspecting Lady Munroe's ailing roses?"

The tone of his voice made her feel very small and self-absorbed. Perhaps she was being somewhat obsessive. She closed her eyes and took a deep breath. When she once again opened them, he had taken a step closer.

"I missed you yesterday." His voice was low.

And I you. Elisa held back the response. His nearness, his size, the way he made her feel very small were provoking her memories of the previous evening. She glanced at the thick lock of hair that had escaped from the queue. That silky lock had been caressing her flesh as his mouth roamed her body…

A shiver wracked her, sending her arms into goose bumps, even as her body tightened in response to the images.

Remember Raymond.

She did her best to look him in the eye and give nothing of her feelings away. "Vaughn, you must cease this pursuit. Especially here, amongst so many people. Rufus already knows you have less than honorable intentions—all he needs is evidence to call you out. And here, in this place...here..." She couldn't give voice to the wretchedness she had been suffering, and how much worse it would be if anyone even suspected their relationship was not what it seemed.

Vaughn's eyes narrowed. "Elisa, hush," he said gently.

Nervously she moistened her dry lips.

"This is something you have not come to understand about me yet, sweet Elisa. I have been playing these games with these people and others of their ilk since childhood. It is as second nature to me as riding a horse. I know exactly how much I can dare under their noses and walk away with my reputation unscathed. I know to the inch. You must trust me in this."

She looked down at her toes.

"Elisa, look at me," he said, his voice low. "I cannot lift your chin for myself when every biddy in that conservatory is probably glued to the window, watching us."

His insight made her smile a little, and she looked up at him as requested.

There was not a hint of amusement on his face, however. "Understand this, my precious beauty. I would sooner shoot myself through the heart than risk you or your reputation. And I will take on any man who does."

"Then you must take on the world."

"Willingly," he answered without hesitation. And he did not smile.

Her heart seemed to freeze for a tiny, shocked moment. She stared at him, unable to assemble a suitable response into words.

Then, finally, he smiled. "Come, we should start walking, or run the risk of shocking our audience."

Elisa knew he was right. The conservatory jutted out into the garden, and gave an all-round view of every path and bed. If they lingered too long in one spot or showed too much interest in each other and not enough for the beds and borders, it would be noted.

They had just stepped onto the cobblestone path when Natasha walked out onto the terrace with Elisa's shawl draped over her arm.

"How convenient," Elisa said under her breath.

Vaughn hissed under his breath. "No doubt her mother felt you would need your shawl...since it is the warmest day of the season."

They both laughed and met Natasha with a smile. The younger woman's cheeks were stained a bright pink. "Madam, my mother thought you would need this."

How Elisa hated hearing the word *madam* from one so young. It made her feel ancient. She took the shawl and wrapped it around her shoulders, despite the fact she was not in the least cold. Natasha curtsied, then turned back toward the manor.

"Why don't you be our guide?" Elisa suggested with a smile, ignoring the sidelong glance Vaughn threw her. "That is if you don't mind..."

"I would love to!" Natasha exclaimed, with a glowing smile. The girl really was beautiful, Elisa thought with honest acknowledgement. Her skin was flawless, her features almost angelic. Truly, she and Vaughn were perfect for each other. They were equals in every way. Both young, both the offspring of the aristocracy, and both with a physical beauty that bordered on breathtaking.

For the next quarter of an hour Elisa walked quietly beside Natasha as the young woman pointed to each plant and rattled off the Latin nomenclature as though she were reciting it from a book. Vaughn didn't say a word, but Elisa could feel him watching her, could feel his impatience with every restless step he took.

"Is this not the most beautiful color?" Natasha asked, picking the best of the infamous purple roses. She handed it to Elisa. "For you. Perhaps you could keep it in remembrance of this day." Natasha looked coyly at Vaughn.

Elisa couldn't stand to be in their presence any longer.

"Thank you, dear." She pretended to stifle a yawn. "I do believe I'll take a nap before tonight's festivities," she said, pulling the shawl tighter about her shoulders. She turned back toward the house.

"I can walk you," Vaughn said quickly.

She shook her head. Those green eyes framed by long, dark lashes were dark with an emotion she knew well.

"That's not necessary. You should stay with Natasha. I will see you both tonight."

It was a way of telling him that whatever had happened between them would have to stay in the past. She had no place in his life. She, with her tarnished reputation, would be the ruin of him. Even if he truly wanted to, he could not take on the world for her sake. She would return to Farleigh hall, marry Rufus, and wait for the one comfort left in her life: her son.

But first she must get through this evening.

As she settled into the chaise lounge to pass the afternoon away, waiting out her incarceration in this unfriendly place, she convinced herself the worst was over. Vaughn's confidence assured her she had been making far too much of the little glances she had caught, and she must have imagined the jibes and snubs of the morning. And her determination to keep Vaughn at arm's length gave her a sense of righteousness.

She knew she could hold her head up amongst the guests at the ball with pride for she had chosen the virtuous course.

She had completely forgotten about the Duchess of Wessex…

Chapter Eleven

Vaughn barely heard, above the orchestra and the chatter, the grandfather clock at the bottom of the stairs strike ten o'clock. He hid his impatience by swallowing another mouthful of the lukewarm champagne. Where was she?

Since leaving Natasha and he in the garden, Elisa had not shown her face. Not at dinner, nor after in the parlor. Rufus had arrived promptly at seven, his voice rising above the others at the dinner table, but he made no apology for Elisa's absence. Vaughn wondered if he had even noticed. He certainly didn't appear to be perturbed by it.

Since arriving, Rufus had not attempted to speak to Vaughn.

Damn him to hell, Vaughn thought viciously. Then he mentally sighed. Why did he let it bother him so? The old man cared so little for him nothing he did seemed to have any impact at all, so why bother? It was a lost cause. Rufus was impervious.

Except when it came to Elisa.

That single exception truly puzzled Vaughn. He showed her less consideration than he did his port bottle, and Vaughn was quite sure Rufus had never shown her any of the gentler emotions at all.

Was it simply that Rufus did not like the idea of anyone having Elisa if he could not? Was it that simple?

Or did he genuinely, secretly, care for her?

Annoyed that he was spending time thinking about a man who would sneer if he knew, Vaughn nodded toward a footman with a tray laden with glasses of whiskey. He exchanged his champagne glass for a tumbler of golden liquid.

"You had best slow down, boy, or you'll be calling it a night before long."

Vaughn turned to find Lord William Munroe at his side. The older man smiled easily and patted Vaughn on the back. "You're not dancing tonight."

"I will before the night is through. "

"My daughter will look forward to it."

Vaughn suppressed another sigh. Innuendos had been flying since he arrived, and he knew by the end of the night all expected him to be formally courting Natasha. Perhaps that was why Munroe had searched him out—to give him a chance to make his case. He was being polite, however, and standing and watching the couples dancing a reel, leaving Vaughn to his thoughts.

Vaughn had been prepared to do whatever it took to stay at Fairleigh Hall, but did that mean he should submit to the pressure being exerted, and formally court Natasha? His life had began to unravel a little since arriving here. He had come to claim Kirkaldy and instead found himself waylaid by a blonde beauty with troubled eyes. It would not be the first time he had been arrested by a pretty face, but if Elisa's resistance had crumbled as most ladies' resistances did when he applied himself, then it would simply have been a slight delay before returning to his original mission: Kirkaldy.

That ambition seemed far distant to him right now. For Elisa *had* resisted him, with far greater determination and doggedness than he had anticipated. And…he had not expected mad desires of his own to complicate the matter. It had become truly a personal challenge now.

How badly did he want to win Elisa? Enough to be a hypocrite and court Natasha? He feared that was what he must do to justify staying on at Fairleigh Hall.

He thought of Elisa, bent over the desk, her flesh golden in the firelight as he had tasted and teased her. Her responses, so uninhibited, told him she could be an equal playmate. Imagining the potential scenarios that might spring from that partnership made his body tighten, and his heart to speed up.

Who was he fooling? Elisa was worth any effort, any cost. He was involved now, and incapable of disengaging until he had taken his sweet prize.

So be it.

But he could not quite bring himself to begin the conversation with his host that would formalize a courtship with Natasha.

Then Elisa arrived and scattered all his thoughts to the wind.

If he'd not known better, he'd have guessed she had hidden herself away all day, and timed her arrival at the ball just to plague him. But Elisa was incapable of that sort of teasing.

Nevertheless, her entrance did not go unnoticed.

She paused at the top of the stairs. Vaughn was quite sure she paused to calm her nerves before entering into the fray amongst the many women here tonight who wore their claws behind perfect manners and polite smiles. But to the world it would seem she had paused for effect.

The effect was worth it.

She was dressed in cream-colored silk. In the candlelight, the silk took on a bright burnish. With her golden curls and flawless skin, she glowed like the sun. Her hair was piled in sophisticated curls on top of her head, but small curlicues were escaping, giving her face an innocent expression.

Not so her gown. The style was shockingly daring in a season when women seemed to be competing with each other to be more conservative than the next. Her shoulders were completely bare—the sleeves of the gown began further down her arms to blossom into the very full style that was popular right now. The neckline swooped, revealing the tops of her creamy breasts, and nestled between them was a diamond pendant.

Vaughn took a deep breath, controlling the desire that raged through him. It was a wonder every man in the hall didn't trip over himself for looking at her. His own hands itched to slide around her tiny waist and pull her to him, to crush her with a kiss that left her panting and her lips swollen.

She walked slowly down the stairs, and Vaughn found himself following her as she made her way across the hall to the ballroom doors.

Inside, she looked around and found Rufus, who sat in a high-backed chair. There was a seat beside him and she took it, folding her hands in her lap. He could sense her nervousness had increased. Her color was a little pale, her shoulders tense.

And he knew why.

Rufus kept her closeted up in the manor, keeping her away from the society that had turned its back on her, and this was the first time she had ventured out among those people since her husband's death.

"She's a vision, is she not?"

Vaughn had forgotten for an instant that Natasha's father had been standing beside him. He must have followed Vaughn across the room. He turned with a smile. "Yes, my father is a very fortunate man."

"I've always liked Elisa. She has a good heart. Too bad about her past, though, hmmm?"

Vaughn knew full well William had had more than one affair in his younger years. He had obviously been forgiven his excesses, yet he was not willing to offer the same forgiveness to a woman.

"She did nothing that deserves a lifetime of banishment," Vaughn answered, and was annoyed with himself for rising to the bait. What would come next? Would he find himself championing Elisa, just as he had teased her he would this morning?

William's brows furrowed into a frown. "She caused her husband's death."

Then Vaughn understood. It was all right for a man to indulge in wild ways and excesses, even to the point of being called out. Eventually, after a few years of discreet behavior, he would be forgiven his sins, and it would all be wiped off as a younger man's adventures. But a woman would never be forgiven such transgressions. In the eyes of the world it was Elisa's fault her husband had died.

"That is utterly ludicrous," Vaughn responded, stung to it by the unfairness of the man's prejudice. "Her husband was in dalliance with the wife of the Minister of Defense, and he had to save face. Was the Minister supposed to ignore the cuckolding?"

William raised an eyebrow. "I did not mean to offend you. Please accept my apology."

Unfortunately, the apology came too late. Vaughn's anger was reaching a fever pitch. "Why is it that Elisa should suffer a lifetime for her husband's inability to keep her happy? Has she not paid by suffering through humiliation of losing her husband because of an illicit affair?"

William was silent for a long moment. "You sound very passionate about it," he finally remarked. "Which I can only attribute to the fact that you accept her as a good mate for your father."

Vaughn took Williams' words as a warning—he must not appear too interested in Elisa. The man suspected something, and if he suspected, then no doubt many others did as well.

He shrugged. "Naturally, I have a peripheral concern for the woman. What if it were Natasha it had happened to?"

William's expression hardened immediately. "My daughter would never be so scandalous."

"What if her husband turned out to be a letch? What if she tried to make him happy, doing anything and everything to please him, even taking on some of his addictions, hoping to win his favor, but to no avail?"

William turned a bright, furious red and began to sputter.

"Hello, Father. I hope I am not interrupting…?"

William's smile recovered as he looked at his daughter. "Why, Natasha, my dear. We were just talking about you."

She dimpled prettily. "That explains why I could not catch Vaughn's eye from across the room. He was listening to you boasting about me, Daddy."

Vaughn clenched his jaw to hide his irritation. Then he remembered he had a role to play. He extended his hand toward Natasha.

"Would you care to dance?"

Her answering smile was dazzling, and as she put her gloved hand into his, she shot her father a triumphant look.

As they gained the dance floor, the music changed from a quadrille to a waltz. Vaughn took Natasha in his arms. He was a little surprised when she tried to press against him and locked his arms against the provocative move.

"I thought you would never dance this evening," Natasha said, looking up at him with wide eyes, her ringlets swinging.

"I didn't have the opportunity to ask you before," he said, feeling like a cad for lying. "Besides, I wanted all the other men to have a chance to dance with you before I monopolized your time."

Her answering smile was luminous, and Vaughn found himself smiling in response. Natasha was surprisingly vain at times—she preferred she, and only she, be the focus of the conversation. It made his chore easier. He would have been taxed far more if he'd had to spend his time talking about himself.

He glanced towards Elisa.

She was watching him. Rufus was in conversation with a group of gentlemen to his left, while she sat unattended and silent in the same seat, clearly forgotten.

Vaughn's fury grew. He looked away for a moment, scouring the crowd. There was a group of women nearby, including Caroline Munroe. The hostess was fanning herself vigorously, her head bent as she spoke amongst the women, who watched Elisa with varying degrees of distaste. Amongst them was the scornful redhead, the Duchess of Wessex.

Vaughn spun Natasha in a circle and looked back to Elisa. She had seen the direction of his gaze, then, for she looked to the woman, then back at him.

For a fraction of a moment, Elisa's polite mask slipped. Vaughn saw bewilderment, hurt and a deep unhappiness pass across her face. She dropped her chin to stare at her hands folded demurely in her lap to hide it.

Bitter, black fury swamped him. He wanted to stalk over to the women bunched about the fireplace and scatter them like a wolf amongst chickens, give them a fright they'd not soon forget.

Every man here who looked down his nose at her — Vaughn wanted to take each one by the scruff of the neck and shake them until they saw sense.

He wanted to do something, anything, to take away that hurt, haunted look in her eyes.

And he could do nothing.

Nothing.

He was forced to dance with the girl in his arms. He must pretend he cared as little as the rest of them lest his interest in Elisa be revealed, and put her in far greater jeopardy.

His helplessness ate at his gut. For the first time in his life he railed at the unbending forces of a society in which he had always found such a comfort.Elisa's cheeks grew hotter with every moment she sat alone on the straight-backed chair. Rufus had not paused to even acknowledge her presence. And now Vaughn had turned away from her, too involved with his pretty dance partner to see she desperately needed his company.

The Duchess of Wessex had taken her revenge for Elisa's failure to leave the dinner table last night, and she was feeling the full effects of it now.

Oh, how she yearned to stand up and tell them all the truth — that her only indiscretion had been loving a man who had clearly despised her, preferring the company of his whores and ignoring his wife and only son. Roger's gossip had taken on a life of its own when he had started the rumors of her liaisons, all of which werefabricated to cover the truth that he was the drunk, the gambler, and the philanderer.

When Elisa had stepped out of her room, and made her way down to the first floor, she noticed all the people wandering about the manor house. She traversed the very wide corridor, taking in the majestic art, hand-carved chairs, and ornate sideboards and settees. Then she made the mistake of looking from a beautiful tapestry to a woman and her escort. The woman's taken-aback expression made Elisa wonder if her dress was somehow indecent. Looking straight ahead, Elisa forced herself to focus on the night ahead, and ignore the whispers behind hands and fans that rippled ahead of her down the passage.

Then she came to the wide landing where many more of the guests were mingling, watching the dancers come and go in the hall below.

Caroline was there, and Elisa felt herself smile in genuine relief. With Caroline, she could be assured at least some pleasant company, and an absence of cattiness.

But the moment Caroline saw her, she started, and her eyes widened. Elisa began to cross the room towards her, but Caroline picked up her skirts. Her face was stony, utterly unforgiving, and Elisa halted where she was. She had seen that expression too many times to misinterpret it. Someone had acquainted Caroline with Elisa's past misdeeds.

Elisa could feel herself begin to tremble, and she looked around, wondering where she might turn and hide, if there was any sanctuary to run to.

That was when she saw the satisfied smile of the Duchess of Wessex, who stood slowly waving her fan from side to side. Cynthia let her smile broaden, then picked up her train, and with a disdainful flick of the black lace, turned and walked away.

Elisa felt as if a hammer had hit her in the stomach. She had not expected such overt hostility—in truth, she had forgotten how truly cruel people could be, and it had caught her unprepared.

How many people had the Duchess favored with the tidbits about her life? Then she remembered the rippling tide of rumor sweeping down the hall in front of her, and had her answer.

Everyone knew.

With legs that felt like lead, Elisa walked to the top of the stairs, preparing to climb down and find Rufus, as a proper wife would. She had paused at the top, trying to scrape together her courage, as well as simply find the strength to descend the steps.

Finally, she took a step down, and then another, and then it became easier. She avoided looking directly at anyone and walked straight over to the ballroom. She sighted Rufus, and an empty chair by his side, and walked over to it. Gratefully, she sank onto the seat and swore she would stay there and speak to no one until she could safely excuse herself and hide away in her room once more.

Until she saw Vaughn with his arm around Natasha, and his keen-eyed glance at the group of women by the fireplace, where the Duchess of Wessex was holding court.

She suddenly yearned for the sanctuary of Fairleigh Hall. She was safe there. She was hidden from the rest of the world. And once she made it back, she would never risk emerging again.

Someone cleared his throat, and when Elisa looked up she found Vaughn standing before her. Her heart lurched. How handsome he looked tonight in his formal attire. The black suit and white shirt had been perfectly tailored, fitting him like a second skin. The jacket served to emphasize the wide expanse of his shoulders. The breeches clung to his muscular long legs.

Seeing him was like a breath of fresh air.

"May I have the honor?" he asked, extending his hand.

Sheer gratitude outweighed her reluctance to cause a spectacle. Vaughn had not abandoned her, after all.

Rufus, who had been busy talking, now stopped and tapped his cane on the floor. "There is a young lady who is vying for your attention, boy. Why do you bother wasting time on your stepmother?"

Vaughn turned to his father, his expression unreadable. Elisa prayed he did not comment about Rufus' use of the word stepmother, as though they were already married.

"I've danced with Natasha, and now I'd like to dance with my *future* stepmother." He turned back to her. "Please dance with me?"

Though her better judgment was telling her to say no, she took his hand. She all but floated out on the dance floor, and when he held her in his arms, she wanted only to get closer. She wanted to feel the beat of his heart against her own. In this room full of strangers and people who disliked her, he was the only one who acknowledged her. But rather than cling to him as she wanted to, she kept a careful distance, every nerve on edge.

"You look stunning tonight." His voice was cautiously low.

Elisa glanced up into his handsome face. His eyes were dark with some hidden emotion, but his smile was warm. "Thank you."

"Are you enjoying yourself?"

She couldn't help the little laugh that escaped her. It had a hard edge to it. "I'd rather be anywhere but here."

He frowned, and she wished she could take the words back. "I mean the ball, not here, this moment," she said quickly.

"I know what you meant," he said quietly, and his firm tone reassured her. Then he hadn't missed her glance at the Duchess of Wessex and her chorus.

Elisa couldn't help but glance at them again. Of course, they were openly ogling her as she dared to dance with a man. It wouldn't matter that he was, in theory, her stepson. They would pounce on the fact that he was handsome and single, and it would be noticed that she enjoyed herself and danced much too energetically.

She tried to look away, but her gaze kept pulling back to the fireplace.

"You're frowning, sweet Elisa."

She forced a smile and looked at his necktie—a neutral view that would not give away her true thoughts.

But Vaughn appeared to read her mind. Very quietly, he swore, and the curse made her look back at his face, surprised.

He shook his head a little, a furrow between his brows.

"Let them talk," he said, his tone harsh. "Let them wonder. I can assure you I'm not the first son who ever danced with his father's fiancée."

"It's not that easy."

"Yes, it is. It's just that easy. Do you really care what they think, Elisa? Do you think Rufus cares?"

She shook her head. "No."

"What could their vicious words do that could possibly harm you?" he asked reasonably.

Because their vicious words took away her son. The truth was so close to bubbling out of her mouth, but she held it back. "You are right," she told Vaughn, managing a shaky smile. "I'm being silly."

His sharp look and the shrewd narrowing of his eyes told her he had seen past her airy acknowledgement, but she kept her smile firmly in place. He did not pursue the matter, although he became quiet after that.

The music stopped and Elisa knew this would be her one and only dance with Vaughn tonight. To dare to take another would only cause speculation, and Rufus would never let her forget it.

"Thank you, Elisa," Vaughn said stiffly, bowing over her hand as he sat her back on her chair.

He turned away and was instantly surrounded by people clamoring for his attention, including Natasha and a good handful of young misses.

Elisa looked away, unable to watch.

Nearly an hour passed when Rufus stood and turned to her. He extended his arm. "Let us partake of the fresh air on the terrace." It was the first time he had looked at her or spoken to her directly since she had sat on the chair.

But Elisa wanted nothing more than to escape the stifling room. She made eye contact with no one, focusing instead on the double doors that beckoned.

Would this excursion outside mean Rufus would want to retire soon? Or perhaps he would sit in for a card game and give her license to retire for the evening.

Rufus opened the door, and motioned her out on the terrace. She breathed deeply of the cool air, hoping it would take the burning from her cheeks. Rufus led her to the low stone balustrade.

Familiar laughter came from nearby.

Elisa's heart jumped a little. That was Vaughn's laugh, the low, intimate chuckle she heard only when she was in his arms.

She peered into the dark, trying to see through shadows. At the far end of the terrace, where wisteria hung in fragrant, discrete bowers, a couple stood locked in a lovers' embrace.

Her pulse jumped. The height of the man, the width of his shoulders, was unmistakable.

It *was* Vaughn.

The woman's arms were entwined around his neck, her face lifted up to his. Natasha. Had she already been kissed, or was she yearning for her first? Vaughn's hands were about her waist, the strong hands and long fingers that had smoothed their way along Elisa's body only last night.

A sickly hot wave passed through her, leaving her dizzy and nauseous. Her heart thudded unevenly, and for a moment her sight seemed to fade. The emotions that wrenched at her were far too extreme to be called simple jealousy. She felt betrayed in the most intimate way possible, and she had absolutely no recourse.

She swallowed against the sickness and tried to keep her irregular pulse even and her breathing calm.

"Look, my dear, we've interrupted young lovers!" Rufus said loudly.

Natasha quickly pushed away from Vaughn and stood with her head down, shamed. Vaughn immediately stepped into the light, away from Natasha and, it seemed to Elisa, a little in front of her. Protecting her? His expression was vexed. He ran a hand through his already ruffled hair.

Natasha was protesting her innocence. "Lord Wardell, I needed a breath of fresh air, and Vaughn was good enough to—"

"Assist you?" Rufus finished for her, a wide smile on his face. "You should go back inside before speculation runs rampant." Rufus sneered at his son. "Unless, of course, that is what you want."

It was then Elisa realized that Rufus had *wanted* her to see Vaughn's arms around another woman. He wanted her to know she would never be anything to Vaughn, that he would one day marry someone younger, more suitable, and…more beautiful.

"My father is right," Vaughn murmured, extending his arm to Natasha. The young woman, with considerable poise, took his arm and allowed him to lead her past Elisa and Rufus without another word.

Elisa watched them return to the ballroom, unable to dissemble and hide her feelings, unable to think beyond the pain of Vaughn's betrayal.

Rufus stepped back to her side. "The young are so careless." He put his hand at the middle of her back. "How typically selfish of Vaughn to fail to consider the consequences of kissing a pure girl right under her father's roof."

Elisa's throat was so tight she could do nothing but nod in agreement. Could Rufus see absolutely everything in her face? Surely he must!

"Shall we return to the party?" Rufus asked, already pulling her along.

"Must we?" She wanted nothing more than to escape to her room. The idea of returning back to the den of those vultures straight after Vaughn's duplicity was too much to bear.

Rufus' hand tightened on her. "You will get in there and face them," he snarled, his voice low. "D'you think I dragged you here just to have you duck out when the water got too hot?"

Elisa felt her jaw sag. "Rufus, I don't understand. What...?"

He pushed her from behind, his hand on her back. "Get in there, I tell you. You will sit there on that chair and take every single slight and insult they choose to give you. You deserve every single one of them, woman. I don't want you moving from that room until you remember how much of a harlot you are, dressed up in your whore's finery."

"Rufus!" She felt herself resisting his hand, sick horror bursting through her. *This* had been his plan. This was his retribution.

He smacked her between the shoulder blades, hard. The slap cracked like a gunshot on the open terrace but would not be heard inside because of the music and chatter.

The whole of Elisa's chest went instantly numb and at the same time felt like it was on fire. She gasped for breath.

"Get inside!" Rufus snarled. "Get in there and remember who it is that gives you a safe bolthole away from all this. Remember that I am the only one who would give you shelter...the only one who cares that you get your son back."

She stumbled inside, dazed and sick with horror, the world tilted and spinning around her. Nothing was as it seemed.

Not even Vaughn.

* * * * *

As soon as it was humanly possible to disengage from the ball without giving offense, Vaughn walked Natasha to her chamber and gave her a chaste kiss on the temple as a good night offering. He knew she would have invited him inside if he had given her any opportunity or encouragement to do so, but he had ducked that issue with bloody-minded ruthlessness. The last thing he wanted was to be delayed any longer from finding Elisa and talking to her. It was already well past midnight and many of the guests had departed already. Elisa and Rufus had left for their separate chambers long ago.

He cursed cruel fate. What had possessed Natasha to attempt her clumsy seduction tonight of all nights? Well, perhaps it was understandable if one considered both Caroline's and William's veiled approval of the match. Perhaps Caroline had even coached the girl on the finer points of catching a man. From all accounts, Caroline had managed to keep a string of beaus panting for her during her glorious debutante season.

Elisa's ill-fated arrival on the scene, however, was no mystery. He'd only taken one look at the delight on Rufus' face to know the cause.

Both those points needed to be explained to her. He had not failed to notice the way her face had blanched and her hands had begun to tremble as he'd disentangled himself from Natasha's clinging arms. After Elisa's evening of fielding barbs and insults, she did not need to be left believing he was the one who had engineered the intimate moment on the terrace with Natasha.

He reached Elisa's door, and looked around. No one was in sight. Quickly, he tried the handle. It turned.

Relieved, he opened the door and slipped inside.

A flickering candle cast a glow upon her sleeping form. He approached, his relief fading as he took in the sight of her. Her pale hair spilled against the pillow, free and abandoned. Her lips were slightly open and pink, full and inviting. Her dark lashes, spiked from tears, cast shadows against her high cheekbones.

His stomach tightened. *Had he made her cry?*

Wondering what she dreamed about, he reached out and lightly ran the back of his fingers along her soft jaw, his thumb grazing her full bottom lip.

She sighed and turned her head, exposing her swanlike neck to his gaze, which shifted lower to breasts that were barely covered by the soft, white silk nightgown. The decadent fabric's dull luster and the way it clung to her breasts, outlining them, caused his breath to catch. He could imagine the feel of the gown under his hand, and the soft breast beneath…

Blood flowed to his groin, filling his cock until it throbbed. He'd had an older woman before, an instructor of French who had showed him the true meaning of a few exotic words. It had been an exciting time in his life, an affair he'd wanted to continue, even though he knew their situation and her marriage had made it impossible. He suspected, though, that Elisa could eclipse the pleasure she'd displayed entirely.

"Vaughn?"

The word was said so softly that at first he thought he'd imagined it. Then he looked up to find himself staring into blue eyes wide with surprise. "What are you doing?" she asked, pulling the sheet up to her chin.

He sat down beside her, the bed dipping beneath his weight. "I wanted to see you before I went to sleep."

"Why?"

"I didn't get to spend any time with you tonight."

She frowned. "We danced."

"Yes, but that wasn't enough."

"You appeared to be adequately occupied elsewhere," she said, her voice little above a whisper.

"I like your gown," he said, pulling the sheet down with one hand while his fingers grazed the neckline of her gown, making sure to stroke more of her skin than the material. He could barely contain himself to that single caress.

Her breath left her in a rush. "Vaughn…"

"Shhh," he said, putting a finger to her lips. "I wanted you to know—on the terrace tonight…that was Natasha's doing."

She shook her head. "Natasha is a child. She knows nothing of what men desire. How could she have known what to do?"

"Every maid dreams of being kissed. That is all she thought to achieve, I suspect. Unlike you, my sweet Elisa. You know what a man needs." He could feel his throat closing down on him, excitement making his voice hoarse.

Her eyes widened in surprise. "You shouldn't be here." She sat up against the headboard and crossed her arms beneath her chest. He wondered if she realized it emphasized the fullness of her breasts even more. "I cannot imagine what would happen if you were caught in here. Marianne will be coming to check on me."

"You brought her with you?" he asked, unable to keep the irritation out of his voice.

"Yes, so you must go at once."

But he could not leave it at that, with his whole body throbbing with need, not when he was alone with her for the first time in days.

He leaned forward and kissed the top of each creamy breast.

She froze, and the pulse in her neck quickened.

"Dear, sweet Elisa, you smell so good…god, how I want to bury myself deep inside you."

She released a ragged breath, but did not push him away.

He kissed a path from her breast to the place in her neck where her pulse raced wildly. There he caressed her skin with his tongue. With his other hand, he stroked her breast through the delicate silk, and felt the nipple grow tight and hard beneath his fingertips. Her breath came still more rapidly.

He felt her surrender, even before her fingers threaded through his hair.

"God forgive me," she whispered, pulling his face up to meet hers.

Chapter Twelve

Elisa woke to the sound of a horrified gasp.

She opened her eyes to find Marianne standing over her, a frown marring her wrinkled face. "My lady, what have you done?"

Elisa's heart pounded as she looked beside her. She gasped, for Vaughn lay there, his eyes closed, ridiculously long lashes fanned against sculpted cheekbones. Even in sleep he was irresistibly handsome.

Her gasp must have roused him, for his eyes opened slowly. "Good morning." His voice sleepy, and his smile completely oblivious to the fact he had just been discovered in his father's fiancée's bed.

Panic raced through Elisa.

Heads will roll for this.

"It's not what it looks like," Elisa said, scrambling from the warm body at her side.

Marianne shook her head, and threw Elisa's peignoir at her. "For heaven's sake, put this on before his lordship comes looking for you. He's been up for hours, and so have the majority of the guests. It's a wonder he didn't discover you himself." With an exasperated sigh she crossed the room and closed the door behind her.

God, what had she done?

"Relax, Elisa. We didn't do anything."

She whirled around to find Vaughn sitting up in bed, with ruffled hair, but fully clothed.

So was she. Granted, she was in her nightgown, but at least she was not naked.

"We didn't?" Her memory was hazy—sleep still fogged her mind, and having been thrown into a state of alarm immediately upon waking wasn't assisting her. Last night she had slept better than she had in years, and the sound sleep seemed to have drugged her mind a little, too.

Vaughn smiled softly. "When a woman cries in my arms, I'm certain that means she doesn't want to make love."

With his words, her memory had fallen back into place.

Vaughn had held her in his arms, his strong heart pounding against her own as he whispered soothing words in her ear. He spoke of the humiliation she had suffered that evening, the pain she must have felt seeing Natasha in his arms, the discomfort of being ignored by Rufus. She had listened with growing wonder, for it seemed he had not missed a single barb or veiled insult sent her way throughout the entire evening. He had observed and remembered them all.

And his fury was unmatched by any man's.

He had dampened his anger, shielded her from it, but she had felt it nonetheless. It had emerged in the words he used, in the way his body grew tighter and harder as he listed each little incident, in the way he swallowed and drew a deep breath after his summary. And finally, he had kissed her temple, and added softly, "I would take all of it away if I could, Elisa. And for what I cannot alleviate, you have my sorrow. They do not understand. I wanted you to know that I do."

The words held a sweetness she had long forgotten—the joy of being desired. Of being thought well of.

The pain and horror of the evening slid from her mind, leaving her feeling light-headed. Never in her life had she known such tenderness and it had moved her to tears.

But why had he not taken her offering? Why had he refrained from making love to her? She would have gladly given him that boon after such an endearing display of concern and empathy. Did he not desire her anymore? Her heart lurched, remembering the pain of Roger's rejection.

He came up behind her and pulled her against him, nuzzling her neck. "You're so beautiful when you sleep," he murmured, his lips tasting her nape and sliding to the edge of her nightgown.

He felt good—all hard, tight muscle, and he was hot where he pressed against her. His arms around her waist were heavy.

The wanton in her stirred, and low in her belly she felt the warm throb of longing begin. It spread out in a slow wave through her body, making her limbs tingle and her breasts, where they pressed against his arms, ache for his touch.

She could detect his male scent and the clean smell of his hair. It enveloped her, and prompted images of him bent over her prone body, his mouth at her breast, and the feel of him hard against her thigh...

"You talk in your sleep," he whispered.

Instantly she stiffened.

He kissed her ear. "Who is Raymond?"

She jerked away from him, pulling her robe tightly about her. All the hot longing in her congealed, and made her head hurt.

He frowned, clearly puzzled. "Elisa?"

Not trusting herself to speak, she shook her head.

His face was puzzled, thoughtful. "He's your son, isn't he?" His voice was quiet.

How did he know she had a son?

"How long has it been since you've seen him?" he asked.

It was as though a wound had been ripped open, the pain was so intense. She turned from him, holding her chest. "I don't want to talk about it."

"Why don't you get him back?"

She turned then, her pain turning to incoherent anger. It gave her an aggressive edge. "Oh, yes, it is so easy. I just get him back." She snapped her fingers. "Just like that." She shook her head, feeling her fury build. This was the first time she had ever spoken aloud of Raymond and her futile efforts to find him to anyone except Rufus. Now the fissure was open, and hot molten pain poured through the rent. "If it was so easy, why is it I have gone months without retrieving him? Why have I agreed to marry Rufus and suffer through solitary nights, dreaming of my little boy?" Her voice suddenly began to wobble. "He's nine years old. He'll be turning ten this year. The last time I saw him, he held onto me, and told me not to leave him. Roger's family has no doubt seen to it that he despises me by now."

She stopped, unshed tears wrenching at her voice and stinging her eyes. Her vision swam. She took a deep breath. All her fury had gone as quickly as it came. She dropped her head, ashamed for attacking Vaughn. "Do you think I would deliberately allow that to happen, if it was so easy to get him back?" she whispered, and each word tortured her aching throat. "A woman has no power in our world, Vaughn. I am innocent. The only man I've every made love to was my husband, and the last time was five years ago, when he was too drunk to realize it was I who had crept into his bed and not one of the servants. I am not guilty of anything, yet I have lost everything I care about—my son, my home, my very character. I should have lived the life I had been accused of living and enjoyed it. After all, no one believes my innocence." She sighed heavily.

"Oh, Vaughn, I've been in hell for so long I had forgotten what it was like to live a normal life. I had settled for that, I could have been content with that. But you've made me yearn for more."

Vaughn remained silent for a long moment, and he stared at her. She knew by his expression she had shocked him. So, he had also thought the worst of her. That knowledge cut to the quick. She closed her eyes in order to stop the tears.

"Oh, Elisa…"

She took a deep breath, battling the sobs that welled inside her at the sound of his deep, sorrowful voice. Wrapping her arms around her waist, she lifted her chin and opened her eyes. "You should go now, Vaughn. I'm certain Natasha and her mother are looking for you."

He took a step toward her, but he did not attempt to take her in his arms. Instead he spread his hands. "Forgive me. I didn't know. I didn't understand how it was for you."

"Please, just go."

But he didn't. Instead he took the other step necessary to reach her and slid his arm around her waist. He moved slowly, as if he was waiting for her to push him away.

She was too drained of energy to resist. His arms came around her, and she was nestled against his chest and shoulder. She stood with limp arms as he kissed one cheek, then the other, before moving to her nose, then up to her eyelids.

Then he paused.

She opened her eyes to find him staring at her lips, which parted of their own accord.

His eyes half closed, and he gave a low groan. "God help me, I want you," he muttered, and brought his mouth to hers. He touched her softly, like a butterfly's wings, then with the pads of his thumbs, wiped away the tears.

And despite her recent anger, despite the tears, the deep weariness that these last weeks had etched into her very bones, she felt her body stirring in response. With no man had she ever experienced such strong needs, desires that never seemed to die fully, but would spring back to life at the merest suggestion of touch, or even thought alone.

"I don't recognize myself anymore," she whispered a moment before she kissed him.

Elisa's low moan goaded him, spearing his gut with aching need. As he plundered her mouth with kisses that grew harder and more demanding, Vaughn pulled her tighter to him and felt the rapid beat of her heart against his own. She wore nothing but the fragile nightgown, and he could feel every inch of her soft, supple body against him. Her hair was slightly scented and tickled his chest where his shirt lay open. She was warm and utterly pliant in his arms, small and feminine.

She was driving him crazy with need.

He bent over her, one hand sliding down to curve over her rounded bottom, and pushed her against him. Their hips made contact, and he could feel the delicious, driving pressure against him.

Her back bowed, increasing the pressure of her hips against him. Her breasts thrust out, almost in offering, and he took one in his hand, caressing it through the warm, soft silk. At once her nipple hardened to a tight little nub. Her responsiveness was exciting him even further. He bent his head to lave the nipple through the silk. His moisture soaked the fabric, and molded it around the dark nipple, displaying her areola. When the material was completely sodden, he blew gently on it, and was rewarded by her gasping groan of delight and the sight of her nipple tightening even more. Her hand was in his hair, and her fist clenched tightly. She was pulling his head down to her other breast, and her uninhibited demand delighted him.

Obediently, he licked and suckled on her breast through the silk, and then pulled back a little to watch her reaction. Her eyes were closed, and a little frown marred her forehead. He looked down at her nightgown. The wet silk was virtually transparent, leaving uneven circles around her nipple virtually transparent. The sight was maddeningly erotic.

He grasped her breast again, smoothing his thumb across the heated tip, and felt her hips push against him again. His shaft throbbed, the blood in his veins thick and hot.

Her hand was sliding down his neck, across his chest, moving restlessly. He found himself holding his breath in anticipation, for this was the first time Elisa had ventured to explore for herself.

The touch of her fingertips on his abdomen, through the opening in his shirt, made the muscles clench and quiver, and drove a sharp spike of pleasure straight to his cock.

Her hand was at his breeches, and she moaned as her hand flattened against his pelvis and moved lower, to the length of his quivering penis, his erection thickening and lengthening with every stroke.

God, he would burst if she continued this way! As her hand stroked him, her kiss grew more urgent, her other hand moving to his hair, her fingers weaving, pulling him closer.

It was too much for him. His fingers found the neck of her nightgown, and he clenched the material in his fist. He pulled his mouth away from hers. "Stop me, Elisa. Tell me to stop, for I cannot stop myself." His voice was thick and unrecognizable even to him.

Her own voice, in answer, was a throaty, low, "Never."

He shut his eyes tight, as the longing in her tone pushed him past the fine edge of control. He ripped the fabric away from her body with a single tug, and threw it from him.

Her naked body, lithe but with full womanly curves, was perfection itself. He covered her with kisses, caresses. He tasted her, his hands and mouth moving over her face, her neck, her shoulders, her breasts, wherever he could reach, as she stood quivering in his arms. Her little whimpers and the clench of muscles in spasms of delight were driving him on.

With a groan, he lifted her into his arms and placed her back onto the bed they had only just left. She stared up at him as he pulled his shirt from him, and leaned over her, an arm on either side of her face. Her hands moved up his arms, squeezing his biceps, before moving up along his shoulders. He moved against her, his erection rock hard, pressing against her mound, the pressure a subtle goad to her pearl. The only thing between them was the fabric of his breeches, and they both knew that soon would no longer be a hindrance.

"Please," she breathed, pushing against him. She stared up at him, her eyes wide and luminous with desire. Her lips were parted as she drew breath into her heaving chest.

He kissed her, long and hard, driving his tongue deep into her sweet mouth. He caressed her lips with his own, and tasted them. Then down the long column of her throat to the small hollow at the base. Her breasts were rubbing against his chest with a sinful friction that sent little sparks of delight through him.

The pressure to tear off his pants and drive himself into her was nearly unbearable. He tortured himself deliberately, wanting to revel in the anticipation of what that first thrust would feel like, the fierce satisfaction in pushing into her and watching her squirm in pleasure, her eyes closing in joy.

He played with her breasts, his long fingers surrounding as much of the soft globes as he could reach, and then drawing them outward, until they met at the nipple, and tugged a little at the erect, rosy flesh. He wanted to push her to the same level of intolerable need he was feeling. As she writhed and moaned, he took first one tight nipple into his mouth, then ministered to the other. He could feel the flat plane of her stomach contract tightly and knew she was reaching the same frenzy as he.

Soon. Soon…

Sweat was beading his brow, and his heart was thudding loud in his ears. At any moment he would go up in flames, so heated was his desire.

But first…

He stroked the skin of her stomach, feeling the telltale quiver ripple through her. He moved down to the tops of her creamy thighs, feeling them tremble and move restlessly. They parted, beckoning.

He caressed the hot, moist folds of flesh edging her cleft, stroking upwards and inwards, and marveled at the incredible heat of her. What would it feel like to slide himself into that molten core?

He realized that he, too, was trembling, as continuous little ripples of pleasure wracked him.

Vaughn slipped his fingers inside her. And as she bucked hard against him, she groaned. She clenched around his fingers, and the power of that spasm astonished him.

He lifted his thumb to rest against the tiny nub of flesh above, and stroked it gently. She gave a gasping cry, and her hand buried itself in his hair, clenching. As he sucked and gently tugged at her nipples with his teeth, he continued the rhythmic stroke, and felt her begin to vibrate against his fingers. The deep, deep wave of release was nearly upon her, and unerringly, he coaxed it closer and closer.

"Yes," she whispered, her voice hoarse, and her breath coming in gasps. Her climax locked her body tight against him, and he held her as she pulsed against his fingers, and her body shuddered.

The need to be inside her at that moment, to feel her clench around him, was all he could think of. But he held himself back, knowing the wait would make that moment exquisite.

She collapsed against him, as if her bones were made of butter, and as he pulled away from her, she did not even lift her head from the coverlet.

"I have not finished with you yet, my sweet Elisa," he told her, and his voice was strained, hoarse with dammed-back desire.

He let his lips trail a path down to her stomach. He laved her belly button, then moved lower, making a precise trail down to her overly sensitive flesh. He could feel her coming back to life beneath him.

"Vaughn," she said urgently and he was not sure if she wanted him to stop or to continue ravaging her.

He lowered his head and tasted her pearl of pleasure, caressing her with his tongue.

She flexed like she had been jolted, and gasped, her dry throat rasping. She moved to push him away, and he grabbed her hands and wove his fingers through her own as he continued the delightful kiss, thrusting his tongue deep into her cleft, then sliding it up, to whirl around the nub of flesh, stroking it.

She raised her hips off the bed, almost involuntarily, offering herself to him.

Vaughn's blood roared in his ears as he tasted her. His body was as painfully sensitive as her own—only a little more stimulation and he would arrive at his own climax. He was shuddering with the need for release.

He had never held himself back like this before. He had never suspected how powerful a stimulant selflessly pleasuring a woman could be. He was drunk with it, and had no intention of stopping until he could truly stand it no more and Elisa begged for release.

Then he heard it. The handle of the door connecting this room with Rufus' was rattled impatiently.

How long had he been trying to get in? How much had he heard?

Vaughn stood abruptly, pulling Elisa with him. Her face was flushed, her stare wild, but as he motioned toward the door she nodded in understanding.

He grabbed her wrapper from the chair at the foot of the bed and threw it to her. As she struggled to put it on, he picked up his shirt and shoes, and stepped over to the armoire in the corner.

"Elisa!" The call was full of fury.

She raced over to the door and shook out the disguising folds of the gown around her naked body. Vaughn pulled the door of the armoire open, and looked back. She had her hand on the key to the door, her wide, frightened eyes looking to him.

He nodded, stepped into the armoire, and shut the door.

Muffled, and effectively blinded, his hearing sharpened.

"I am sorry, Rufus. I was asleep."

"For god's sake, woman. Why do you dally about in bed all day?"

"I did not sleep well last night." Her voice was shaky, husky.

"Have you seen that son of mine?" Rufus' voice was coming closer. "He's not in his quarters, and it doesn't look like he's been there at all during the night."

"I haven't stirred from this room since you escorted me here last night," Elisa said. Truthfully. "Perhaps he left the manor last night," she added. "He did not seem to be happy about being interrupted on the terrace."

"His belongings are in his room."

"Maybe he spent the night with another?"

Vaughn smiled to himself in the dark. Elisa had a wicked sense of humor.

There was a pause, and he strained to hear what was happening, but no sound came.

"Why do your thoughts turn to such an unfit subject?" Rufus asked softly.

Vaughn rubbed his temple. What was the mad bastard working up to? The quiet way he'd phrased the question made imaginary hackles rise on Vaughn's back.

"I...I don't know what you mean." Elisa's voice was full of sudden wariness. She saw the menace, too.

"Is it not enough to be shamed and humiliated in one evening, but you must also insist upon my correcting your attitude the next morning?"

"Rufus, it was simply a suggestion. Vaughn is a young man, after all."

"Such an idea would never have occurred to a true lady," Rufus responded.

Vaughn closed his eyes. It was too late. No matter what she said now, she was condemned in Rufus' eyes.

"I am truly sorry, Rufus. I am trying to behave properly."

Her contrite voice, the ringing note of honesty should have swayed him. It was a valiant try to coax him into a more jovial mood. But it was Rufus, not any other man. Such feminine wiles would not work with him.

Vaughn squeezed his temples between thumb and forefinger as his other hand reached out for the door of the armoire. He heard the slap from inside the cupboard. It sounded loud and shocking even from in there. Elisa's gasping cry stabbed into his heart. He gathered himself to burst out into the room, and halted, his mind whirling.

He could not reveal himself, even to save Elisa this moment's pain. If he were to show himself to Rufus, Elisa would suffer far more than a single slap.

An image of Rufus stumping up to the screaming horse and shooting it without hesitation flashed through his mind.

Sweat broke out on his forehead, this time provoked by fear.

He had to bide his time. He must wait.

There were things he had to set in motion, first. Safety measures. Contingency plans.

And Kirkaldy, the very place he had considered his sanctuary would become Elisa's. In that moment all claim to his mother's Scottish estate ended. Elisa *needed* Kirkaldy.

In the dark, he bowed his head, and silently cursed his helplessness as Elisa sobbed softly.

* * * * *

She did not hear Rufus leave, or the door close behind him. She heard nothing, until she felt hands on her arms, lifting her up from the floor where she had fallen.

"Shhh, I am here," Vaughn whispered, and his big warm arms wrapped around her.

She smothered her sobs against his bare chest.

"I'm sorry, Elisa. Forgive me—but had I stepped out to confront him, he would have shot us both on the spot. The man always carries a gun. " He gently brushed her hair from her face, and she realized his hand was shaking.

She shook her head a little. "You have nothing to apologize for. I would rather you live, too. It was only a blow. It will pass. Rufus is under a lot of strain right now."

His arms tightened around her. "Then stay away from the monster."

She sighed. "My life is such a mess." She hesitated, then spoke the words anyway. She had passed far beyond such rudimentary caution with Vaughn. "He pays for agents to look for my son. I don't have funds to do that, and he is the only one who will."

Vaughn grew very still. "I don't believe he has done such a thing. It is unlike him to help anyone," he said, his voice low.

"But it is true," she declared swiftly, defiantly. "He has given me reports of their activities."

"And in what…five, six months, they have been unable to find a single trace of a small boy?"

She stiffened. "Raymond's father's family are very cunning. He has been moved—every time they come close to finding him."

Vaughn lifted her chin and stared into her eyes, as if he were looking for something there. Then he nodded. "I see," he said quietly. He shifted a little, moving her in his arms. "If you must go back with him, promise me you'll meet me at the pond tomorrow at noon. I'll come straight from here so there will be no speculation. Tell Rufus you're going for a ride and you'll return shortly. Tell him you have to buy a bonnet or some such frippery."

Reluctance made her hesitant to agree. "Vaughn, we must be realistic. I am to be a married woman, and you—"

"No, Elisa!" He gave her a little shake. "Promise me," he ground out. "Be at the pond."

She shook her head a little. "If Rufus knew —"

"Then you must be careful. But promise me you will meet me there." She felt him draw breath. "Please, Elisa."

There was a quality to his voice she didn't understand. It was as if he knew something about Rufus that she did not, which was strange. Rufus and Vaughn had been practically strangers until a few weeks ago, and their relationship had not grown any closer since then.

"All right," she agreed. "I will meet you."

He let his breath out with a harsh sigh, and got to his feet. Gently, he lifted her to hers, and gave her a hard, quick kiss on the lips. "Until tomorrow," he assured her, and strode to the bedroom door. He pulled the door open, looked about for observers, and left.

How brazen he was!

Elisa made her way slowly back to the bed and sank gingerly onto the mattress.

Tomorrow…

Her heart thrilled at the possibilities.

Chapter Thirteen

"My lady, what can you be thinking?" Marianne demanded. She stood with her hands on her hips, watching Elisa with an expression that would make most people cower.

A day ago, Elisa might well have cowered, but not today. She turned towards the mirror and gently touched the bruise over her cheekbone, high up next to her eye.

"I'm thinking how wonderful it feels to be desired," she told Marianne.

"He wants only one thing from you."

The words sent a little shiver down her back, caused by shades of doubt. This was obviously Marianne's intent, for she watched Elisa with a lifted brow.

"You know I'm right, don't you?" Marianne insisted.

Elisa grabbed the brush and began running it through her hair. "You are wrong," she said as steadily as she could, but in the corner of her heart, she wondered. Vaughn had never professed love, or any of that emotion's cousins.

But...the look in his eyes when he was making love to her—she could not doubt that. A man could say anything he wanted, but his physical actions, especially when he was in bed, were the truthsayers. It was not simply a matter of sex, she was sure of it.

But Marianne was clearly not so sure. Since returning to Fairleigh Hall last evening, she had been following Elisa around like the nursemaid she once was. Elisa knew Marianne was genuinely concerned and trying to protect her, but she resented the intrusion on what little happiness she'd found since Roger's death.

Because Marianne meant well, Elisa tried to speak the truth as she knew it. She looked at Marianne in the mirror.

"I know that I want him just as badly, and I cannot bear being without him."

The direct answer silenced Marianne, who let out an exaggerated sigh. She went to the wardrobe and threw open the doors.

"I need a riding habit."

"You are riding…again?."

"Yes, I am."

"You're going to meet *him*, aren't you?"

Elisa remained silent. She turned on the stool and studied Marianne, waiting for the other woman's reaction.

Aside from shaking her head, Marianne made no further comment.

Elisa turned back to the mirror, planning her escape.

Just as he had told her, Vaughn had not arrived home last night. He would meet her at the pond at midday.

And today she would make love to him.

Rufus' manhandling of her yesterday, and his powerful retribution at the ball, had removed her conscience in this regard and made the decision for her. She would allow herself the very private pleasure of making love to Vaughn. She would revel in it. And she would refuse to bear any guilt for indulging in the one thing in her whole life that made her happy. It would be a secret she would carry to her grave.

A thrill raced through her, knowing that soon she would be in Vaughn's arms.

An hour later Elisa walked down the stone stairs and swung around the newel post to head for the French doors and the stables at the back of the garden.

She wore a formal navy riding habit. It was a severe cut and style—a high collar, and a long row of tiny pearl buttons all the way down the front of the bodice were its only decorations. The skirt had a train, as usual, but lacked any other decoration. And her hair was caught up in a very simple bun. The removal of a single clip would bring it all tumbling down, and it was a style she could easily recreate herself, and without the aid of a mirror and brush.

The gown was not her favorite at all, but it had two virtues: it disguised the fact that she was completely naked beneath — she wore no stockings, no garments of any sort. The second advantage was that once the row of buttons were released the bodice fell away, and the skirt was unfastened with a single button at the back.

The many buttons she did not foresee as a problem — she knew Vaughn would delight in the slow revelation of her nakedness as he undid the buttons one at a time.

Oh, wicked, wicked Elisa! the voice of her conscience whispered. She smiled to herself, her heart already picking up speed.

As she approached Rufus' study, the last door off the foyer, she saw the door was open. Her heart sank. She hoped he would not notice her pass.

It was too much to hope for.

"Elisa." His voice was sharp.

She swallowed hard and retraced her steps, stopping at the door. "Yes?"

He sat back in the oversized chair, and looked her up and down. "Where are you going?"

"For a ride."

"Alone?"

Reluctantly, she nodded.

"Why don't you stay home today?"

"The weather has been so fine. I wanted to enjoy it." Clenching her gloved hands into fists at her sides, she remembered something Vaughn had told her to say and forced a smile. "I thought I might stop by the village and order another bonnet. I promise I won't be long."

He frowned. "I thought the festivities had tired you?"

"I slept very well last night, and now I'm restless."

"Perhaps I should accompany you."

His words startled her. "On horseback?" she asked.

"You think I am not an accomplished rider?" he responded, his eyes narrowing. "I was an excellent hunter before the bloody gout took me."

It was hard to imagine Rufus physically active. She resisted the urge to refuse his suggestion for it would only cause more suspicion on his part. Instead she prevaricated. "Is this not the time you usually take a nap?" An idea occurred to her. "There is a second bottle of the port Vaughn imported from France—in the dining room. Shall I have Joshua bring it to you?"

Rufus straightened up in his chair, patently trying to hide his eagerness. "Well, perhaps just one," he said.

"I'll tell Joshua," she said.

"And buy me a cigar!" Rufus called as she left the room.

With deep relief she went back to the kitchen to rouse Joshua, before hurrying to the stables.

* * * * *

Vaughn stared at surface of the pond. It was a hot, still day and the water was smooth, silvered. Flat calm. Not so his soul. He had tried sitting while he waited, but his seething nerves would not allow it.

He wondered what was keeping Elisa. Since leaving Munroe Manor early this morning, he had ridden at breakneck speed for York, to complete his business there, then hurried back to the pond. He had barely made the appointed hour himself and had fully expected Elisa to be here, half out of her mind worrying whether he would keep the appointment or not.

A horse's neigh brought his restless pacing to a halt. He spun to face the grove of trees where the sound had come from.

A moment later Elisa appeared, her color high, her eyes brilliant as she greeted him with a warm, open smile that made his blood surge.

"You made it."

"Did you think I would not?" Her smile was playful.

"I thought perhaps you would choose not to." He studied her anew, his heart quickening. There was something different about her this day. It was not physical, but it affected all of her. Her speech, her face, was more alive and open than he had ever seen it, and if he had not known she was incapable of teasing, he would have thought her expression and tone one of banter.

"Indeed, though it was more difficult than I had anticipated. I told him I was going to the village to pick up a bonnet. He suggested he come with me." She gazed at him with a clear-eyed stare and a soft smile on her face. She was utterly beautiful, a confident woman. But then he saw the bruise beside her eye and remembered the truth — she was also vulnerable and still young. She had been hurt. He reached out and gently touched the ugly bruise.

Her smile faded. "Don't," she whispered, and tried to push his hand away. Her own was small against his and strengthless.

He cupped her jaw. "Why not?"

"Here, today, is not the place to talk about him. I do not want him spoiling the day."

She closed her eyes and leaned into him with a sigh. Her lips grazed his wrist, and a fire raced through him at the fleeting touch. He pulled her to him, his fingers brushing her slender back. Her heart pounded hard against him, matching the rhythm of his own.

"I've never wanted anybody the way I want you," she whispered against his lips, a moment before she kissed him. In that moment he wondered who was the seducer as her arms entwined around his neck and she pressed herself hard against him, as though she were trying to make them one.

Her bold statement reminded him of dozens of well-trained maids, who played the game of seduction well, but expected an offer of marriage before giving themselves to him. This was not such a woman.

Suddenly she put him at arms length, her breath coming in gasps as she stared at him. There was such a fire in her eyes that it stole the breath from his lungs. Her hands were fumbling at his jacket, sliding it off. He allowed her to remove it, standing passively, although his heart was anything but passive, shuddering along under the heavy burden of an excitement he'd never experienced before. Elisa was seducing him. A woman was making her desire clear and intentions direct and active, and it acted on him like the opium drug that could take a man's mind and possess it to the exclusion of all else.

Her small fingers were working at the buttons of his shirt, tugging at the tails, drawing it from his breeches. He stirred a little, reaching for her shoulders, but she shrugged out of his reach, and pushed his hands away. "Not yet," she murmured.

A small smile lifted the corner of his mouth. "What is it…?"

"Shhh…" she breathed. She slid the shirt from his shoulders. It snagged on his arms halfway down, but she seemed in no hurry to remove it completely. Instead, she drew very close to him, so close he could feel her hot breath fan across his chest, down across his belly. It was an astonishingly arousing sensation. It combined with the wisp of a breeze skimming off the water beside them, to run cool fingers across his bared chest and shoulders. A deep shudder ran through him—but it was a shudder of delight and an excitement he had not felt in…years.

Her lips touched his chest. Hot, soft and moist, they anointed each of his nipples in turn, creating hard nubs of highly sensitive flesh. Her tongue flickered out, lapped at each of them, and he took a deep breath.

"Elisa—"

"Speak not a word," she murmured, not even looking up at him. Her tiny hands flattened themselves against his stomach, and his muscles quivered in reaction. Her warm fingers slipped down across his flesh, and slid beneath the band of his breeches. He groaned low in his throat, the sound ripping from him involuntarily, as his stomach clenched.

She did look up at him, then, with a smile that spoke of womanly delight. She clearly reveled in her power over him. "Look at you," she murmured. "You are like a work of art...perfection." Her fingers, just inside his breeches, were so close to touching his throbbing cock...just an inch or so lower. He squashed the impulse to ask her to do so. Let Elisa play out the role she had chosen today. Let her reveal the goal she had in mind.

The delicious tension of not quite knowing what would come was adding to the level of pleasure building in him.

She was fumbling at the fastenings of his breeches, the small fingers working at the buttons and ties.

"You intend to strip me bare?" he asked, and was surprised at the raw note in his voice—he sounded like a man pressured beyond endurance.

"Perhaps," she answered, her voice remote. Then a small frown puckered her brow. "If only I could conquer these dratted fastenings."

The prosaic problem made him chuckle a little. "One would think you have never before done this service for a man."

And, astonishingly, she blushed. "I have not," she admitted, her eyes downcast.

"But...your husband?"

"He always came to me...undressed," she said.

He let the information be absorbed into his mind. "Then you have never had the pleasure of a seduction, have you? You have never..." He shook his head, trying to clear the surprise, his bafflement. "You have never had a man make love to you, have you?"

"No." Her voice was almost bodiless, so soft was her answer. Her hands were at her sides now, and still.

"Just a dry marriage bed, with wifely duties," he surmised.

"There was pleasure there," she said quickly. Too quickly.

"Not the sort of pleasure I will give you," he assured her, and was delighted to see her blush re-bloom in each cheek. "Elisa, yesterday was the first time you have climaxed, yes?"

Her blush deepened. "You mean that...moment...when I..."

"When you climaxed," he said firmly. "Then it was your first."

"I have never felt that before."

"You most assuredly will feel it again," he promised her. "I will give you more pleasure than even yesterday." Again, he was rewarded with her small smile.

He went to take her in his arms, but the forgotten shirt, still draped around his shoulders, locked his arms in place by his side.

Elisa stepped back a little, her smile broadening. "You are trapped," she observed.

"Hardly." He took a breath and flexed himself, feeling seams give and the costly fabric tear. In a moment he was free, and he flung the useless garment aside. Elisa backed up a step more as he approached her. "Nothing you could do would stop me from reaching you," he promised.

"If only I allow it," she returned.

His smile broadened. "We shall see," he promised her, and lunged for her.

She skipped out of his way, the hem of her gown flicking across the soft chamomile growing by the banks of pool, leaving him empty-handed.

He studied her a moment where she stood close by the flat rock where he usually lay in the sun, spinning dreams. She would be cornered if she backed up a little further, he realized.

He took another step toward her and she stepped back. Quickly he moved to trap her between the rock and the trees behind it, wrapping his arms around her waist and drawing her to him.

She reacted quickly, but not quickly enough. Her tiny fists flailed lightly at his shoulders, and she tried to push and pummel her way out of his grasp. Her wriggling put pressure on his already taut groin, and the friction set up an aching, needy throbbing. He tightened his grip on her with one arm, and sought to capture her chin in his hand. Her struggles didn't subside even when he brought his lips upon hers. His fierce kiss contained little passion, for it was intended to control and subdue. Yet at the taste of her lips, he could feel his excitement leap and coherent thought start to tear apart. The need to slake himself grew swiftly stronger, blotting his mind of all other concerns.

Even the resistance of her hands and the straining motions of her body against his carried their own excitement. God, but the woman was driving him beyond endurance! So swiftly was he reaching that point...what was her magic?

Elisa's hand lodged against his shoulder, and she gave a hard thrust, hard enough to dislodge his hand from her chin and for his hold around her waist to loosen. Quickly, she pulled herself from his arms.

She stepped away, her breasts rising and falling swiftly, her breath ragged. Her eyes were a little narrowed.

"You dare...!" she murmured, but there was a hint of challenge in her voice.

"Enough," he declared. "Play time is over." And he reached for her.

She took another step, but he had no intention of allowing her to continue the game. His body would not allow the torture. Swiftly, he snatched her up in his arms, holding her tight. Her hands beat their small tattoo on his shoulders again, which made tackling the fastenings of her clothes more difficult.

With a curse, he bent at the knee and lowered her to the chamomile lawn, then captured her wrists in his left hand, leaving his right hand, his lips and body free to pleasure her as he wished. To quell her struggles he threw his thigh across her hips which added a delicious pressure to his groin. Her hips pushed against his thigh.

He reached up to the long row of buttons on her bodice, but his hands were thick with pounding blood, clumsy. With forced patience, he attacked each tiny button, unhooking it, knowing that the release of each one brought him a little closer to seeing the bounty he knew lay beneath. He pushed the bodice aside, and grew still, looking down at her, his breath catching.

She was bare beneath the bodice. Her perfectly formed breasts, adorned by tightly crinkled nipples, were exposed to his gaze, to his hand. She was still, watching his expression, judging his reaction.

"And the skirt?" he asked, his voice hoarse.

"The skirt only. One button is all that stands in your way. Nothing else." Her own voice was just as husky.

The groan he uttered was pulled from the depths of his soul. He lowered his head, and took her nipple into his mouth, sucking and licking it. She bucked hard against him, a small gasp sounding as she threw her head back. He took advantage of her movement, and slid his hand beneath her waist to flick open the single button. The skirt loosened, and with impatient tugs he removed it and flung it away. He removed her bodice, too, leaving her completely naked.

She was the picture of femininity. Her waist was tiny, her hips flared and curved down to long, shapely legs. He studied the thatch of blonde hair at the apex of her thighs. His shaft throbbed.

Moving quickly now, he turned from gazing at her pale, flawless figure to kiss her deeply. He tugged at his breeches. "Elisa, I cannot wait a moment longer. I must have you. Now."

"Yes," she breathed, and the single confident whisper was another sensual stroke to his aroused emotions. He at last freed himself from the breeches, and his penis jutted, swollen and proud. Feeling his heart beat thundering in his temples he slid between her thighs, and probed for entry, almost clumsy in his haste.

Her sweet thighs parted, and he was enfolded in her flesh. With a gasping groan he thrust into her. Her channel was tight, gripping his cock with a hard caress.

Elisa's head fell back, and her whole body lifted, her hips thrusting, as she gave a low cry of feminine satisfaction. The sound was a goad.

He was too close to the edge, he realized, with a tinge of amazement.

With another single, deep thrust he climaxed, with a powerful surge of pleasure that ripped from his toes and tightened every sinew in his body. He threw his head back, as the waves of sensual delight pounded through him. His whole body was locked into stillness, wracked by the tremors.

When he could draw breath once more, he released a shuddering sigh, and propped himself up on one arm.

Elisa was watching him still, and he could see the signs of her own excitement in the redness of her flesh, her open mouth, the frantic pulse beating visibly at her throat, just by the sharp, delicate curve of her jaw.

He kissed the pulse, feeling heat and sampling her bouquet with a delighted in-drawn breath.

"You seemed…hurried," she murmured.

"That I was," he assured her. "You drove me to that haste, Elisa. You, with your perfection and sensuality. You are unique. But don't worry—I will take care of you in a moment."

"Take care…? You mean, like yesterday?"

He smiled. "Did you think to halt here and leave me still wanting?"

"But that is *my* pleasure, not something that you would want." She licked her lips, confused. The tip of her tongue touching her reddened lips was a tiny pleasure of its own.

Her coyness delighted him. She may have been married, but she was virtually untouched and completely uneducated to the joys of lovemaking. What a treasure!

"But...you have spent yourself," she managed.

He thrust his hips a little, for he was still resting inside her. He let her feel him. He was already swelling, stirring, tingling with renewed vigor thanks to the heat and touch of her body.

"Spend myself and leave you wanting? Only a cad could consider it," he assured her. He fitted his hands around her waist, and rolled on to his back, bringing her with him, still joined.

She gasped a little as she settled against his hips. He was still buried deep inside her. He lifted her hips, showing her how she could ride him for herself, and she quickly found a rhythm that made each stroke a breathless joy. He reached up to cup her breasts as they swung a little with her movements and she caught her breath.

The sight of her straddling his hips, her sweet body taking him in, her long flowing hair lifting a little in the breeze...already he could feel the inevitable moment racing closer as he watched her enjoyment mount.

He slid his hand to the juncture of her thighs, to the slip between the flesh to find the tender pearl there, and stroked. She gasped, her head rolling back, and her hair trailed down to brush his thighs. Little shivers of pleasure ran through him at the light touch, a counter-point to the deep waves of excitement building in him.

Her rhythm grew faster, but her smooth motion faltered a little. Her growing excitement was destroying her concentration.

And he realized that he was already skirting the edges of control once more. Unwillingly to perform a short duty yet a second time, he flexed himself upright, sitting up with Elisa in his lap.

She looked at him, a little startled, her eyes wide and her breath ragged. "What is it?"

"You, my dear Elisa, are far too much woman to suit my equanimity. You are a sweet tease...far too sweet."

"I do not understand," she confessed.

"If we were to continue, I would spend myself a second time, and leave you disappointed."

"Oh..." and she smiled a little, his meaning suddenly clear to her. "Should we rest, then?"

"Not at all." He lay her on the fragrant chamomile, and kissed her swollen lips, his tongue exploring the warm taste of her mouth. Her hands were in his hair, caressing his back, and he wondered if she was aware of their restlessness, of the pressure they were applying to bring him closer to her. Elisa had an untapped sensuality—and he was responding to it with rare potency.

He kissed his way down to her belly, laving the indentations beside each hip with his tongue, and her hips lifted in response. Her legs moved restlessly as his lips moved onto the creamy flesh of her inner thighs.

"Vaughn, what do you intend now...?" she began. He lowered his mouth to her mons and slipped his tongue inside the folds to stroke her heated, swollen nub.

She gasped, and her hands buried themselves in his hair, clenching tight. "Oooh...!" she gasped, and he delighted at the sound, knowing from her reaction that no man but he had ever done her this service before. He caressed her with his mouth, and slid his fingers into her channel, and stroked and played the flesh there, feeling spasms and ripples of excitement pulsing through her. Her breath was coming in tight little gasps, faster and faster. Her whole body was quivering, shifting under his ministrations. He could feel the peak of her pleasure building, approaching, and coaxed her to that point with every skill he had learned.

Elisa climaxed, a screaming gasp locking her throat, and her body tightening into a stillness that seemed to spin out for an eon. She shuddered, waves rippling through her. Her hands tightened convulsively against him.

Her pleasure was intoxicating. He was responding to her even without direct stimulation. Once more he marveled at the effect she had on him.

Finally, the surge ceased, and her body went limp. Elisa licked her lips, her eyes heavy lidded with languorous satiation.

He lay down beside her and stroked her soft skin—gently, without provocation, allowing her to recover. She rolled on her side, and her legs entwined with his own. Her heart was beating a thousand miles an hour…like his own.

He looked down at her upturned face. Her eyes were closed, a soft smile on her face. She was a woman who'd been pleased.

With a sigh she opened her eyes and smiled. "My bones have melted."

"Good," he murmured.

"That is what you meant when you said you could give me even more pleasure?

He smiled a little at her curiosity, which held no taint of coyness or fake prudery. "That is what I meant," he assured her. "It will serve?"

"Oh yes!" Her lips curved in a glorious smile. "Only…" She blushed deeply. "Until this moment I believed I was experienced in the ways of men and women. I thought I was a wicked woman because what I knew of these things left me unhappy—"

"You mean unsatisfied, do you not?"

She bit her lip, considering the question. "Yes, but Vaughn, you must believe me when I say that I did not know all of it. Until yesterday, I did not know of this, that I was capable of…climaxing. Vaughn, is this something that every woman can experience? Or is it just the women that men call whores that do so? Is that why they are whores? Is that why men seek them out?"

His laughter came from the bottom of his belly, and it felt and sounded like *good* laughter—bereft of any of the cynicism that had colored it of late. "Elisa, my sweet, I believe that all women are capable of what you just achieved, but many, many of them will never experience it because they will not open their minds to the possibility. They think it wicked and will not consider it."

"Yes, I know many women like that. Most of the women I know are like that. I always thought…" and she paused, a frown puckering her brows. "I always thought there was something wrong with me, that because I found the little experience I had with my husband not enough to…satisfy me, that I was…perverted."

"You are a delight, Elisa. How could that be perverted?"

"Men have tried to…seek me out." She looked up at him from under her brow. "I know what they say of me, Vaughn. I thought that I was truly a whore and that was why they sought me."

He could feel the distress behind her simple words.

"Yes, they call you whore and worse, but it is just a name, Elisa. Just a name that comes easy to their lips. I believe that men can sense you are capable of enjoying yourself, and that makes them eager to experience it with you."

"It does?" She was startled by the idea.

"Certainly. Oh, they may not understand this themselves, but I know that I enjoy making love with you because you enjoy it yourself. It is not an odious duty to you."

She lifted herself up on one elbow. "Truly? You do not think less of me because of it?" She was watching his face, missing nothing.

He took a deep breath. "Truly, Elisa. I do not think less of you. More, if anything. Far more than I believed a month ago." And he realized he was speaking the utter truth.

She continued to study him carefully for a moment, then visibly relaxed. A slow smile curved her beautiful lips. "I see," she said.

And he knew that she did see, that she understood intuitively far more than their simple conversation encompassed.

She glanced over her shoulder towards the pond. "I believe I will bathe." She didn't wait for him to answer, but came slowly to her feet and walked toward the water, completely uninhibited. He stared at her backside, her heart-shaped buttocks, her long legs, her beautiful back. As the water lapped around her ankles she turned to him with a smile. "Come, join me."

She didn't have to ask twice.

Coming up behind her, he wrapped his arms around her and pulled her against him, nuzzling her neck. His hand captured one breast, and he rubbed his thumb over the upright nipple. She gasped, with a tiny catch in her throat, then gently pushed him away.

With a sweet laugh, she walked further into the water, then plunged beneath the surface. A moment later she emerged at the other side, her hair—dark now it was wet—slicked back off her face, showcasing her fragile beauty.

He followed her, the cold water taking the breath from his lungs. But at least it helped to ebb the fire that burned within him. While she paddled in the water to keep herself afloat, he found he could touch bottom. He pulled her into his arms and she wrapped her legs around his hips, her smile wicked as she pressed her breasts against his chest. He lifted her higher, taking a rigid peak into his mouth, laving it, suckling hard.

She shifted and impaled herself on his still rigid cock, gripping his shoulders as she ground against him. The motion washed water around her neck, so he moved forward a few paces until they were in shallower water, and he could control her movements. He held her hips and thrust into her with slow strokes. Despite the coolness of the water, he was responding with the same overwhelming reaction as before. Her newly released inhibition was a glorious coercion.

He found himself thrusting compulsively, the primal need washing conscious thought from him, driving him to the delicious pinnacle once more. She must have sensed it, for at that moment she pushed away from him, with a little laugh, and climbed back onto the bank.

Water streamed from her as she turned and looked at him. She did not beckon to him, but her stance, the small smile, were beacon enough, and he found himself emerging from the water, moving towards her.

He reached for her but she pushed on his chest a little. "Wait," she murmured, her hands on his chest. Her lips replaced her hands. Soft butterfly kisses dotted his chest and down his stomach, which clenched tight as she fell to her knees.

She moaned low in her throat before she took him into her mouth. Vaughn's head fell back on his shoulders. His hands fell to her shoulders, clenching as she suckled him. She was not an expert, but she could read his responses and very quickly learned what was the most effective—her lips encircling the swollen head of his cock, slipping wetly against the sensitive ridge of flesh; the teasing stroking of her tongue against the tight ridge of flesh on the underside of the head; sucking strokes, little flicks of the end of her tongue against the tip. He opened his eyes and looked up at the blue sky. If she did not stop, he would lose control.

"Elisa," he said, the words coming out strangled.

She clenched his buttocks with her hands, pulling him closer to her.

Finally he pushed away the slightest bit. She looked up at him, her eyes dark with a passion he was becoming to know well.

"Enough," he said, drawing her up to him. The feel of her soft body against his hard one was exhilarating.

Perhaps sensing his eagerness, she coaxed him to the ground, to lie between her thighs. Her legs came up around his hips. She looked up at him, her expression one of complete surrender. He entered her with a single hard thrust.

Her mouth opened with a soundless gasp as he buried himself to the hilt. God, she was so tight! It must have been years since she'd taken a man. The thought made him lengthen. He began to move, and she along with him.

He tried to hold on, keeping his movements slow, but it seemed she would have none of that. She clenched his buttocks, pulling him closer as she lifted her hips in a rhythm that would have him spent long before planned.

"Take me," she whispered in his ear.

That's all it took. With a savagery he'd not known he possessed, he thrust harder and still harder, until she moaned loudly. As she squeezed him tight, he came with a ferocity that left him trembling.

* * * * *

Later that afternoon as Elisa slowly dressed and arranged her hair, she glanced up to find Vaughn watching her. He sat on a nearby rock, already dressed, his eyes dark with an emotion that she was beginning to recognize as passion.

Despite making love five times, he still wanted her. And she could feel herself respond to his thoughts. Even though he had reassured her he accepted her passionate nature, welcomed it even, she wondered if her need of him did not constitute an obsession. Despite the hours that had just passed, she knew she wanted him again.

And what if he did not feel the same? What if he left for London as he had been threatening to do for a week? What if he became engaged to Natasha?

"I don't want to go back," she said, speaking before she could doubt the wisdom of such candor.

A small frown marred his forehead. "Then don't," he said.

"You know it isn't that simple." She dropped her hands from the row of buttons on her bodice.

"I know I hate the thought of him touching you. How could you entertain the idea, Elisa?"

"You know why."

"I know the reason he gave you," he muttered, standing abruptly and striding to the water.

"You hate him, don't you?"

His answer took a moment. He glanced at her. "Do you think he'd be a good father to your son?"

She shrugged. "I would hope so."

He laughed without mirth. "That man doesn't know what compassion is. Not once did I ever receive a hug. Not even a pat on the head for any accomplishment. He has always hated me, hated everyone...except for my mother. And when she was gone, he had no use for me. You want that for your son, Elisa?"

She was silent, unable to form an answer. She had not considered her life beyond the moment when Rufus restored her son to her. She had been so focused upon finding Raymond and winning him back.

"I know Rufus is the only one who has given me any hope of finding Raymond," she answered truthfully. "I cannot jeopardize that." She glanced at the long shadows on the ground. "It's late. I must return before he becomes suspicious."

"He always wins, doesn't he?" Vaughn growled. "I make love to you, but he wins because you're running back to him."

His words struck a chill in her heart. "What did you say?"

He was scowling at the water, occupied by his thoughts, but he must have heard her for he sighed and ruffled his hand through his hair. "He wins," he said bitterly. "Although..." His frown smoothed itself a little. "It occurs to me that I have had my revenge upon him this afternoon, haven't I?" And he looked at her with a twisted smile.

The breath left her in a rush. He had not seduced her because he was attracted to her at all! He had seduced her to revenge himself upon the father who had turned his back on him.

Hollow nausea gripped her throat and stomach. "You lied to me," she whispered.

He turned then. Her voice must have given away her horror. "Lied?" he repeated.

She finished fastening the last of her buttons with hands that trembled violently.

"The men that sought me out because of my s-s-sensuality — they at least were direct. They did not have hidden motives."

"Elisa, what on earth...?"

"You used me in a way they never did," she spat. "Congratulations, Vaughn, you have truly turned me into a whore."

She turned and ran, not caring that she left her hat or that Vaughn was yelling her name.

Chapter Fourteen

When she returned to the manor, Elisa was enormously thankful to learn Rufus was resting in his bedchamber. It saved her the complication of more lies. More importantly, she could avoid Rufus' scrutiny before she had a chance to bathe and wash the sins of the day from her flesh. As it was, by the time she reached the cold marble hallway dinner was barely an hour away. She had little time to take a bath and dress.

Marianne was unusually quiet. No doubt her maid was disappointed in her for giving into temptation. Though Elisa had kept her silence about the afternoon, it was as though Marianne could read the imprint of every forbidden caress upon her face. The Frenchwoman poured water with a sad, repressed air that seemed almost sorrowful.

No one could be more sorry than Elisa herself. She had let herself down, broken faith with her personal vow to win her son back, and worse still, wanted the man who'd used her so blatantly.

Damn Vaughn to hell with the rest of mankind!

As she dressed, she squirmed under the raw knowledge that Marianne had been right all along, that she had been a pawn in a man's game and meant less than nothing to him personally. As a result, she found it impossible to make eye contact with Marianne. If she could not deal with Marianne directly, how could she possibly look at Rufus without giving herself away?

With a final look in the mirror, Elisa took a deep breath and headed downstairs, repeating hollow reassurances. Nothing had changed. No one could see anything if she did not speak of her guilt aloud. No one would know. No one would ever know. She would bury her foolishness and her guilt deeper than a corpse.

She would just behave as always.

Despite her funereal pace, the double doors of the dining room rushed to meet her. Inside, she could hear Rufus ordering a servant about, his voice booming. A chill raced down her spine.

How she hoped Vaughn would make excuses and not attend dinner! She knew he'd arrived home shortly after she did—she had heard the sound of servants heading for the opposite wing. They always did flock around him whenever he returned to the hall. They adored him and fussed over him and she could hear their conversation as Vaughn walked down the passageway, the light, bantering tone he used with them. She prayed he had the sense to stay in his room rather than show his face.

Her hand trembled as she pushed the dining room door open. Her heart sank to her toes when she saw Vaughn sitting in his usual spot, across from her seat at Rufus's right. His glass was halfway to his lips, and as she entered he set it down without taking a drink.

She quickly turned her head away and smiled at Rufus. Her lips trembled, so she pressed them together.

Tonight she had dressed in her most conservative gown, one with a high lace collar and modesty panel. It had seemed prudent at the time she'd chosen the gown. She realized now her guilty conscience had prodded her into covering her shame with a false modesty that would deflect any attention. Now she realized she had garnered attention instead by changing her style of dress too swiftly.

"Do you mean to tell me you've already worn all the gowns I bought for you last week?" Rufus asked as she sat down.

Folding her hands in her lap, she clenched them together, gathering control, before replying as steadily as she could. "I fell asleep and when I awoke it was late, so I donned the first item in my wardrobe."

"I see." He lifted a brow while motioning the footman to refill his glass. "Did you get my cigar?"

Her heart leapt a little. "I'm sorry, I completely forgot your request, my lord."

He took a swallow of his port then set the glass down harder than necessary. "And did you forget your bonnet as well?" His voice was laced with sarcasm.

Though she schooled her features, she could feel heat rise up her neck and stain her cheeks. "Actually, I did. I apologize again. It is simply that I enjoyed my ride so much, I didn't wish to stop in the village. I rode all the way to Caroline's, instead, and called on her to thank her for her hospitality the other night."

Vaughn's silence was like a shout. He was not supporting her, not providing help in any way. She could feel his gaze on her, but she refused to look his way, for she knew one glance would be the undoing of all her courage. How could she make it through dinner without revealing her guilt in some way?

The footman moved forward, filling Vaughn's glass to the brim. From the corner of her eye she watched Vaughn lift it to his lips and drain it.

"You're thirsty this evening," Rufus remarked, his attention neatly diverted from Elisa.

"As a matter of fact, I am," Vaughn replied, motioning the footman over again. "You may as well leave the bottle, my friend."

The footman obliged, settling the craft to Vaughn's right.

Rufus cackled. "What a lively group this is. You look terrible, boy."

"I'll consider that a compliment, coming from you."

Rufus' eyes narrowed. Elisa held her breath, knowing the fury to come.

Vaughn lifted a dark brow. "Come, father. Tell me the sins of drinking, since you have so much experience."

The veins in Rufus' head grew pronounced as he leaned forward and leveled his son with a glare that would make most men tremble in their boots.

Vaughn was completely unaffected.

Whatever Rufus had been about to say, Vaughn's indifference changed his mind. He picked up the fork he had dropped. "Come morning, you will leave my home."

A sharp pain lodged in her heart. Leave? Vaughn could not leave! She opened her mouth, a protest at the ready. Rufus' order abruptly dislodged the afternoon's betrayal from her mind, relegating it to a insubstantial memory. She rallied words to her defense, phrases that would mollify Rufus and make him retract his order.

Vaughn beat her to the deed, drawling, "Father, how can I properly court Miss Natasha from jolly old London?"

A slow smile spread across Rufus' mouth. "So that is your interest in staying on at Fairleigh Hall."

"What else could there be?" Vaughn returned, pouring himself another glassful of port. His casualness, the dismissal, stung the core of her soul. Indeed, what else could there be now he'd had his way with her? She had been a tool he had used and could now dismiss from his attention.

The shame of the afternoon surged in her anew, and she clenched her fists. She had experienced unparalleled bliss in his arms and on the same day he spoke of courting another. She wished she could convince herself he did this merely to prolong his stay at Fairleigh Hall in order to be with her, but there was no conviction in the wish, for she knew the truth, now.

"You've asked William and Caroline for their permission to court their daughter?"

"Not yet," Vaughn returned.

"Tomorrow, then," Rufus said matter-of-factly, his good mood returning once more. "Morning tea would be the earliest appropriate moment."

"Yes, that would be quite suitable," Vaughn replied. "I find I am quite anxious to see her again." He looked at Elisa. "Perhaps you would accompany me, madam? You could help me persuade Caroline and William."

Her indignation at the arrogance of his suggestion evaporated under his intense stare. There was a message in his eyes — words she could not quite read, for her soul was churning with the hot mixture of shame and anger that had been burning there since the afternoon, blinding her. Yet she knew that she must understand what he was trying to tell her. With a deep breath she let go of the emotions, and opened her heart to his unspoken message.

He cared for her. Perhaps it wasn't love, but it was desire. Even now her insides clenched, remembering the feel of him within her. Her fingers tingled, recalling the touch of his tight, smooth olive skin. She remembered how the muscles of his shoulders and arms bunched as he thrust within her time and again, his whole body swept up into the primitive need to take her, make her his. She could see now in her mind the feral, haunted look in his eyes as he spilled his seed within her. And her whole body thrummed with the remembered sensations, tight with renewed tension. The raw, replete flesh of her cleft, her abused nub of pleasure throbbed in response.

"Can you not respond?" Rufus remarked, bringing Elisa out of her wicked thoughts with a small jump.

She cleared her throat and looked Vaughn in the eye without difficulty. "I would be happy to assist, though I doubt you will have difficulty. They are enamored of you already."

"Thank you," he said, relief not only in his voice, but his beautiful emerald eyes as well.

Conversation halted as the main course was served. Rufus attacked a healthy portion of lamb and vegetables smothered in gravy. Throughout the meal Elisa could feel Vaughn watching her and knew he wanted her to look at him, but she forced herself not to respond. The setting was too intimate. There were no guests to distract Rufus tonight. He would see far too much if she gave in to the emanation of Vaughn's will silently reaching out to her across the table.

When she felt a light touch on her ankle, she quickly tucked her feet back beneath the chair, out of Vaughn's reach. She would not give in so easily. She knew now that theirs had been a mere tryst. It had ended just as all things ended, and she would emphasize that point to Vaughn.

Tomorrow she would tell him.

Rufus stood abruptly, with a belch, and a thump to the chest to clear his wind. "Time for a cigar. Come Elisa," he declared.

Her plate was still untouched, but Elisa willingly rose to her feet.

"She's not finished eating," Vaughn pointed out.

Rufus looked at the untouched plate, then back to Elisa. "You're getting much too thin, my dear. Come, play for me." He extended his arm.

Elisa glanced at Vaughn, lounging in his chair with one hand on the goblet of wine, then tucked her hand under Rufus's arm and allowed him to lead her from the room.

Vaughn stayed at the long table while the servants cleared the two untouched plates and the remains of Rufus's hearty meal and silently wiped up the slops from his glass. While they worked, a soft melody trickled from the piano in the parlor. An hour went by while Vaughn finished off the bottle of port and music filled the manor. He envisioned what was happening in the other room and considered opening another bottle. Elisa would be playing the piano, wooing her fiancé to sleep, hoping he would pass out and not bother her.

Trying to avoid attention had been a hallmark of his own schooldays, he recalled, and his stomach twisted at the thought.

The life he'd experienced in school wasn't so different from the life Elisa would live, married to the monster he had the privilege to call "Father".

How could she consider submitting to that life for even an instant?

For a moment he entertained the delights that would come from taking her from here. Spiriting her away—to Kirkaldy, his estate on the Scottish border over looking a field of heather, Kirkaldy, that his mother had loved, where she had been so happy. They would have a good life there, away from the ghosts.

He ran a hand down his face, as he realized where his thoughts were straying. Dear lord, he had drank far too much tonight! He had come to despise drunks thanks to his father's example, and yet he had allowed himself to become intoxicated and his mind to wander like a befuddled old fool's.

The music stopped in the next room and he waited, listening for her footsteps. There they were—small feet climbing the cold stairs, the noise echoing off the marble walls. The whisper of steps along the carpet of the old wing corridor, then the distant closing of a door.

Vaughn forced himself to movement. He crossed to the drawing room and peeked in. Rufus was sprawled in a wing chair, his head fallen against one shoulder, snoring loudly, his mouth ajar. He would sleep until morning.

Vaughn shut the door, and blinked a little, clearing his head. The fool's visions of domestic bliss in Kirkaldy were still wreathing his thoughts, sliding into his mind. Where had they come from?

Beckoned on by the seductive urgings, Vaughn climbed the stairs to the second floor and turned right, heading for the wing where she had just gone.

At her door he listened, but heard nothing. He tried the handle and found it unlocked.

Surely she had left it open for him?

Encouraged, Vaughn slid inside the room, but the moment he entered, she turned on the stool she sat upon before the dresser, her eyes narrowing.

"Get out," she spat.

"I know you don't mean that."

"Marianne will be here any moment to help me undress."

"I'll help you."

She shook her head. "You've been more than enough *help*, thank you." Her narrowed eyes were filled with a light...with anger, he realized with a jolt.

"You're angry with me?"

"You used me!" she declared.

"You used me as well," he shot back.

"That is a lie!"

"Really? Tell me that you did not for one moment feel some satisfaction in betraying that pig of a man you intend to marry. Tell me that there was not the smallest degree of revenge in your soul when you lay with me and thought of him. Tell me that."

Her mouth opened in disbelief, and she rose to her feet. "You insufferable bastard!"

He smiled, understanding the guilt that forced her to deny the truth of his words. He took a step closer, within arm's reach. "Do you hate me so much, then?"

Lifting her chin, she swallowed hard. "I have been hurt before, Vaughn. I know the cruelty of men, and you would think by now I would have learned my lesson. Yet I allowed myself to be led down that road once more and this time I have only myself to blame. Therefore, I will bear responsibility for ending this affair. I would ask you to leave."

He reached out, his finger tracing the curve of her neck. She flinched, but didn't push him away. "Do you really want me to go, Elisa?"

Her breasts strained against her gown, and he could see her eyes turn dark with the passion that had driven her that afternoon to wanton acts that fired his blood even in memory. But her voice remained calm and she did not sway towards him in response to his touch. "I will not be betrayed again," she said. "If you do not go now, then you *will* betray me in the end."

"I want you."

"You want only to hurt your father."

"To hell with the old man," he snarled.

She watched him intently, as though if she looked hard enough she would find the answer she sought.

He attempted to explain himself a little better. "I knew you were an equal, and not the plaything others assumed you to be."

A blush raced quickly up her neck. "A plaything?" she replied.

He shrugged, hoping to disguise his discomfort with such disclosures. He caressed the upper swell of her breasts above the dress, through the delicate lace. God, just standing this close to her was making him throb with need for her, for the sweet release he had enjoyed that day. "You are no plaything," he added. "I could take you a dozen times and it would not be enough."

She pushed his hand aside and slipped past him, moving to the bed. She sat on the edge and leaned down to push off her slippers. Her breasts, lush firm globes of pale flesh, pushed at the lace—he could see the dark valley between them, and the sight brought a silent groan to his lips.

She looked up at him. "Leave me. I need to sleep."

He could now add headstrong to her long list of traits. "I can think of more exciting things to do than sleep."

Her expression was cold, but he could see her eyes darken, the lashes lower. She was angry, but still aroused at the thought.

A knock sounded at the door. "Marianne," Elisa said under her breath. "You have to go."

Vaughn crossed his arms over his chest and leaned against the wall.

She shook her head. "Hide then."

Dutifully he found a good hiding place behind a chest of drawers that once graced his mother's room. He crouched down and waited.

The conversation between the two women was light. Each one of Elisa's words were clipped and curt, signaling to the other woman she was in no mood for conversation. After endless minutes, the light went out and the door closed behind the maid.

He stood, finding his way by the light of the full moon that escaped through the sheer drapes. It occurred to him that it had been a full month since he had been struck speechless by her angelic appearance in the library the first night he had returned here. "Does she tuck you in every night?" he asked, sitting on the end of the bed.

"Yes."

Even in the darkness he could feel her anger. "I apologized, Elisa."

She sighed heavily. "I know, but it doesn't change what happened. You knew I would give into you. You knew I would not be able to resist your charm."

Had he known that? Yes, he had been confident that sooner or later she would give in to him. It had never occurred to him that she would be able to resist.

He ran his hand up her leg, wishing it were her flesh and not the coverlet he felt.

"You want me," she said.

"Of course."

"Lay down beside me," she whispered.

His heart beat in double-time with almost schoolboy glee. He obeyed with alacrity, realizing that she had forgiven him somewhat. He had an inarticulate hope that her forgiveness would be total.

"Your boots. Take them off," she ordered.

Again, he obeyed her command, enjoying the little game.

"Take off your shirt."

Unable to hide his smile, he threw the shirt on the floor.

She held the covers aside and he slipped into the warm bedding. Her thigh, wrapped in silk, came to rest over his breeches, and she cuddled up to his side with a sigh.

He stroked her leg through the silk, his fingertips tingling with the touch, while her hands moved up along his arms, curling around his biceps. "I am more than a plaything, then?" she asked.

"Yes," he agreed, puzzled. Hadn't he just told her that?

She sat up then, straddling him, and in the moonlight, her silk shift rode up high, revealing the pale, slender length of her thighs.

"I see," she murmured, and moved her hips in an enticing, lustful way.

His erection, already painfully engorged despite the drink he had consumed this evening, grew thicker and longer as she rubbed against him. She leaned toward him, and her breasts, gleaming in the moonlight, were mere inches from his lips. He swallowed dryly and reached for them, but she caught his wrist in her hands and pulled his arm over his head, until it brushed up against the iron bed frame. The movement brought her breasts breathtakingly close to his mouth.

Distracted so, it took him a moment to realize that she had slipped something warm and soft around his wrist. It was only when she caught the other wrist in her small warm hands that he felt the tug of the restriction on the other.

"What...? Elisa, what are you doing?" he asked, trying to move his head around so that he could see.

"Shhh, plaything," she murmured. "You need to learn your place." Even as she spoke, his other wrist was moved to the other corner of the bed head and anchored.

He tugged at the bonds experimentally. They were quite secure. Straining his head to one side he could glimpse a hint of bright colors around his wrists. Bending his fingers inwards allowed him to feel the sensuous touch of silk.

"What is this? Elisa, where did you get these?"

"They are scarves. Silk scarves from the Orient. I put them under the pillow just now when Marianne helped me to bed." Her voice seemed distant, as if she were concentrating on other matters.

Scarves or ties, it did not matter. The tight weave of silk meant that if she had tied an adequate knot he would never break the bonds. His tugging told him the knot was adequate.

"Elisa, enough of this. I apologized. Let me loose."

She didn't say anything. Instead, she slithered down the length of his body, her breasts grazing his flesh, brushing past his groin, and he realized her next target. He moved his foot out of her way, but she was quicker. A loop of silk was whipped around the other ankle, and cat-quick, she looped the other end around the bedstead, and fastened it. That left one remaining limb free. By the simple expedient of sitting on his thigh, her round warm bottom anchoring his leg, she tied his ankle to the other side of the bed frame.

He was utterly helpless.

She turned around, and in the moonlight he could see her small smile. She ran her fingers lightly down his arms, and then his sensitive side. She moved further down his body, her hair tickling his belly, and then his groin. Her lips followed the same trail and soon he was straining against the bonds.

"Elisa, I want my hands free."

Her teeth flashed white in the darkness of the room. "Not until you've learned your lesson."

"God's teeth, Eliza, I apologized. And I explained — revenge upon my father was…an afterthought. A sweet bonus."

"Yes, I know. But that is not the lesson."

"Then…I don't understand," he confessed, a little confused. Although her lips on his flesh were causing some of the confusion, too.

"Exactly. You need to understand."

She reached across him towards the side table, her breast again brushing his chest. His flesh rippled beneath the fleeting touch, sending spears of feeling into his groin. He caught his breath. There was a degree of enjoyment at being completely at her disposal, he realized. The novelty had cleared his head of the last of the port, too.

Then she straightened up again, her knees on either side of him, the negligee again pushed high up by her hips. This time, though, she wielded a knife.

Fright touched him. "What do you intend to do with that?" he demanded. Surely…she had forgiven him, yes? Or did her anger run deeper than he had suspected?

"I thought I might want to have a weapon for protection." She waved the knife, the blade gleaming dully, catching the direct reflection of the moon in ghostly flashes of light that caught his attention, and held his gaze. The blade looked ridiculously long.

"What is it that you want?" he said, keeping his voice as even as possible.

"You," she answered, her voice ethereal.

"Elisa —" he began as she lowered the knife towards his stomach. He held his breath, bracing himself, as the cold blade slide beneath the top of his breeches. "Elisa," he tried again, and then, abruptly, she flexed her arm, and the tough broadcloth parted with a soft tearing sound, from waistband to hip, split by the knife. She pushed the raw edges aside with the knife, then used the point to tickle the extremely sensitive flesh right next to where his shaft reared against his belly. She seemed thoughtful, absorbed in her task.

He flexed against his bindings. "For God's sake, Elisa, let me loose."

"No."

"Let me loose, or I'll—"

"You'll what?" she asked, lifting her chin to look at him. The knife had stopped its tickling and rested alarmingly close to his groin and the master vein that throbbed there.

"I'll…you'll pay for this."

"I have already paid. Clearly, you still don't understand." She pushed the knife down the leg of his breeches, which was still relatively whole, then turned the knife sideways so that the edge of the blade lifted the fabric. The broadcloth gave way with another quiet rip. Slowly she worked her way down the leg of the trousers until the fabric lay on either side of his now bare leg.

He lay still, his heart beating with a mix of puzzlement and astonishment.

Still in thoughtful silence, she tore the other leg of his breeches from his body, leaving him completely naked, with his limbs stretched to the four corners of the bed. Despite his demeaning position he was painfully aroused.

Still holding the exceedingly sharp knife, she leaned down towards him. He gritted his teeth as her lips encircled the tip of his penis. "Elisa…"

She ignored his helpless protest and instead suckled him until he was writhing beneath her. He fought to maintain control, to stay on top of the powerful swell of pleasure building in him, sensing it would be an acknowledgement of her power in this position if he were to climax.

But that was not her goal, he realized, when she sat up on her heels and looked down at him. She brought the knife up to rest between her breasts, and slipped the tip inside. The blade split the fine material without effort, and the insubstantial nightgown fluttered down onto the bed, leaving her glorious body naked and awash with the glow of the moonlight. Her nipples were hard and erect. Her hands came up to cup them, and her fingertips played with them.

"What is it you want, Vaughn?"

"You."

Her hands dropped to his thighs. The fingers ran up both thighs, coming to a stop right at his groin. She skipped over his throbbing, hot member and caressed his stomach, then chest.

"I cannot hold out against you much longer," he warned.

"You have no choice," she responded. "That is your lesson." She leaned over him, and this time her breast caressed his chin. The tip nudged his lips. "Take it in your mouth," she commanded.

He took the proffered nipple and suckled it, flicking it with his tongue, deliberately doing his best to arouse her in the hope that she would release him to finish the task properly.

Her soft moans were indication that he was succeeding. After a few moments, though, she moved so that the other neglected breast was presented to him.

"Again," she commanded.

He doubled his efforts and this time he could feel her moving against him, her hips rubbing in tight little circles, pressing against him and sliding up and down the length of his shaft. Warm moisture from her slick cleft anointed his cock, making it leap in response.

Then she was pulling the breast away, straightening up, positioning herself over him. Then slowly, inch by inch, she lowered herself onto him. Her progress was so slow sweat began to bead upon his forehead. He could feel every inch of her channel slide down over the sensitive tip of him. She was obviously enjoying herself, extending the sensations for as long as possible.

That was when he understood with growing wonder: *She was using him.* Using him for her own pleasure.

Just as slowly as she had lowered herself she began to rise once more. She had learned much since this afternoon for now there was no faltering in her motion. She was regulating the motion with deft precision for her complete pleasure. But it was not his complete pleasure, it was not exactly what he needed.

For many minutes she continued to pleasure herself upon him. If he gave any sign that he was close to climaxing she would halt her motion, denying him the release. His breath grew ragged and harsh, and his body wound tighter and tighter as he sought with the limited means at his disposal to find a release despite her. Unable to stand it, he thrust upward.

She immediately grew still, and put her hands on his chest. "No. I am in control here. Do you understand?"

The need for release was like a scream in his mind. He could think of nothing else. And Elisa held the power to give that to him. He could deny her nothing. He nodded.

"Excuse me?" she coaxed.

"Yes," he breathed.

"Yes, what?"

He took a deep breath, an attempt to make his voice behave normally. "Yes, you have control," he said.

"And the lesson?" she demanded.

A trickle of sweat rolled from his temple to the linen beneath his head. He swallowed. "The lesson?" He was appalled at the croak in his voice.

She moved her hips a little, and he felt her clench around him. "I want you to remember that from now on, when you come to me, when you make love to me…it is because I allow it. It is because I want it."

"I understand." He shifted his hips and once again she stopped.

"Vaughn, I don't want to have to say it again."

He clenched his jaw. Once she untied his hands, she would get a lesson she would not forget in a hurry. He would take her over his lap and spank her bare bottom. He groaned. The image did not help matters.

"I cannot wait much longer," he said between clenched teeth. His whole body was now covered in sweat with his efforts.

She began to move, a slow, sensual rhythm that soon gave way to a frenzy. He urged her on with soft spoken words, and struggled against his bonds to no avails. Then it happened, her body visibly tightened, her sheath squeezing him tight as she cried out his name.

With a single thrust, he followed her over the edge, his seed spilling into her with a single hard spasm that left him utterly spent.

A little later she recovered enough to lift herself away from his body. The soft brush of her against him made his deeply sensitized body leap, but he was still tied and the movement was aborted. Every nerve end in his body felt raw.

She rose to her feet and walked over to the bedroom door and startled him by locking it and pulling out the key.

"What do you plan now?" he asked as she walked towards him, the sweet hips swinging in small circles.

"I plan to sleep. It has been a long day."

"Sleep sounds good," he admitted.

She picked up the knife from the floor beside the bed and slipped it beneath the strained bindings around his wrists and feet, severing them with a sharp tug.

He rubbed his abused wrists and watched with a touch of surprise as she picked up his shirt and sliced it in half with the knife.

"Elisa…!"

"Time for you to leave," she said calmly.

"What do you mean?" He smiled a little. "You just locked the door."

"That's right. You can go out the window just like any other lover would."

"The window…?" He looked out upon the moon-flooded garden, one storey below the window. "You just cut up my one remaining item of clothing."

"Just a small reminder of my control, in case you didn't quite understand the first time."

He shrugged. "Then I'll sleep here."

"No."

Just the one word, but he saw the iron will behind it. And then he really did understand. Whatever power he had held in their relationship was gone now. They were equals, and she was now exercising her power. He could refuse to submit, but that would end the relationship immediately.

He stood. "No more playthings, hmmm?" he murmured.

"Exactly," she agreed.

"And if I'm caught out there, Elisa?"

"There's only a small likelihood of that happening. You're quick and strong."

"You would take such a risk?"

"It is you who takes this risk. I will swear that you must have been having your way with my maid, next door, and Marianne will support me in this. And your clothes will be found in her room."

"They will not believe that."

"Why not? It's well-spread gossip in the servants quarters that the maids all adore you." There was a touch of dryness in her voice.

"Why, Elisa? Why this?"

"Because I want you to taste the possibility of what it would be like to be thought badly of. I wanted to force you to submit to me and risk everything, just as you forced me to."

He caught her head in his hands and gave her a thorough, long kiss. "Good night, sweet Elisa," he assured her, and went to the open window to begin his risky trip back to the safety of his bedchamber without further protest.

The price of potential embarrassment should he be caught abroad stark naked in the moonlight was worth it.

Chapter Fifteen

"I need a word with you."

Elisa set the cup of tea down on the table and turned her attention to her fiancé, who had just entered the drawing room.

Sitting back in her seat, she folded her hands in her lap. "Good morning."

Rufus walked to the mantle and leaned heavily against it, looking up at the elegant picture of his great grandfather, a man to whom he bore absolutely no physical resemblance. He turned to her. "You lied to me."

White, hot fear raced through her. "Lied?"

"Yesterday you said you visited Lady Caroline, yet my man was there and he did not see you, nor was it mentioned that you had visited."

Elisa kept very still, her heart sinking. That damned story she had concocted at the last minute! Surely that would not be her undoing?

Deep in her heart she had known that sooner or later the lies she was sowing would eventually catch up with her. She just hadn't expected it to be this soon. What of Raymond? Rufus had indicated that Raymond would be returned to her before too long—she had to play for more time!

"I...didn't want you to be angry with me."

He planted both hands on his hips. "Why would I be angry?"

"You don't like me to ride, and I—"

"Stop it!" His voice cut straight through her words. He was upon her in two strides, taking her by the arm and lifting her up toward his face, so close she could smell his stale breath on her cheek. "You were with him, weren't you?"

She swallowed hard. "With whom?"

His bloodshot eyes pierced hers. "You spent the night with Vaughn. You were with him yesterday as well. That is why your gown has dirt and grass stains."

She winced as he twisted her wrist painfully. How had he learned of her ruined riding habit? Was she surrounded by spies?

"I want the truth. Now!"

"You're hurting me!" She tried to pull away, but he was unrelenting.

He thrust her from him, and she fell into a table. "Now, Elisa!"

"I had Marianne with me yesterday. And I fell from my horse. That is why I had grass stains."

"You took Marianne riding?"

"She is an excellent horsewoman, and I thought it more respectable to go calling upon neighbors and retail establishments with a maid to accompany me."

"You are a lying whore!" Rufus declared.

Above all she knew she could not rise to the bait in his insult. She could not afford to break off her relationship with Rufus yet. She must placate, must play for time. And then she realized the train of her thoughts, the idea that Vaughn had planted yesterday: once Raymond was back with her, she would leave this odious, dangerous man without a backward look and consider her debt to him paid in full.

Play for time.

"Why don't you ask Marianne yourself and put this behind us?" she told Rufus. She crossed the room and pulled the bell-pull.

It was a huge gamble she took, hoping Marianne would back her without coaching, but it would buy her more time than a less risky gambit—*if* Marianne played along.

Jacob appeared almost immediately, making her wonder if he had been hovering by the door, listening. "Yes, my lord?"

"Send Marianne to us right away," Rufus said, before Elisa could request her maid attend for herself. He threw himself into the nearest chair. "Then we'll get to the bottom of this."

Afraid her legs would give out, Elisa sat in a high-backed upright chair and waited for her maid. She kept her hands in her laps and fought not to wring them anxiously. A few silent moments passed before a knock sounded on the door.

"Come in," Rufus said, sparing Elisa a quick glance before they both turned their attention to the maid.

Marianne looked terrified. Elisa prayed she wouldn't fail her.

Rufus stood abruptly, nearly overturning the chair in his haste. Marianne visibly cowered as he approached her.

"Tell me what you did with your day yesterday," he demanded.

Elisa's stomach clenched tight and she thought her heart might burst through her chest, it was beating so hard. Rufus had asked an open question! How could Marianne possibly provide the correct answer?

"Why, my lord, I went riding with my lady Elisa," Marianne said, her tone puzzled, as if she couldn't see the point of the question.

Elisa nearly sobbed aloud her relief. Marianne had found some meager clue that told her the lie she must give.

"Really? Was it a pleasant day?" Rufus asked with oily concern.

"Pleasant enough in this chilly countryside, m'lord. But...the lady, she did fair ruin her riding habit. I've despaired over the cleaning of it."

"So say you. How did she ruin it?"

Elisa knew Marianne could not possibly answer this one correctly.

"Well?" Rufus demanded when Marianne did not answer straight away.

"My lord, Miss Elisa would not want me to reveal that, I am sure."

"I am her future husband, woman. If you wish to keep your position in this household you will answer me at once."

"I understand, my lord. My lady prides herself on her horsemanship, so she will not like me telling you that she fell from her horse."

Elisa bit down on her lip, and did not bother hiding her reaction when Rufus whirled to face her. She could not believe her good luck, and judging by Rufus' red, blotched complexion, he did not believe it either. His fury was almost palpable.

He turned back to Marianne, and his movement put Eliza in a position where she could see her maid once more. Marianne did not so much as glance at Elisa. She held her chin up and her shoulders square, proud and elegant.

"Did you look in on your mistress last night?" Rufus asked.

Marianne answered without hesitation. "Yes, my lord, I did."

"What time was it?"

"I'm not certain. It was the middle of the night, and I thought I heard something."

"It is not your custom to check on her?"

"Not usually, my lord. My lady used to sleep peacefully until of late."

"And why is that?"

"She's been worried about you, my lord. She told me you appeared tired, and she feared your attending the Munroe's ball may have been too taxing."

Instantly Rufus' shoulders relaxed a bit, and he turned toward Elisa. She forced a soft smile.

"Is this true?"

She nodded. "Yes, my lord. You slept much of yesterday — longer than usual, and last night you seemed — "

"Exhausted," Marianne finished for her.

The frown left his features instantly. "That will be all Marianne. Thank you."

The maid left the room, and Rufus turned his full attention to Elisa.

He watched her several minutes, saying nothing, leaving her with nothing to do but watch him in return. She must look completely innocent. She must carry this out. Marianne had done her part.

He approached her, and took her hand in his. With the other hand, he traced a line from finger to wrist. Slowly he brought the hand to his lips and kissed where he had so furiously twisted it. Already the skin was turning black and blue. "I didn't know you were worried about me."

The urge to rip her hand from his grasp was near overwhelming, but she resisted. She did not believe the gentleness of his tone was a true indication of his thoughts. "How can I not be?" she responded. "You've taken such good care of me."

"It pleases me you understand your place in this household, woman. It appears I was wrong about you and that wretched son of mine, which is just as well — " He twisted her wrist the slightest bit, causing her to cry out. "It saves me the bother of killing you both."

He let go her wrist, tossing it back into her lap like damaged goods, turned on his heel and left the room, slamming the door behind him.

Elisa remained seated until the violent trembling subsided.

She was not fooled by Rufus's words. He had not thought he was mistaken at all. He had fallen back for a short time because he had no proof, and that was all. The last words had been a direct threat: he knew about Vaughn and her. If he found any proof at all, he would follow through on his promise and kill them.

* * * * *

Vaughn walked amongst the old ruin of what in Henry II's day had been a grand castle protecting the county from French marauders. Now it was nothing but a heap of old stones, sitting upon on a cliff overlooking the ocean.

It seemed like a lifetime has passed since last he'd visited this spot. The last time he'd kicked at these stones had been before his mother's death. They had picnicked beneath the enormous oak that had once graced the bailey of the great fortress. While waves pounded against the cliff, he'd listened to her soft voice as she told him about the brave knights who had lived in the castle and protected it from enemies.

Everyone had an enemy, she'd said. Kings and beggars, thieves and queens. At the time he'd wondered who his enemy was. He found it fitting that his enemy was his own father, in keeping with the Greek tragedies his schoolmasters had once forced him to learn and recite in perfect ancient Greek. A tragic stage seemed to fit his mood, but what didn't suit him at all was that most of the characters in Greek dramas ended up dead.

On his real-life stage they were all helpless players in the plot that was unfolding. This morning Marianne had woken him hastily, warning him that Elisa might be in danger. She had hurried from the study straight to his bed to inform him of the interview Rufus had put her through.

After clearing his mind of sleep, Vaughn tried to put the pieces together. "How on earth did you know what to tell him?" he asked Marianne.

"Because Jacob listened outside the door and told enough before I got in the door to let me know what my lady had told the master," Marianne answered him as if it was perfectly clear and logical.

He was surprised at the maid's complicity in this matter when she had made it perfectly clear that she thought Vaughn a no-good scoundrel. "You hate him that much?" he asked.

"He is a stoat in human clothing," she declared calmly. Vaughn liked the analogy. Stoats were small, vicious creatures that attacked without provocation. They would take on a man if he got in the way and could do considerable damage. Fatalities were not unheard of. Luckily, there were very few of them left in the world.

He'd penned a note and handed it to Marianne with instructions to hand it to Elisa as soon as possible. Then he dressed and went straight to the stable to collect his horse and ride here to the ruins. He would wait all hours of the day and night until she came, if that was what it took. Rufus would think he was out wooing Natasha as he had ordered.

Vaughn spared a passing thought for the young girl. True beauty she was, yet she compared not at all to Elisa. By giving into his seduction, Elisa had managed to entwine her presence ever more firmly into his mind. Taking her to bed had not cured him of the obsession, but merely intensified it. How could he have thought it would be easy to walk away from her?

How could he possibly leave her with *him*?

The sound of an approaching rider brought him to his feet. Even before he could make out the features of the rider he knew it was Elisa. Her gown was tucked up to her thighs, her hair, coming lose of its chignon, flew behind her as she raced toward him as though the very devil were on her heels.

Was she being followed? He looked behind her, but the long flat plane that lead to the brink of the cliff was empty of all but Elisa. He released the breath he'd unconsciously been holding.

For a moment he thought she intended to ride him down, for she showed no signs of stopping or even slowing. But at the last possible minute she reined in and brought the mount to a stop in a flurry of sods. Without pause, she slithered from the saddle, straight into his arms.

Her words were almost a jumble, so quickly did she speak, her voice trembling.

"He knows, Vaughn. He knows! Marianne lied for me — god knows how she knew what to say, but she stopped him for the moment — but only for a moment. I could see it in his eyes. He knows, and he waits only for proof. Vaughn, he warned me he would kill us if he found us together. You must leave Fairleigh Hall."

He put her at arms length. "Shh, Elisa. Calm down, sweet one. Marianne told me what happened. There is nothing to fear yet. He is only guessing, or he would have taken his retribution this morning."

"He waits only for proof!" she cried. "Somehow he knows."

"No, he only suspects. He would like it to be true so that he can kill me with a clear conscious, but that is all."

"You must leave then, before he decides he'll kill you anyway." Glancing over her shoulder, she scanned the horizon before turning back to him. "We'd best tether our horses and keep hidden."

They walked the horses into the only standing structure left: the great hall, where it was rumored Henry and Eleanore and their feuding sons had once held court. One day he would tell Elisa all the stories his mother had shared about the castle's past, but now she needed assurance, not talk of enemies or Greek tragedies. Yet he could not speak reassuringly here amongst the ghosts of another family that had torn itself apart through petty jealousies and squabbles. Taking her hand, he led her back outside to the shade of the old tree.

When he tried to take her in his arms, she shrugged out of his reach and took his face between her small hands. Her expression was resolute. "Vaughn, you have to understand. You must leave, or he will kill you...and me as well. He told me as much."

"It's just an old man's bluff. Elisa, he knows nothing."

She released him, and shook her head. "We've only been together once at the hall and he learned something. He even knew I hadn't visited Caroline. For all I know I could have been followed that day at the pond. He appears to have spies everywhere."

Vaughn's attention was caught by another matter entirely. He reached for her arm, and pushed back the loose sleeve cuff to see for himself. Purplish bruises covered her wrist, and the flesh appeared swollen. Anger rushed through him. "Did he do this to you?"

"He was angry—"

"You defend him?" His voice rose. "That son of a swineherd's bitch!" He started toward the horses when she stopped him by grabbing his hand.

"No, Vaughn. Forget him. For a little while. For now. Let us enjoy the time we have."

He stood locked to the spot by helpless fury.

"Make love to me," she whispered. Stepping into his arms, she lifted her face to his. "Please, Vaughn."

He could not respond to her request. His anger was too great. She covered his face with a flurry of kisses, and he tried to move his mouth away from hers, although he could not bring himself to actively push her from him. She caught his face in her hands again, and this time she managed to capture his mouth with hers. Her tongue slipped inside, exploring his teeth and tongue. She pressed herself up against him, her breasts flattening against his chest. The yielding swell of them and the protruding nipple told him that beneath the cotton of her dress she was again naked. Indeed, he could feel the mild rise of her mound pushing with gentle insistence against his thigh, bereft of any intervening petticoats.

He knew that if he was of the mind, he could slide inside her with three quick movements and experience once again her hot, moist sheath. The thought caused him to stir, even though his anger had not subsided.

Her hands were fumbling at his breeches, and she proved yet again how quick a study she was. Within seconds she had the fastenings undone, and the breeches sagged around his hips, then her hands were inside, closing around him.

His resistance broke, and with a growl he lifted her and pinned her against the tree. She gasped at little at the contact, but reached eagerly for him, wrapping her legs about his hips as he lifted her skirt out of the way. With the one thrust that he had conceived of, he buried himself inside her and groaned aloud his satisfaction. But she goaded him on with words and cries of pleasure, and he thrust into her again and again in a venting of frustration, rage and obsession. He poured it all into each hard thrust. He freed her breasts from the low bodice, and partook of them, feasting upon them with his mouth and hand. He rubbed a nipple with his thumb while suckling on the other, drawing it into his mouth, and circling the tip with his tongue, flicking it, lapping at it.

Her head fell back against the tree in ecstasy.

The mating was frenzied, Vaughn setting a pace that was both savage and desperate in its intensity. Her fingernails raked into his back through the shirt as her climax began to build within her and explode. He gritted his teeth, the chords of his neck straining, and he moaned low in his throat as he came within her.

* * * * *

She rearranged her skirt as Vaughn dressed. He appeared calm again, not so apt to ride off wildly. He kissed her forehead. "You deliberately distracted me, Elisa. While I can't gainsay the distraction, I won't be deterred."

"I don't know what you mean," she said, but she couldn't look him in the eye.

"If I am to leave here, I will not leave without you."

She looked at him, and swallowed. This was what she had been afraid of. "I cannot," she said quietly.

"I will not leave you in the lair of that monster, Elisa."

"Where would we go?" she asked practically.

He shrugged. "Who cares? London. I know lots of people in London. They would love you."

Tears stung her eyes. "London? I can never return to London."

"Why not? It's not like you'd have to mix with the people you knew before. My townhouse is right by Hyde Park. The neighbor on the right is a good friend of mine—Henry Fitzgerald. And Jonathon Wright, on the other side, I went to school with. Oh, and Jonathan's wife is about your age. You should get along marvelously. She has a wicked sense of humor."

He was growing visibly more excited as he planned ahead, but Elisa could feel her heart sink with each sentence he spoke.

"Tell me," she said quietly. "Henry Fitzgerald, if I remember correctly is the earl of..."

"Sussex," Vaughn responded.

"And Jonathon Wright—I know his name, too."

Vaughn frowned. "He's the grandson—no, nephew, of the Prime Minister."

"Vaughn, listen to yourself. These people would have even less reason to accept me than those who pushed me out of London in the first place."

"That's ridiculous. They don't know you."

"They know who I am. I was banished years ago, yet you saw the way I was treated at the soiree. The people there knew me as well as your neighbors do. I could never return. Not ever!"

He considered this, his head down, impatience thrumming through him, communicated by the tense set of his shoulders. "Fine. Kirkaldy then. Wherever. I truly do not care, Elisa."

The tears that had been prickling her eyes for moments now finally escape to roll down her cheeks, and she dashed them away with the back of her hand. "No, I cannot," she repeated.

"Elisa, what happened in the past is exactly that…the past. Would you rather stay here with him?"

Her heart ached as she watched him. He was so certain that everything could be fine, but she was old enough to know better. "You know that's not the case. You know what society thinks of me. You've seen it for yourself. Even you have said my past is not sterling. A plaything, you called me."

"I said that out of anger."

"I know, but you can't possibly understand what it's like to lose everything and then be branded a whore. Your father was the only person who stood up for me."

Vaughn shook his head. "I will not leave you here."

"You have no choice."

He looked at her then, pain in his eyes. Just moments ago he had made love to her, and already she missed him. How could she live without seeing him every day, knowing his touch, hearing his voice…

"Then we'll stay away from society," he announced. "I could sell my estate in Scotland, and we could move to the—"

"Vaughn, stop." For six years she'd been kept away from society and she had hated it. She wouldn't let him do that to himself. She put a finger to his lips. "This is madness."

He shook his head. "Elisa, we could do this."

With every ounce of her being she wanted to go with him. There was only one reason to stay here, but it overrode any of the considerable arguments Vaughn could make. Besides, she had spoken truly; she couldn't return to London, or society, and she wouldn't make him sacrifice his home on her account. He would only resent her.

"Vaughn...he can give me my son back. I will not—I *cannot* give up the chance of finding Raymond again."

She could see in his eyes he could not counter this objection, as she had known from the beginning.

He sighed. "At least do not go back there without me, Elisa. I don't trust Rufus."

She gave him a reassuring smile. "I left word with Marianne I was riding to Caroline's to speak to her on your behalf just as we discussed last night. We'd best go there before Rufus comes to check on us, as I have no doubt he will."

* * * * *

Vaughn lifted Natasha's hand to his lips. "You look beautiful today, Natasha."

The girl beamed as she looked up at him, adoration sparkling in her dark eyes. A quarter of an hour ago he'd arrived with Elisa on his arm and asked to have a word with Caroline and William.

His request to court their daughter had been answered with wide smiles, and William's "yes" had been completely without hesitation. Throughout the short interview, Elisa sat nearby, her face pale, her smile forced. She had donned a pair of delicate lace gloves, conveniently hiding the bruises that marred her soft flesh. He had thought it impossible to hate his father before, but the bruises had indeed taken his loathing for the man to a higher summit.

Now he walked in the garden with her, thinking of things to say, wishing he were still at the ruins with Elisa. Perhaps if they hurried here, they could return and spend the afternoon making love.

"Who could that be?"

Vaughn followed the direction of Natasha's gaze and saw one of Fairleigh Hall's footmen walking up the long tree-lined drive.

"I believe that is Harlan, one of my father's servants. Perhaps he's come to escort my stepmother and I home."

She stopped in mid-step. "Oh! You don't have to leave already, do you?"

"I'll stay for a short while. If you'll excuse me, I'll see what he is here for."

Vaughn met Harlan at the front door. "What is it, my good man?"

Harlan took the steps two at time. "His lordship has requested his fiancée's presence at Fairleigh Hall. I've come to take her back."

"I can do it."

The servant lifted his chin. "No, sir, I'm afraid I have the strictest orders to return her myself. Plus, he said you would no doubt want to stay with Miss Natasha."

It was the last thing he wanted to do, but he couldn't deny it without causing speculation. "Very well, I'll get her for you."

Vaughn found Elisa in the parlor with Caroline and William, having what appeared to be a celebratory toast, for three glasses of champagne sat on the table.

"Toasting my future, I see," he said, stepping into the room. All three of them turned to him, but he was automatically drawn to Elisa. She was still far too pale, and her lip trembled when she did not press them together. When she looked up she smiled a little when she saw him, but the smile evaporated when she saw Harlan beside him.

"It seems Father wants you home," Vaughn told her. "Harlan has come to escort you."

She stood abruptly, knocking the table and spilling the champagne. "I'm so sorry," she said, righting one of the glasses. "How clumsy." Her hands were shaking.

"It's quite all right," Caroline assured her, and called for the servants.

Vaughn went to Elisa, and extended his elbow. "I'll walk you to the door."

"I will call on you later this week, if that is to your satisfaction," Elisa added politely.

"That would be lovely," William declared, and Caroline, who had clearly received the full details of Elisa's supposed sordid past, murmured something that Vaughn did not catch. For the sake of seeing him married to her daughter, it appeared that Caroline would suffer a whore in her parlor. The hypocrisy of high society never failed to amuse Vaughn, but his amusement had a bitter edge now.

Vaughn had offered to escort Elisa to the front door as a means for talking to her about this abrupt summons back to the hall. However, Caroline and William followed them to the hall, all the way to the front door, where Harlan already had Elisa's high-fettled horse waiting.

As Vaughn helped Elisa up into the saddle, which she settled into as if it was a sidesaddle, with one knee around the pommel, he squeezed her hand tight and murmured up to her. "I'll be right behind you. Stall Harlan if you can."

She nodded, looked up and smiled at Caroline and William then settled the reins. Harlan was on foot, and that would slow them somewhat. Vaughn knew Elisa had a head for intrigue— she would find a way to take forever to reach the hall, which would give him time, he hoped.

She glanced at Vaughn once more before kicking the horse into a slow walk, and he saw pure fear in her eyes. It kicked him in the gut. Suddenly, he knew he could not allow her to return to the hall alone. He did not care that she had refused him, that she had made her choice. Instinct was screaming at him.

But before he could so much as turn to ask for his horse to brought around, William was at his side. The older man clapped him on the shoulder. "Come. You and I will go to my study and lock ourselves in with one of those excellent bottles of port you sent over to me and the chessboard. We have things to discuss, away from the women."

Vaughn glanced back over his shoulder, to where Elisa was already at the end of the drive, Harlan's hand on the horse's bridle.

At the top of the steps, Caroline was smiling at him.

He pushed himself into a jovial smile. "Wonderful idea," he lied.

Chapter Sixteen

Elisa glanced over her shoulder. It was ridiculous to hope that Vaughn would catch up with them, despite every delaying tactic she had been able to conjure up, including a desperate plea for a private moment behind a bush, which she had spun out for long minutes. Despite the knowledge that Vaughn could not possibly be that close behind her, Elisa found herself looking over her shoulder constantly, hoping to see him.

Yet for as far as the eye could see there was no one. Just she and Harlan, and within minutes they would be at Fairleigh Hall.

Please, Vaughn, hurry.

They reached the gravel driveway, and Harlan helped her dismount. The great manor rose above her. Each step she took up the stairs toward the front door felt like her last. The mahogany door with its huge brass knocker loomed. She glanced back at Harlan, who stood at the bottom of the steps watching her. What was he doing? Did he fear she would run?

With a trembling hand, she opened the door. Every nerve on edge, she took a deep breath, and stepped into the front entrance foyer.

It was empty. She relaxed a little, then reminded herself that Rufus would hardly await her arrival in the front foyer.

"I see you've made it!" Rufus' voice boomed, startling her. That booming, echoing quality meant he must be in the circular stairway hall.

Her heart racing, she walked to the end of the foyer where the archway gave on to the marble floored hall. The sun was spilling through the high windows at the back of the house, flooding the hall with light that bounced off the shining marble surfaces, dazzling the eye, and making the hall glow with a false warmth. She had always thought the hall a cold place, empty of heart.

She stepped onto the marble, looking around for Rufus, and came to a halt, barely a pace into the hallway, with a hand to her mouth.

Rufus sat on the fourth step. Between his feet was a nearly empty decanter. The half-inch of liquid at the bottom was golden yellow. Rufus had exchanged his usual port for stronger spirits. His face was red, his hair wildly disarrayed — it looked as if he had been ruffling it with his hand, or perhaps he had simply rolled out of bed this morning without pause to complete his normal toilet. His tiny eyes were blood-shot and bleary. But it was not his demonical appearance that halted her. It was the pistol in his hand.

Everything within her screamed at her to run. The door was still open behind her...in two steps she could be racing down the foyer and out across the open field.

Except Harlan stood guard at the front door.

"Rufus, what is this?" she asked, wincing as her voice broke.

He got to his feet slowly and stood swaying. Then, with a pause to perhaps consider his next movement, he stepped down to the stair. His toes barely missed the decanter. Another step. "Come here, woman!" he bellowed. "You have made me wait for too long."

Though she knew it would infuriate him, she made no move toward him. It felt as though her legs were encased in lead.

"Did you not hear me, whore?"

She flinched as though struck, and bit the inside of her cheek rather than respond.

He stood a step toward her. She took one back.

"Do you fear the man you are going to marry?"

Swallowing past the hard knot of fear in her throat, she replied, "I fear the anger in your eyes. I fear the fact you have a weapon in your hand."

He lifted the gun, a smirk on his cruel lips. "Do you fear I will use it on you? Or do you fear for your lover…my son?"

Before she could move, he was upon her, grabbing her by the same wrist he had twisted earlier that day. She winced under the pain, but refused to cry out.

"Harlan's son went for a walk this morning. He went to the ruins."

Which meant he had seen her and Vaughn making love beneath the tree. There was no way she could deny it. And she knew he wouldn't believe her denial anyway. Time had run out. Just like that.

"Vaughn will be back soon," she warned Rufus.

He laughed—it was a twisted noise that shocked her. "Of course he will. That whoreson has been sniffing around you from the moment that he saw you. I knew if I sent for you, he would coming running. I counted on it."

Horror burst through her in wave of hot and cold. Vaughn would be walking into a trap! She must find some way of disarming Rufus.

He was waving the pistol at her, and she swallowed dryly. "You counted on it?" she repeated. "I assume, then, that Harlan's son didn't spontaneously decide to go for a walk this morning, either. You set him to follow me."

"But of course," Rufus snarled. "Did you think I'm addled, woman? I could smell that whoreson's stink all over you. I knew that if I watched you, sooner or later you'd go running to the bastard."

"Congratulations, then. You've acquired exactly what you wanted. Although what has it got you, Rufus? You don't look like you're enjoying yourself right now."

He slapped her so hard it split her lip. Her entire jaw went instantly numb, but she could taste blood in her mouth. She accepted the blow calmly. She had deliberately baited him, after all.

The slap served another purpose, too. It gave her an idea. Rufus was clearly waiting for Vaughn to arrive before he used the gun, or he would have pulled the trigger a moment before.

Disarming him physically would be beyond her meager strength, but there was another way to disable a pistol: fire it. There was no powder horn nearby that she could see, no shot. If she could anger him enough, she could perhaps get him to shoot the pistol. He was too good a shot to hope that he would miss her, but at least he would not be armed when Vaughn came upon him. It would give Vaughn the slender advantage he might need to overcome Rufus.

So. Elisa eyes Rufus, judging him carefully. He was no fool. She could not immediately begin baiting him and expect him not to see through her strategy.

"Rufus, listen to me. I'm the one who started the affair. I'm the one who pursued Vaughn. He's a young man who simply took what I offered."

The vein in Rufus' temple looked ready to explode. The blood-shot eyes narrowed. "You lie for him."

"Why would I lie now? Ask Harlan's son. I'm sure he gave you lots of detail. Ask him if I seemed at all unwilling this morning. Ask him who it was who pressed their attention upon the other."

She knew she had scored a hit, for his fingers bit into the skin of her arm.

"But you already know, don't you?" she said quietly. "He did not spare you a single detail. I'm sure he delighted in the retelling."

"No!" Rufus shook her arm. "He despises me as much as I despise him. He wanted to hurt me, and he thought seducing you was the way."

"Of course a man with a heart as cold as yours could never be hurt by an emotion as petty as love," Elisa taunted.

Rufus's cackled laughter made the hair on her arms stand on end. "All he got for his trouble was a well-used whore. How quick you are to return to your wicked ways."

"For my trouble, I learned how deeply your hatred of me truly extends, Father." It was Vaughn's voice.

Rufus' pistol swiveled immediately to the left of her. She whirled, to see Vaughn leaning against the doorframe of the French door that led to the back garden and the stables. His arms were crossed, and he looked not at all concerned about the pistol Rufus held.

"Elisa will be coming with me," Vaughn said, straightening up. He took a step toward her, but Rufus cocked the gun. Elisa smothered a little shriek with her hand, but Vaughn seemed not to notice…or care as he held his hand out to Elisa.

Rufus waved the pistol. "Hands off her!"

"Vaughn, don't—he'll kill you," Elisa breathed.

"It's time for you to leave," Vaughn said. "I learned some interesting news a few moments ago. I received a letter from Lord Arden in London." He reached into his jacket, but Rufus snarled and he aborted the movement after glancing at his father.

"Don't talk as if I'm not in the room, boy," Rufus added.

Vaughn turned his head. "You have been dead to me since the moment I read the letter." He made the pronouncement as one would announce breakfast. There was no drama, no emotion there. Vaughn looked back at her. "I've had my letters directed to William's estate as I didn't trust the security of any correspondence that arrived here. It's just as well. My agents in London reported back to me about a matter I asked them to investigate a few days ago."

"London?" Elisa repeated, dazed. What was all this? Did Vaughn not care that a pistol was pointed at his back? Did he not realize that every second he ignored Rufus, the little man's choler rose higher and higher? She licked her lips, her mouth and throat drier than a sand dune.

"This man you agreed to marry, Elisa, the man who told you he would get your son back for you has never lifted a finger in the attempt. No one was ever hired to find Raymond. He merely told you that in order to keep you with him. Rufus has coveted you for a long time...not long after you married Roger, he vowed you would one day be his. No-one took any notice because most of the men in London swore they would have you one way or another. But Rufus was quite serious in his intention. He coaxed Lord Arden into calling your husband out when Roger was caught in his wife's bed. And it was Rufus who encouraged Arden to twist the events. Arden was desperate to save his wife's reputation—he is particularly influential in the House of Lords, and this would have destroyed his career. By claiming that he had been caught in your bed, Elisa, Arden gained the admiration of every man in London, and his wife was protected."

"But...why would Rufus do that?" Elisa asked, bewildered.

Vaughn grimaced. "That is the truly evil part, Elisa. He wanted you cut-off from society—to the point no one could help you...except for him. Arden's claims worked perfectly. You were ejected, shunned. Vulnerable."

She looked at Rufus. She should have known, she realized. It was in keeping with the rest of his scheming. It fit his twisted personality—bending people to his will in whatever way proved most effective, regardless of the hurt and damage it would do elsewhere.

But the truth hurt. It wounded her, and she realized then that she had been clinging to her false hopes because she couldn't bear the thought that nothing was being done to find her son, that she had absolutely no hope at all.

She had been willing to walk away from Vaughn to live with that false hope.

She had been an utter fool.

Some of her thoughts must have shown on her face, for Rufus laughed at her. "You are so incredibly gullible. Do you realize you have spent your entire life being manipulated by men? First your blessed sot of a husband, then me, and now my son delivers the *coup de grace*." He mangled the French, making it sound coarse.

"Elisa, come with me," Vaughn said, taking a step closer.

"Stay right there, boy." Rufus waved the pistol again. This time the barrel pointed directly at Vaughn's head. "You're both tainted with the same sin. You cannot save her any more than you can save yourself."

"You would actually kill your own son?" Elisa breathed

"*Son?* Vaughn isn't my son. His whore mother took another man's bastard seed. The same man she was running to the night she was killed."

Elisa turned quickly to look at Vaughn, to see how he received this news. Vaughn's mouth had opened a little, but as she watched he nodded, as if a suspicion long held had now been confirmed. "So you sent me away," he added.

"No one gets away with betraying Rufus Fairleigh. Your bloody mother found that out the night she died."

"You killed her," Vaughn said softly.

Elisa felt invisible hackles rise on the back of her neck. The *danger* in Vaughn's voice!

Rufus gave a chuckle. "With this very same pistol. Fitting, hmmm?"

Vaughn leapt at Rufus, and Elisa heard herself scream in reaction, for the pistol was already pointed in Vaughn's direction. He stood no chance. None at all.

The pistol fired, and Vaughn fell to the cold marble with a cry and lay still.

She went to her knees beside Vaughn. His eyes were closed. Blood was already pooling on the floor beside him, collecting at the bottom of the stone stairs.

Rufus dragged her up by her hair and released her with a shove. She staggered towards the arch that led into the front foyer. Escape lay in that direction, and now Rufus had no gun.

"Take another step and I'll shoot you now," Rufus said from behind her.

She glanced over her shoulder, in time to see him reach beneath his jacket and withdraw a second gun—the twin to the first, that lay by Vaughn's still body. She halted instantly. Of course, a dueling brace.

"This one is loaded, too," Rufus assured her and cocked it.

She backed up a few steps and found her back was against one of the cold pillars. It was one of the pair that she and Vaughn had stood between one night—eons ago.

Rufus pointed the gun at her breast.

"Kill me, Rufus, and you will never have a plaything of your own." It was a last desperate gamble.

"Your use has expired, whore," Rufus growled. "You're not worth the trouble and upkeep."

Behind Rufus she saw a shadow of movement and her breath caught. Was Vaughn still alive? Suddenly, she found herself babbling inanely, speaking any sort of drivel, in an attempt to keep Rufus' attention upon her. It was utter nonsense, and perhaps that was what tipped Rufus off—or perhaps he saw her glance behind him.

Warned, he spun around to guard his back.

But it was too late. Vaughn's hand, holding the solid crystal whiskey decanter with the heavy base, smashed into Rufus's temple as he turned, and Rufus dropped to the marble like a stone and lay still.

Hysteria and relief roiling in her, Elisa skirted the still body. Vaughn stepped back a little and reached out blindly for the newel post behind him. He propped himself up against it, and held his side. His shirt beneath the black broadcloth was bright with blood, and he hung his head a little. His face was an alarming shade of gray.

Elisa reached for him, and he held up his hand, covered in blood. There was a trail of it behind him.

"I thought you were dead."

"It's still undecided," he whispered. "Elisa, you must get me somewhere safe, far from here."

"Vaughn?"

He collapsed forward, into her arms.

* * * * *

Elisa stared out the window, though she could see nothing through the rain that streamed down the glass. The lack of reflection forced her to deal with her thoughts instead. For nearly two weeks she had not be able to think beyond the immediate moment. For all of that lengthy fortnight she had been fighting to preserve Vaughn's life.

Tonight, for the first time since she had seen his still body on the marble floor, she knew for certain Vaughn would live. He was clear of any infections that might have plagued him because of the wound. No one had found them at the small inn a few hours away from Farleigh Hall.

She had no idea if Rufus lived or had died, and cared less, save that if he lived he might have people out looking for them both. She had stayed tucked up inside inn, caring for Vaughn, taking barely any food or drink herself. In her worry over Vaughn's condition, her appetite had completely disappeared.

That awful night she had called out the servants and loaded Vaughn into a covered carriage, she had planned to flee far from the hall—as far as she could get the coachman to take them. But her frantic ministrations to Vaughn's wounds in the carriage had told her that with every mile they traveled Vaughn would become weaker. He needed attention she could not provide in a moving carriage. Seeing the small inn tucked away beside a bridge, she had decided that until Vaughn could travel that was where they would stay.

Aside from visiting a nearby mercantile establishment for supplies and food, Elisa had stayed at Vaughn's side. The first night she'd wondered if he would see the dawn. She couldn't bear to close her eyes for a moment during the first forty-eight hours. Then the fever had overtaken him, and her fear was renewed.

Yet the fever had also subsided and now his face held color, and with each day he grew a little stronger. Tonight he slept peacefully.

If only she could sleep, too! Every time she closed her eyes an image of Rufus appeared. Every day she feared he'd find them and finish what he'd started.

Tonight she was free to wonder if Vaughn had killed him, but knew if that were the case, word would have reached them. Rufus was the richest man in the region, and stories of his death would surely make the rounds, even in this small place.

Elisa wished she could turn back the calendar by five years and return to the time when Roger had first died. Had she known what she knew now, she would have taken Raymond and run far and fast. It wouldn't have mattered that they would be poor, just that they were together.

But she could not go back, and just like five years ago, she now faced an uncertain future.

Her gaze was drawn back to the bed, as it had constantly since she had taken lodging in the room. Vaughn was asleep, his long lashes feathered against his high cheekbones. His dark hair was unruly, sleep tossed. His body was leaner from lack of nourishment. Her heart clenched as she stared. He was so young. She should release him, give him back to the world and let him find his way. Now he knew the truth about Rufus, perhaps he could search for his real father.

She had to leave him. She would only destroy his life—had nearly destroyed it already.

Just then his eyes slowly opened. Elisa caught her breath. He was awake! He blinked a little, and looked at his pillow and the canopy of the bed above him.

"I'm alive," he said to himself. The croaky voice did not hide his surprise.

"You most certainly are alive," Elisa said.

He turned his head to look at her. A soft smile formed on his lips. "Come here," he said, motioning to the space on the bed beside him.

She sat on the very edge of the bed, not willing to disturb him more than necessary. "How do you feel?"

He reached for her arm, gently pulled her down to his level and kissed her. "Better now," he said with a smile.

The smile turned her mind to wicked thoughts. The sheet had fallen back to his waist, leaving his torso with the white bandage revealed, the olive skin gleaming in the dull light from the candle.

Her stomach clenched tight. It had been two weeks since they'd made love, and though she knew he was hurt, she wanted him. She looked at his strong chest, then his abdomen and the line of hair that disappeared beneath the sheet.

"Join me," he said.

Elisa looked up to find him watching her, a heat she recognized in his eyes. Excitement tingled along her spine. "You're hurt."

"My wounds have patently healed."

"But what if—"

With a growled he lunged for her and pulled her on top of him, proving that although he was wounded, he was not at all incapacitated.

Through the sheet she could feel him against her, hot and hard. She pressed her hips against him, sending heat to the very core of her.

"Take off your clothes, Elisa." Vaughn's eyes were dark, his lashes lowered. That he wanted her was very clear. By his tone she knew he would not brook delay.

Rather than disrobe as he demanded, she slid her gown up about her hips, slowly revealing her nakedness beneath. Though he had lain unconscious or in a stupor all these days she had kept herself bare and ready for him beneath the dress. She would recall his request—his low voice asking that she make herself so for him, and him alone, for no one else would know, so she would leave off her underclothes and hug the secret to herself as something she shared with Vaughn only.

As she revealed herself, she heard him draw a deep breath. "Ah, but I have dreamed of this," he murmured, and his hand smoothed its way up her thigh.

She pulled the sheet aside, revealing his already erect member, and straddled his hips, as he tugged on the strings that held her bodice together, loosening it. As he pulled the bodice apart, baring her breasts, she sank down on his shaft, taking him slowly within her body.

Once his cock was fully embedded within her she began to ride him, the tempo intentionally slow. His hands were on her breasts, caressing the nipples, stroking the soft round swell of flesh around them, as she moved slowly around him.

He grinned, as though knowing what she had in mind. "You test my stamina."

She shook her head. "No...I'm testing my own." As she shifted her hips, rotating in a circle, he held onto them and thrust. He had been too long without her, and his body betrayed him. A groan ripped from his throat as he filled her womb with his seed.

Elisa stared down at her lover's face. Vaughn's eyes were closed, his lips slightly open, his chest rising and falling as he filled his lungs with air. Slowly he opened his eyes, and she smiled down at him, loving the feel of his thick, heavy member within her. "That didn't take long," she teased, shifting her hips the slightest bit.

Immediately his shaft filled with blood and he grew hard once again. She arched a brow, the side of her mouth lifting. "I believe you've made a quick recovery."

"I am eager to please my lady."

My lady. The words were said like a caress and she felt it all the way to her soul. Did he truly feel that she belonged to him? Did he love her, as she loved him? For she knew without a doubt their relationship had grown from lust to love—at least for her.

"Take that blasted gown off," he said, his hands impatient as he stripped her of the gown and threw it aside. "That's better."

She attempted to give him a look of pure innocence. "And now what will you do with me?"

He flipped her on her back, and beneath him. "I'm going to ravish you," he said against her lips, his mouth hovering close, teasing her. But rather than kiss her, he wandered lower, his hair falling against her breasts. He teased relentlessly, kissing her breasts, yet ignoring her nipples that were hard and sensitive. How she wanted his mouth there, sucking, tugging, laving her until she couldn't stand it.

Her breath caught in her throat as he proceeded downward, his tongue circling her stomach, then lower still. Her abdomen rippled in anticipation, for his breath blew hotly against her thighs. She looked down at him and found the sight an erotic one: his dark hair bent at her mons, his large hands cupping her hips, pulling her toward his mouth.

He kissed the fold lightly. She moved her legs, opening her thighs for him as a silent urging to stroke her properly. She saw his smile and then his tongue caressed her pearl, tickling, stroking, flickering against the sensitive bud. She grabbed hold of the headboard, biting down on her lip to keep from crying out.

Vaughn felt a hot triumph as he watched her writhe beneath him, opening herself up fully to him. He knew she came to him completely without reservation this time, unshackled by any commitments. She was his in every sense of the word. His erection was near bursting, but he held himself back, controlled it, wanting her to experience the same joy she'd brought him. He took her breasts in his palms, teasing the pink colored aureoles.

She moaned low in her throat and he felt her climax grip and release her.

"Vaughn...make love to me," she whispered, pulling him toward her.

On his knees, he probed her with the head of his erection. She shifted her hips, trying to take him in, but he held back, studying her gleaming, welcoming cleft, the engorged folds of flesh, and the little spasms and movement of her hips. "You're so wet for me."

"Yes."

He filled her with a single thrust, and she cried aloud her pleasure, her head thrown back, her throat extended. With a smile, he lifted her legs, and thrust into her a little further, causing her to gasp once more. But the little movements inside her tight sheath were already pushing him to close to his climax. He kept his grip on her thigh, and with shortened thrusts, little movements of his hips, dammed the climax back.

This time he would wait for her. He wanted them to come together, to experience that rare mutual pleasure. Concentrating on reading her responses, tracking her growing excitement, he found his own pleasure was not building with the direct, swift climb to the peak, but was lifted up by a deep well of sensation that was more intense, more overwhelming than any he had ever experienced. Perhaps his profound pleasure communicated itself to her—he didn't know if it was possible, for this was a new experience for him—but Elisa was moving with complete and utter abandonment, pushed towards that same exquisite peak. She was tightening around him, her body tensing as the moment drew closer. Then she arched hard, and clenched about him, and the internal caress sent the cascade of rippling, convulsing joy through his body.

As he spent himself within her, he kissed her, wishing they could stay like this forever.

* * * * *

It was nearing three weeks after the shooting when Elisa knew it was time to discuss the future. They could not spend the rest of their lives hiding away in the small forgotten inn. Decisions must be made, actions taken. She knew it was time for such a conversation, for Vaughn had spent the majority of the morning away from the inn. He didn't tell her where he'd gone, but she could tell by his quiet manner that it probably had something to do with Rufus. That he did not share his morning with her was unsettling. She could not let the matter rest without discussing it. If she had learned anything from her pathetic marriage it was that secrets between people could fester and rot.

She would tackle the subject over lunch, she decided, as the meal was laid out upon the table in the corner of the room. Vaughn was washing the dust of his travels from his face and hands.

But when they sat before the modest repast, her courage failed her. After all, what was her place in Vaughn's life now? Did she have any right at all to demand an accounting, a settling? The possibility that she did not kept her silent.

Until, finally, he pushed his plate aside. "I need to go to London," he said, turning to her, his expression undecipherable.

Her heart lurched. He had said *I*, not *we*. Was she meant to stay here? "When will you return?" she asked.

He swiveled to face her properly and took her hand in his big warm ones. "I'm not certain. I do know this much, however. I want us to marry."

She laughed without mirth. "Vaughn, you know that's impossible."

"It would work, Elisa. I know it."

The words held such conviction, she wished she could believe them. But she shook her head, and shifted her gaze from his steady examination of her. They could not continue to live like this, closeted away from the rest of the world, that was true. But...marriage? "No one would ever accept us," she said softly. "The moment we revealed ourselves, we'd be shunned by all of society. I know how that feels, Vaughn. I won't put you through it."

"I have done nothing wrong," Vaughn said. "I intend to marry a woman who has been previously married. It's done all the time."

"I was your father's fiancée. I still am, in society's eyes. And you're courting Natasha. Our relationship is forbidden, and you know it, Vaughn. They will crucify you, as they did me."

The trials of the past made her think of Raymond. "I would lose any hope of seeing my son again." Tears burned the back of her eyes and she quickly looked away.

She heard him move, the chair scrape back. Then she was picked up. He took her over to the bed and laid her down as though she were as fragile as crystal. Just as delicately he undressed her and made love to her. When he was within her, she allowed her tears to fall, anointing what might be the last time they ever made love.

Chapter Seventeen

As he hurried into the inn, Vaughn's thoughts turned to Elisa. How he'd missed her these past five days. Every waking hour he thought of her, wondering what she was doing, praying she would still be there when he arrived. Her refusal to consider marriage hadn't surprised him, but it reinforced his understanding that Elisa, unlike any woman he'd ever met, was an independent person. He remembered the lesson she had implanted in him in that regard — the bonds and the knife and the control she had exerted over him. If Elisa was still in their room when he arrived, he knew it would be because she had chosen to wait for him rather than leave.

Why she would choose to stay was a matter that puzzled him in the moments when he had the courage to examine it. He had spent the last five days trying to earn that privilege. He would soon find out if he was too late.

He had to force himself not to run into the inn. It was quiet inside — no late customers tonight, either. The door to their room was closed and when he tested it, proved to be locked, too. He pulled out the key from his pocket and turned the lock, cracked the door aside, took a deep breath and stepped inside.

Elisa sat in a chair, her back to him. She appeared to be reading but she didn't turn as he entered. Her stillness made his heart race. Rufus was not far away — he might have found her while he was not here to protect her…

He hurried to the chair to face her, and his gut loosened with hot relief when he saw that she was merely sleeping, the novel she'd been reading in her lap. Her elbow was propped on the arm of the chair, her hand holding up her head. She was still dressed in her day gown, and by the way her body slumped in the chair, she was still without a corset.

His heart ached. She had endured too much of the cruelty life could deliver, yet appeared untouched by it. Her naturalness, her candor, and the tiny line between her brows that dug deeper whenever she insisted her demands be met…he had much to do with the emergence of these qualities, but the world had created Elisa, full of promise and potential and he had been lucky enough to watch her flower to full bloom.

"Please make her stay," he breathed to the same world that had delivered her to him, then ran his fingers down the side of her face and kissed her lightly.

Her eyes fluttered open, and the open, radiant smile that emerged made his blood heat within his veins.

"Vaughn," she said on a sigh, throwing her arms around his neck and holding him tight against her. "I was so afraid something had happened to you." She put him from her. "Let me have my fill of you. I'm starved…five days you've been gone, and not a word."

He was startled to see tears in her eyes despite her smile, and realized then that she had been dealing with her own fears. He had selfishly focused upon his own affairs. "Elisa, my love, my dearest love, I'm sorry," he said, and heard his own words with a small spurt of surprise. The surprise fled when he realized that he had spoken truly.

Her eyes widened. He saw doubt, then a deep glow seemed to fill them. Happiness, he realized, and felt a giddy joy that he had put that happiness there. Would loving her keep her by him?

"Truly?" Elisa whispered.

He took her hands within his own and brought them to his lips. "With all of my heart."

She pulled her to him, kissing his neck, his ear, his jaw. Soon she was reaching for the buttons on his shirt, but he held her hands fast. "First I want to tell you about London."

He saw the wariness in her eyes as she sat back. He pulled the other chair closer, took a seat, and once again picked up her hand. "Weeks ago I organized a group of men to look into Raymond's whereabouts."

Her throat convulsed as she swallowed hard.

He smiled, hoping to calm her fears. "They found him, Elisa, and I went to him."

Tears welled in her eyes. "Why did you not tell me?"

"I wanted to see for myself what had happened in the years you've been separated. I wanted to talk to him, to hear what had transpired."

"But why…?"

"Elisa, I lived Raymond's life. I was separated from my mother at a very young age, given no explanation for her departure and no hope of her return. She loved me and would have kept me by her, but there were times when I resented her for the pain her absence caused in me—so much at times that I felt I hated her. If she had suddenly appeared before me during those times, I would have struck out at her with all the despair and pain that I had in me."

"Oh Vaughn…" she breathed.

He shook her hand a little, to take her focus away from him. "I did not want you to be greeted by that reception, if by some enormous stroke of luck you had got past the front door of his home."

"But you did get past?"

"I am not without…influence."

"How did you find him?" she asked, and dread was thick in her voice.

"He was lodged with distant members of Roger's family. They are not as well as off as you. He has a roof over his head, but it is not the life he would have had with you."

She closed her eyes for a moment. "Did he ask about me?"

"Elisa, look at me."

She opened her eyes. The guilt, the torment of a mother who feels she has failed her child—Vaughn could read it all in her eyes. "He showed me a well-worn leather book, with silk stitching and hand-drawn lettering, *St. George and the Dragon*. He said you used to read it to him every night before he went to bed. He keeps it upon his bedside table."

"My father gave me that book. It is very old, from a monastery near where he grew up. Oh, Vaughn, he still has the book? Then...he does not bear me ill-will?"

Hope was emerging now. He rejoiced at its appearance. "That is what Raymond told me about the book, too. Elisa...he believed you were dead."

Her mouth opened and her eyes widened. "Dead? How could he—"

"Rufus," Vaughn said simply.

She stared at him, her eyes widening even more.

"Rufus arranged it through intermediaries. That's how I eventually found Raymond—money always leaves a trail. This decrepit wing of Roger's family did not want the boy, but with the annual stipend Rufus gave them, they accepted both the discomfort and his instructions that the boy must not learn where you were and try to reach you. The easiest way to ensure that was to tell him you were dead."

She sunk into her chair, shaking her head a little. "Vaughn, I knew Rufus was a little mad, a little cruel in his methods of acquiring what he wanted, but I cannot believe the depths of his depravity. This is...this is a wretched thing he has done."

"He wanted you to himself, Elisa. He lied to ensure you were tied to him."

"My poor little boy..."

Vaughn couldn't quite suppress his smile. "No longer, madam. I made sure he knew the truth."

"You spoke to him?"

"I did better than that. He waits outside."

Her eyes widened as she looked to the door, then back at him. "You jest?"

"In this matter? Never. I am giving your son the one thing I yearned for as a child…The chance to see my mother again."

She began to tremble and he stood and took her in his arms, comforting her. "Elisa, be calm. He is as nervous as you."

"I should change."

"No. Let him see you as you really are. The way I see you." He put her from him. "Are you ready?"

She nodded, biting her bottom lip doubtfully.

"Stay right there."

Elisa could hear her heart thudding in her temples and her ears, the organ jumping against her chest. She gripped the back of the chair tightly as Vaughn crossed the room to the door.

For years she had worked only to have her son returned to her, and suddenly, without warning, the moment was here—her crowning ambition completed. Steadying herself, she folded her trembling hands together and waited.

The door opened once again. A tall child stepped through, Vaughn just behind him.

Raymond.

Elisa's breath left her in a rush. He was a young child no longer, but a boy on the brink of adolescence. He reached to Vaughn's shoulder already, his dark hair a little unruly, but curly just as Roger's had been. His eyes, so like hers in shape and color, stared back at her with disbelief.

"Mama?"

The word was wrenched from him as he flew across the room and straight into her arms.

Sobs racked her as she held him tight. She couldn't let him go. She would never let him go again.

She saw over Raymond's shoulder that Vaughn stood by the door. He wore a small, satisfied smile. When he saw her glance, he placed his hand over his heart, gave her a short bow, and closed the door behind him, leaving Elisa and her son alone.

* * * * *

The following morning Elisa was first to wake and lay staring up at the bed canopy, enjoying the peace in her heart and mind. It had been many long, turbulent years since she had woken to a day with nothing in it to dread.

She glanced over at Vaughn, who slept soundly beside her, and then her heart gave a little leap as she glanced across the room to the settee where her son lay, his even breathing telling her that he, too, still slept.

Elisa eased out of the bed, drew a wrapper about her nakedness and crept to the settee. Going down on her knees so she could study him more closely, she took her fill. Her heart lurched with love and pride for her son. Awkwardly she lifted a hand to ward off the curl that fell over his brow. He was so handsome. In ten years time he would have every woman in England after him.

She had lost more than six precious years with him, but she would make up for them.

He stirred slightly, sighing, his lips curving into a soft smile. She smiled as well, smoothing the blanket over his side. "I love you, Raymond," she said softly.

"I love you too, Mama," he murmured, not opening eyes, but snuggling into the blankets.

This was a happiness she had thought unattainable, a pleasure so deep she feared it would end quickly, for no one deserved such unadulterated joy—especially wicked Elisa. But Vaughn had paid off Raymond's aunt and uncle, so she had no fear of someone taking him away from her. Raymond, too, now he was older and understood the fears and motives of adults better, would also fight to remain in her life.

Elisa turned toward the bed and the man who had made it all possible.

He was awake, propped up on his elbow watching them, a soft smile on his handsome face. She went to him and lay down beside him, her back to him, cuddling into the warmth he gave. He held her close, his fingers weaving through hers as they watched her son together.

"He has your eyes."

She smiled, and glanced over her shoulder. "I know."

"A handsome young man as well."

"You need not remind me," she said, pleasure filling her at his words.

He laughed lightly, wincing as she glanced over at Raymond, his soft breathing filling the air. "Shhh."

"I forgot, our son is sleeping."

Our son.

She studied him closely. "Do you mean what you say?"

"Why would I not?"

"He is not your flesh and blood."

"I would marry you and spurn your son?" He shook his head.

Elisa turned onto her other side so that she was facing him. "You can't marry me."

"Do you refuse my proposal?"

"Yes."

"Because you do not love me?"

"Love is for romantics. You're a lord of the realm, Vaughn. You cannot simply marry whoever you please. You certainly can't marry me."

"I certainly can. The only reason I will accept for your refusal, Elisa, is if you can look me in the eye and tell me you do not love me."

She looked away, knowing he would read the truth in her eyes. "I will destroy your life."

"You've already done that, sweet one."

She looked back at him quickly, shocked.

"You have completely changed the way I look at my life, Elisa. And part of that change is a refusal to be influenced by what people think I should or should not do. So I will marry whomever I damned well please."

"If you do this, you will never be accepted by society again."

"We don't need them."

"But…Raymond will need them when he grows to adulthood," she said. "We cannot spurn them and allow them to cast us out. It will cut Raymond off from the opportunities he should be entitled to—an education, a home, an income that will let him support a wife and children."

"And if you do not marry me, Elisa, will you be able to provide him with every item on that list?" Vaughn asked.

Tears pricked her eyes and escaped to roll down her cheeks. She knew Raymond's life would be bleak if she were to take care of him by herself. Her only comfort would be that she could surround him with love, unlike the last six years of his life.

"Shhh…Elisa," Vaughn crooned. He lifted her chin, wiped off her tears and smiled at her. "I know how to solve your dilemma."

"H-h-ow?" she asked.

"Trust me," he said. "I have a plan."

* * * * *

Elisa looked from Vaughn to the expensive ball gown laying across the bed.

"*Natasha's* ball? We're to go?" Elisa repeated. "Vaughn, you're supposed to be courting the girl. You appear at her ball with a widow and her nearly-grown son on your arm, and announce…what you intend to announce…Vaughn, good lord, they'll kill us!"

Vaughn laughed a little. "What of it? We agreed, did we not? No more hiding away. No more hypocrisy. We stand up and claim our lives for what they are, and hang the consequences."

She bit her lip in indecision. They *had* agreed, but faced with the real prospect of confronting people who wielded the power to destroy her life and the lives of those she loved… "The doing is much harder than the stating of it," she confessed to Vaughn. "The people that will be at Natasha's ball—they are the same people who turned their backs on me when Roger died, and at the ball a few weeks ago. I know these people, Vaughn. They have no conscience, no qualms…"

"Shhh…" He took her shoulders and kissed her temple. "Remember what we said. We know what is going to happen…We must face it this once, and then it will be all over, and we can live the life we want."

She realized she was shaking. "Yes, that is what we said," she agreed, and her voice shook too.

Vaughn pushed at the fabric on the bed. "Besides, I insist I have the pleasure of seeing you in this dress and dancing, Elisa. My imagination must pale in comparison, I'm sure." He held up the dress, displaying it for her. "Do you not itch to wear it, hmmm?" he asked, with a wicked smile.

Elisa looked at it and sighed a little. Vaughn had returned to their room just a short while ago, bringing the hint of cold weather breezing in around his boots, the big box under his arm. He had moved straight over to the bed, without even a greeting, thrown the lid of the box aside and let the delicate layers of silk and lace spill out upon the counterpane. The gown was an extravagant creation made of Tussore silk, and even in the dull afternoon light it glowed almost with a light of its own. It was a beautiful gown, made to draw the eye toward it.

"I bought it in London. A French countess ordered it, then decided against it later."

"It's too expensive," Elisa said, her fingers grazing the soft material. It would feel wonderful against the skin.

"I want you on my arm and dressed to suit your true station in life, Elisa. I want you dressed like a queen," he said, coming to her and pulling her into his arms. He pressed his hips against hers, his hands holding her against him. "Raymond is out riding with Henry again?"

Raymond had found a friend in the innkeeper's son, a boy in his early teens who loved to ride as much as Raymond.

"And what if he is?" she asked, lifting her brow.

"Then I will take advantage of the moment," Vaughn told her. With a slow smile, he turned her around so her back was to him. She felt him lift the skirt of her dress, and against her bare cheeks she felt him rub his erection against her. He was still encased in broadcloth, but immediately a warmth built in her, shifting low into her belly and lower still. She became moist and warm.

His hands slid up her torso, to cup her breasts through the fabric of her gown. His thumbs caressed her nipples as they crinkled hard. Her hips thrust forward involuntarily as the ripple of excitement tingled through her, arrowing straight down to her cleft, to the nub there which began to throb. Her bottom was against Vaughn's hips and she could feel his member, thick, hard and beating against her. He groaned, a deep sound that tightened the building pressure inside her a degree more, and one of his hands slipped down to push at her hip, to drive her more firmly against him. The tips of his fingers were only a little way from her mons, and her pearl of pleasure, and she ached for his touch there. She found the hem of her skirt and lifted the front of it in her other hand, while she guided Vaughn's hand to the place where she wanted it. The long fingers slid into her hot, moist cleft and stroked knowingly. She gave a small cry as the delicious surge of pleasure ripped through her and her head fell back against his shoulder. Her body quivered against his hand.

She could feel Vaughn's heart beating frantically against her shoulder, could hear his ragged breath. There was an added satisfaction knowing he took enjoyment from pleasuring her, too.

"Yes," she breathed out a sigh.

He bent her over the chair, her hands on the arms, and her skirt over her waist. His hands stroked the tender flesh of her bottom, then she heard the quiet whisper of cloth against cloth as he unfastened his pants. The little silence was agonizing as she waited for him to enter her, eager for that first thrust that always gave her such enormous pleasure. She felt the blunt tip of his cock against her and then he thrust hard, filling her completely. He held her hips tight, grinding against her at a rapid pace, then slowing, withdrawing almost completely, driving her crazy with need.

He leaned over her, kissing her neck, his fingers seeking her pearl as he thrust within her, then slowly withdrew again.

Time and again he did this, slowly withdrawing, then filling her to her womb. The pressure built within her, to a point she could no longer take it.

Vaughn, perhaps sensing her need by her quickening movements, the tremors wracking her, and her building gaps and shortened breath, thrust three more times in quick succession, sending her over the edge, and as she cried aloud her pleasure, she heard Vaughn's hoarse voice join her own, and his hot seed spill inside her.

Chapter Eighteen

Elisa smiled as she looked out the carriage window and saw the blazing lights of Munroe Manor in the distance.

"I would have thought a frown or fear would appear on your face when you looked upon that manor," Vaughn drawled from the corner of the carriage. "Hardly a smile. What *are* you thinking, my wicked Elisa?"

"Not what you would like me to be thinking, I am sure," she said, with a quick smile in his direction before returning to study the limestone manor with the dozens of carriages and people milling about the steps.

"The way your mind works never ceases to astonish me, so perhaps I wouldn't be disappointed at all. Tell me," he coaxed.

"I am thinking how much I love you and how, as long as you are with me, nothing of what the night holds for us can touch me. Vaughn, I cannot believe how I feared these people only two days ago. And perhaps I might fear them again in a few minutes, but at this moment, here with you, I have no fear at all. I am invulnerable. I don't know what I did to deserve this happiness, this peace. I hope it never ends."

He leaned forward and took her chin in his hand. The swaying carriage made his fingers move restlessly under her chin. "I promise you, Elisa, I will do everything in my power to make this last for the rest of your life."

She looked into his eyes. In the dim carriage the green of his eyes darkened. There was no devilish light there, no wicked humor. She smiled softly at him, as the carriage came to a swaying halt.

He pushed the door open as a footman unfolded the steps, climbed down to the ground, and turned to help her from the carriage.

Elisa took his hand, took her first step out of the carriage, and looked around. There were a multitude of guests moving about the gravel drive, heading for the wide steps of the manor, and some of them turned to look at Vaughn. One woman's face lit up with a smile of delight, then turned to inspect Vaughn's companion. When she saw who it was that Vaughn was helping to the ground, her mouth opened and her eyes widened. She dug an elbow into the side of her own companion and quickly raised herself to whisper into his ear. The man was swiveling his head to look at them as they were swept up in the tide of people moving through the wide double doors of the manor.

Elisa swallowed a little. Her fear had already returned, shattering the glorious moment she had enjoyed in the carriage.

Vaughn's hand pressed hers. "Remember, Elisa," he murmured.

She looked up at him, and he shook his head a little. "Remember what this night will give us," he said, his voice low. "Don't let them hurt you. It's all meaningless in the end."

She drew in a shaky breath and nodded her agreement. She took another breath, and looked around. Waltz melodies could be heard faintly in the air—the party was well under way. Waiting carriages were parked in the lane and on the lawns. Many people had obviously made the journey from London. Caroline and William would be sheltering them all for the night.

"After you, my dear," Vaughn said, motioning toward the steps and the manor's front door.

They began the long walk, and Elisa kept her gaze firmly on the doors, not willing to test her resolve a second time by watching people's reactions to her appearance on Vaughn's arm.

Then they were inside, and a butler was standing by while Vaughn helped her take off her cloak.

Elisa could feel tension tighten even more inside her, because until this moment, Vaughn had not seen her in the dress he had acquired for her. She had insisted upon it, hoping to give him a small pleasurable surprise here at the manor amongst what might be larger, less enjoyable shocks. Now she worried that if her appearance was not to his taste, then she would simply be adding to his burdens this evening.

She turned to face him, and found Vaughn was standing quite still with her cloak in his hands. The butler had his arms raised, ready to take the cloak, but Vaughn was too busy staring at her to notice.

She smoothed the silk at her waist. "What is it? Is something wrong?" she whispered.

Then behind her, she heard a gasp, echoed swiftly by another, and the run of murmured gossip that she remembered so well from times past. She had been noticed. But she spared no attention for anyone else except Vaughn.

"Vaughn? Is it...wrong?"

The ball gown was indeed fit for a queen, and Elisa had been extremely nervous about wearing something so beautiful and so daring in cut and styling. The woman for whom the dress had originally been made had a wider waist and smaller breasts. Elisa had spent two days taking the waist of the gown in with delicate stitches that would not mar the beautiful golden cream silk, but she could do nothing about the shaping for the breasts. She had tried it on with the help of the innkeeper's wife, and found that she could not possibly wear it without a corset to help hold up the almost indecently cut bodice. Her breasts now pushed against the top of the bodice, swelling against the silk. The bodice was tight, cinching in her waist and falling to a point at the front. The sleeves were giant puffs of silk, ending at her elbows with ruffles of pleated chiffon edged with satin ribbon and finished off with satin bows.

The skirt was attached to the bodice with hundreds of tiny pin-tucked pleats, which allowed the skirt to fall into a full, flattering bell shape over the top of many layers of starched petticoats, making her waist appear even smaller. Across the bodice and sweeping up the sides of the skirt in a pattern of points were delicate German lace pieces adorned with beads and bows to resemble sprays of flowers, in the same golden cream color as the silk they were attached to.

Elisa had studied her reflection in the small mirror the innkeeper's wife had produced when she'd tried the dress on, while the woman had sighed. "Madam, with your coloring, your golden hair and your beautiful skin, you look like you are lit from within. With candlelight reflecting on you, your gentleman would be a fool if he thought there was another woman there to match your beauty."

"Thank you, Mary," Elisa had murmured then, a little reassured by the woman's fulsome praise. But now she held her hand against her bodice, staring at Vaughn, for he still had not spoken. Her heart was racing.

Finally, Vaughn shook his head a little, then smiled, the smile slowly growing wider. "Elisa, you are truly stunning," he said, handing the restless butler the forgotten cloak. Then he shocked her a little by stepping forward, sliding his hand about her waist and kissing her on the lips.

She was not the only person to feel that shock. She plainly heard the indrawn breaths and gasps about the hallway, where people were climbing up and down the sweeping stairs and were lingering at the second floor balconies and about the lower floor where the ballroom doors were. There were perhaps fifty people in the hall — all of them must have seen his kiss, to judge by the buzzing conversations starting up around them.

Vaughn stepped back, touched her lips with his finger. "Remember," he murmured, and held out his arm to escort her to the ballroom.

The ballroom was near to bursting with people. Pausing at the top of the stairs, she glanced at Vaughn. He squeezed her hand, and with a smile that melted her heart, he took the first step down.

She would follow wherever he led her. The destination did not matter, nor did any challenges along the way so long as he was with her.

While Vaughn looked about for a pair of vacant straight-backed chairs, Elisa watched the crowd slowly become aware of them. It began as a pinpoint of realization, when a man quite close to them turned and recognized Vaughn, then looked at Elisa and widened his eyes almost comically.

She stared back at him calmly. He turned back to his companions with a whisper. Slowly the realization rippled outwards across the room. One by one the crowd turned toward them, their faces showing their astonishment at seeing the two of them together at such a public place.

Perhaps sensing her need to turn and run, Vaughn pulled her tightly to him and whispered in her ear, "Tonight we speak our minds. Tonight we put the past behind us and start anew."

She tried to smile at him, but knew that even this tiny intimate exchange was being noted by everyone who watched them. It would be torn apart and examined in conversation for weeks to come. *Did she really let him kiss her? They spoke to each other like they had known each other for years—perhaps they have!* Every little movement they made tonight would generate endless speculation and gossip.

But Vaughn's smile did not falter, and she felt her fear slip away as she stared into his eyes. The side of his mouth quirked a little. "It will all be over soon."

Elisa turned back to face the room. She lifted her chin, and forced a smile to her lips.

"Here comes Caroline," Vaughn warned her under his breath, his hand on the back of her waist, a silent signal of support.

Caroline approached them, her fan waving furiously. "Elisa, how…interesting it is that you join us tonight."

The thick group of guests on her left, huddled about the chairs by the ballroom entryway, tittered behind their fans and hands. Elisa felt their hate all the way to her bones.

Vaughn's shoulder edged between her and Caroline. "Caroline, Baroness Munroe," he said, holding out his hand so that she was forced to give her his and allow him to bow over it. "I was most flattered by your invitation to tonight's affair. I have been looking forward to the opportunity it has presented me since I received the invitation. I must thank you for providing me this chance."

Caroline's eyes narrowed as she looked up at Vaughn, studying him. She did not absorb what he was saying, for her mind was fully occupied on her own concerns. "We heard that Rufus has not been well lately, and we have wondered what happened to you both."

"As you can see, we are both in excellent health," Vaughn replied.

Elisa wondered why he was playing with Caroline when they had agreed that they would not descend to the level of petty, veiled insults that society seemed to use to keep each other in their appropriate places. Then she saw the look on Vaughn's face, and realized he was not playing at all. His tone was flat. Blunt. There was no lingering trace of a smile on his face. No hint of poorly hidden amusement. He had truly discarded the shield of facile charm. Vaughn stood with her hand tucked firmly in his arm, defying everyone in the room simply by wielding the truth.

Pride swelled in her, and she suddenly knew that Vaughn had been right: this was what they must do to preserve any sort of a life for themselves.

She lifted her chin and stared at Caroline, who was quivering with indignant anger, yet was incapable of speaking it aloud.

"Rufus has remained silent on the subject of your whereabouts, although your presence tonight affirms rumors I have heard—whispers only, that you are, that you two..." She could not finish the sentence.

"We are to be married," Vaughn said flatly.

This time, Elisa had no difficulty hearing the collective gasp of shock emanating around the room. Truly, every pair of eyes and ears must be trained upon them by now, although the musicians continued to play, the waltz echoing horribly around the room now that no dancers moved to its beat.

Caroline's jaw unhinged a little, her lips parting. But her eyes narrowed, glittering with repressed emotion.

"You cad!" she cried. "You are courting our daughter!" And she lifted her hand to slap Vaughn across the face.

He caught Caroline's gloved wrist well before her hand made contact with his face, and held it in mid-air. "For any hurt I have delivered upon your daughter's feelings, you have my apologies."

"Perhaps you should address those apologies to me," William said, hurrying down the steps to get to his wife. Elisa saw that he was not as angry as Caroline, and his tone sounded much more reasonable. She had often noticed a bond between men that allowed more forgiveness. Vaughn nodded to William. "I initiated the courtship because I was attempting to smooth things over and maintain a peace that did not suit me. But no longer will I be a party to a mockery that covers up lies, sins, and pure evil."

"Sins in plenty, it appears," Caroline spat.

"Evil? That's a bit strong, isn't it?" William said.

Caroline looked down her nose at Elisa. "Had I any idea of your past, I would never have befriended you."

The words wounded her despite being braced for such attacks. She flinched at the fury in Caroline's eyes. Before could she find words to respond, Vaughn remarked, "I know of a married gentleman who had a mistress. She was a beauty, a stage actress who had men vying for her attention, but she adored her lover. He agonized over his relationship with the actress, and when he got her pregnant with a son, he thought he would lose everything…for his family would not accept a bastard as heir—"

"Say no more," Caroline replied, her face as white as a sheet. Elisa realized with growing wonder that the man Vaughn referred to could only be William, and that Caroline was aware of her husband's sordid past.

"You *knew!*" Elisa breathed.

Caroline glanced at her, and Elisa saw real pain in her face.

"And you condoned it? What of the child? Did you not think—"

"Enough!" William declared, his voice low. "This is not the place for such a discussion."

"You chose the place, William," Vaughn replied evenly. "And it's high time truth was aired in these halls. Burying it has encouraged the roots of this country to rot away beneath the surface." He looked at Caroline. "His son went to school with me. He's a good man, though he despises his father for abandoning his mother." Vaughn tilted his head slightly. "So you see, Lady Munroe, everyone has a secret, and everyone has a past. If you can forgive your husband for the greatest betrayal of all, certainly you can forgive a friend the injustices she's been dealt since she took Roger as a husband at the age of sixteen."

Caroline abruptly snapped her fan shut and leveled Vaughn with a daunting stare. "You will leave my home at once," she declared.

"With all due respect, Lady Munroe, I will leave once I have spoken with your daughter and apologize for the deception I involved her in."

"Not while I draw breath," Caroline declared.

"And I must also speak with Rufus," Vaughn said as if she had not spoken at all.

"Your father is ill enough without—" Caroline began.

"He is not my father."

This time her lips parted fully, and her eyes widened and kept widening as the implications of his simple declaration made themselves clear.

But Elisa found her attention was drawn to the middle of the ballroom floor, where Natasha, the Belle of the Ball, stood surrounded by beaus, yet stared at Vaughn with a hurt, bewildered expression.

Elisa tugged on Vaughn's arm, drawing his attention to the young woman.

She looked lovely, her dark hair piled up in curls on top of her head, making her look older. Her dress was a deep purple watermarked taffeta, which made her blue eyes darker and set off the fine, youthful skin. Altogether, Natasha was a prize and it was easy to understand why so many men were vying for her attention.

She wondered if Vaughn had any regrets.

He turned to Elisa, picked up her hand from his elbow and kissed it. "I must leave you here, Elisa. I will be but a moment," he told her.

"I will be fine, now," she assured him.

Vaughn stepped around William and Caroline, who seemed dazed by the rapid presentation of indigestible truths, and walked over to their daughter. The men around her bristled protectively, but Natasha stepped forward, away from them, and toward Vaughn.

He bowed over her hand, and spoke to her quietly.

Elisa realized that the music had halted, and now even the musicians were watching the drama unfolding in the middle of the ballroom with undisguised curiosity.

After a moment of looking at Vaughn steadily, Natasha finally dropped her chin and nodded. Vaughn patted her cheek as one might a child, and she glanced up at him once more before he turned and headed back to where Elisa stood before Caroline and William. Elisa could see tears sparkling in her eyes, when Natasha glanced at her. But there was not enmity there. No anger.

After a moment, Natasha turned and made her way to the back entrance of the ballroom. The door there led to the service rooms and the servants staircase leading to the private rooms on the next floor. She was making her escape.

Elisa was glad to see the girl's shoulders were square and straight and knew Vaughn had kept her pride intact.

When he reached her side, he picked up her hand. "Come with me," he said, his voice low. But the resounding silence from the avid witnesses in the room meant his every word was quite audible.

He led her around the Munroes towards the other end of the ballroom. People made way for them without a word.

Elisa looked past Vaughn's shoulder and stiffened. Rufus sat in the corner, in the same spot and possibly on the same chair upon which he'd sat at the soiree. This time, though, there were no fawning associates about him. He sat entirely alone, and he looked quite ill. His face was flushed its usual red from excess drink, but he was much changed. The bones beneath his wattled skin seemed to have shrunk, leaving the skin loose. Where it was not touched with red, the flesh had an alarming gray pallor that looked not at all healthy. Even his hair had lost its iron constitution and lay in wispy silver strands about his head. His hand on the top of the cane shook even with the support.

Rufus had become an old man.

Elisa almost felt sorry for him, but when his eyes met hers she saw a loathing so intense, she shivered.

Rufus shifted in his chair as he watched their approach. He glanced about, patently unhappy with the unavoidable confrontation in such a public place.

He would have killed us both, she reminded herself.

"You whore!" he swore at her as soon as they were within a few feet of him. "You would come here and humiliate me in front of my friends with your immorality?"

"Rufus, you will speak with a civil tongue," Vaughn said. "Or you and I will reach an agreement right here on this spot. Not outside, but here, where there can be no doubt about the outcome or the methods used. Do you understand me?"

Rufus glowered. "Yes," he spat.

"Elisa…" Vaughn pulled her to his side, and closer to Rufus. "He will listen now," he assured her.

She looked down at Rufus, but the shrunken old man stared down at his breeches, refusing to meet her eyes.

"I know what you did to hold me to you, Rufus. I know that you lied about looking for my son. I know that you told my son I was dead."

"You lie!" Rufus declared, and glanced around the room. That told Elisa that he made the accusation not because he was afraid of what she thought, but what everyone else in the room thought.

"You poor old fool!" she railed at him. "Did you really think Vaughn would not find him? Raymond is with me, now, and he does not lie. We know you paid to have him hidden from me. You failed."

"You should know, Rufus, that I intend to marry Elisa at the soonest possible opportunity," Vaughn said. He did not speak with any sort of intensity, but the whole room seemed to draw a shocked breath in reaction.

Rufus's head lifted quickly. "I could have your title taken away," he said, his teeth clenched.

"I could have you put in Newgate Prison," Vaughn shot back. "Shall I show everyone the fresh scars beneath my shirt? The scars left by your pistol?"

Rufus swallowed hard, his narrowed eyes finding Elisa once more. She blanched under his stare. "He will leave you one day, when you are older and he is still a young man."

"You tried to kill us both, Rufus, because you're an unhappy man who can't abide joy in anyone else, and all I feel is pity for you. You'll die a lonely old man."

Rufus looked back at Vaughn. "Take her then," he said. "I care nothing for her. But I can strip you of your title, lands, money."

"If you want to let the world know I am not your son, then so be it. I don't need a title. I have my mother's home, Kirkaldy, and that is all I want. You are not my father...and for that I thank God."

Rufus looked down at his lap once more, and Elisa realized that his sting had been pulled. The last shot he had thought to be such a powerful one had had no effect whatsoever. Again, facing the truth squarely had disarmed the enemy.

Vaughn took Elisa by the hand. "One last thing," he murmured. He led her to the middle of the dance floor, and everyone again silently moved out of their way. Vaughn walked a full circle around her, confronting everyone, before halting to face them all.

"My name is Vaughn Wardell, Viscount Rothmere, and this," he said, motioning to Elisa, "is the woman I intend to marry."

"You all believe Elisa a wicked woman, but she has been wronged by all of you who refused to consider the truth because it is unpalatable. Her husband was murdered, her son taken from her, and her reputation ruined. She was cut off from the world she knew, shunned by all. And for what?" He scanned the room. "Because her husband had been unfaithful."

"For god's sake, man, this is not the place!" a man called out. "There's women here, innocents..."

"They more than anyone else here need to hear this!" Vaughn shouted back. "Every man here already knows or suspects the truth of what happened to Elisa's husband, but you have turned your backs on that truth because it was easier to believe the story that was concocted instead. Elisa was innocent of all but loving her husband. All of you here know that Roger was a blatant womanizer."

There was a feminine gasp at this outrageous statement, but Elisa noticed that Caroline and other women of her age did not gasp. They knew, or suspected, the truth.

"We all know the woman in whose bed he was found, and we all know the husband that was forced to take up the duel against him. When Roger conveniently got himself shot for his efforts, the husband found it would be less embarrassing if he claimed that it was he who dallied with the lovely, untouchable young wife—Elisa—rather than admit his own wife had strayed. And you, all of you, supported him in this effrontery! You did nothing while this young woman lost everything. She did *nothing* to deserve such cruelty." Vaughn spun on his heels, pointing at them all. He was furious—the tendons on his neck straining as he shouted at them all.

Elisa saw that some of the men were nodding. And she realized with a welling sorrow that Vaughn had it right: the men, many of them, knew the truth, or suspected it. They had let her be cast out from their world in order to support their fellow man.

Vaughn shook his head. "I'm going to marry this woman," he said, lifting her hand to his lips. He smiled warmly. "I don't care if you approve or not. I'm marrying her because I love her, and you can all go hang."

He smiled at her, and tugged her gently toward the door. "It's over," he murmured to her. "We can leave and never look back."

The silence that followed them was deafening. It was a roar and Elisa held her breath, half expecting a bullet to shatter that silence.

But what did shatter it was a single clap. Vaughn stopped in mid-step, as did she. They both turned, seeking the source of the clap, as another clap sounded.

Behind them, walking the length of the ballroom floor towards them, was Natasha, slowly clapping her hands together, a fierce, determined look on her face, her tear-stained eyes glittering with intensity.

Another clap joined hers. Elisa spun to find the source and saw Caroline had joined her hands together. Tears streaked her face, too. Next to her, William also began to clap.

The clap was taken up by others, more and more quickly, until it had spread about the room, gaining in intensity until they turned to face a crowd that no longer condemned, but who had obviously, by their acclaim, accepted them for who they were. The clapping grew to a thunderous applause.

Vaughn turned Elisa around to face him, and before the entire room took her face in his hands and kissed her thoroughly.

Enjoy this excerpt from

SEDUCTION OF COLETTE

© *Copyright Claire Thompson 2004*

All Rights Reserved, Ellora's Cave Publishing, Inc.

"My lord, you can't be serious!"

"Of course I am. She's mine, I can do as I please!" Claude Rousseau shook off the restraining hand of his friend, Andre. It was after midnight at the Court of Versailles in the French countryside, and many of the parties were only just getting started. Rousseau had been drinking hard, as was his habit, and for a while had been winning steadily at Le Poque, as the game of poker was called at Court. The year was 1678, and King Louis the Fourteenth had reached the zenith of his career. All Europe bowed before the nation of France, and the country itself had been brought by skillful tyranny to admire and obey the Sun King as sole sovereign over all.

The splendor of the Court lay in the beautiful palaces constructed at huge expense under the careful direction of the King, as well as in the luxurious furnishings of the apartments, the lavish dress of the courtiers, the sumptuous entertainments, the fame of the men and the beauty of the women drawn there by the magnets of money, reputation and power.

The morals of the Court included discreet but constantly present sexual dalliances, extravagance in dress and gambling, and passionate intrigues for prestige and place, all carried on a rhythm of external refinement, elegant manners and compulsory gaiety. Nobles and their ladies consumed half the income of their estates on clothing, lackeys and equipage; the most modest had to have eleven servants and two coaches, some of the richer dignitaries had seventy-five attendants in their household, and forty horses in their stables.

Gambling at cards was a chief recreation and Louis again gave the lead, bidding for high stakes, urged on by his mistress Montespan, who herself lost and won four million francs in one night's play. The gambling mania spread through the Court, and Claude Rousseau was no exception. This evening he had consumed several bottles of wine, and his hand now shook as he made what would turn out to be his final bet of the evening. Liquor had colored his ability to judge the skill of his bluff. The pile of coins he had started the evening with had dwindled to nothing, and still he went on. His old friend Andre shrugged, tired of arguing with a man who was about to give away the thing he should have held most dear.

Across the table Philippe de Valon silently surveyed the gentlemen. He noted Rousseau's wig was askew, and rivulets of sweat made little lines down the white powder on his sagging jowls. The man was desperate, and drunk, and not in a position to be making the wager he now made. And yet, who was Philippe to stop him? It was a curious wager indeed, and Philippe was not at all uninterested.

Lord Philippe de Valon, master draftsman, shipbuilder, heir to a huge fortune in the northern port of St. Malo, was at present one of the King's favorites. Though he would rather have been home in his own province, tending to his businesses and seeing to his properties, the King had bid Philippe to stay at Court, and continue to design lovely buildings for him. Of course, he was also invited to partake in the elaborate excesses of food, wine and, most especially, women.

Philippe had thought by now he had seen it all. But this latest bid by the Duke of Lyon was extraordinary, even measured against the cynical sophistication of the Court. It must be a bluff, surely.

But again Rousseau said, "As you can see, I am out of coin, but so confident am I in my hand that I am willing to risk the person of my daughter as collateral for my wager. You win, you get her. I win, I get the all the gold that has changed hands tonight, as well as two of your horses and a carriage. Fair?"

"More than fair," nodded Philippe, mentally calculating the value of this man's daughter to her father in his own head. It seemed a paltry price to pay for another human being! Especially a lovely young virgin. And did the father have the authority to hand over another human being? Yes, technically he did, as she fell under the estate of Le Duc Rousseau de Lyon. Still a man of some influence in the kingdom, Rousseau's once sizable holdings had been dramatically reduced by the King's taxes and forced 'gifts', as well as the duke's own mismanagement and neglect.

The duke's daughter, Colette, age eighteen, would surely be considered by most fathers to be a most prized possession. The duke, however, was not a sentimental man, and certainly not a loving one. For him, his three daughters had come down to a matter of gold. Each had a cost, since their father was expected to provide a sizable dowry to get them properly wed. Colette's two older sisters had just been successfully matched, and the cost to the duke had been substantial indeed.

Colette was, at the moment, asleep in her chambers in one of the smaller houses on the King's huge estate at Versailles, blissfully unaware that the course of her life hung in the balance over a game of cards.

"Well, then. Top this, if you can!" With a flourish, Rousseau spread his cards on the table. Philippe studied them carefully, and then slowly, his expression inscrutable, revealed his own cards. Rousseau's hand had been reaching for the pile of gold even while Philippe had been laying down his cards, so sure was he of his bet.

Now Andre, turning pale, shouted, "Claude! You imbecile! You've lost! You do not have the winning hand! Lord de Valon has outwitted you again! And now you've lost Colette! You fool!"

Rousseau spluttered and swore, his hands falling away from the gold as his face reddened, the words of his friend finally penetrating the thick fog of wine in his brain. "No! He cheated! It's impossible! I had the perfect cards! No!" Rousseau stood, pulling and fumbling at the sheath that held his sword. Fashion demanded that every gentleman sport a sword, and this was sometimes a dangerous state of affairs, when tempers were frayed and judgment blurred by alcohol. Philippe also stood, his hand on his sheath, not yet drawing. Several men at the table constrained the old duke, who fell back against his chair, his face now pale and sweating.

"A bet is a bet," intoned one of the men, and they all nodded. Rousseau seemed to age suddenly before their eyes, slumping in his chair and dropping his head into his hands.

Philippe took his own hand from his sword, though he remained standing. He decided to ignore the older man's insult that he had cheated. A duel with the old fellow would certainly lead to Rousseau's death, and Philippe had no desire to kill a man, especially not a drunken old sot like Rousseau.

"Gentlemen," he said, "This has been quite an entertaining evening. Unfortunately, I find myself quite exhausted and would bid you good night. Lord Rousseau, I will be by your chambers in the morning to collect my prize. Good night." Gathering the stack of gold in front of his place, Philippe bowed gracefully to the gentlemen at the table, the plume of his hat grazing the winning cards.

Also by Julia Templeton:

Now and Forever
Kieran the Black
Dangerous Desires
Hometown Hero

Also by Tracy Cooper-Posey

Winter Warriors
Red Leopard

About the author:

Anastasia Black is the pen name for a writing partnership between two Ellora's Cave writers: Julia Templeton and Tracy Cooper-Posey. Anastasia Black writes Regency and Victorian historical romances.

Julia and Tracy welcome mail from readers who write to them c/o Ellora's Cave Publishing at 1337 Commerce Drive, Suite #13, Stow Ohio 44224.

Why an electronic book?

We live in the Information Age—an exciting time in the history of human civilization in which technology rules supreme and continues to progress in leaps and bounds every minute of every hour of every day. For a multitude of reasons, more and more avid literary fans are opting to purchase e-books instead of paperbacks. The question to those not yet initiated to the world of electronic reading is simply: *why?*

1. *Price.* An electronic title at Ellora's Cave Publishing runs anywhere from 40-75% less than the cover price of the <u>exact same title</u> in paperback format. Why? Cold mathematics. It is less expensive to publish an e-book than it is to publish a paperback, so the savings are passed along to the consumer.

2. *Space.* Running out of room to house your paperback books? That is one worry you will never have with electronic novels. For a low one-time cost, you can purchase a handheld computer designed specifically for e-reading purposes. Many e-readers are larger than the average handheld, giving you plenty of screen room. Better yet, hundreds of titles can be stored within your new library—a single microchip. (Please note that Ellora's Cave does not endorse any specific brands. You can check our website at www.ellorascave.com for customer recommendations we make available to new consumers.)

3. *Mobility.* Because your new library now consists of only a microchip, your entire cache of books can be taken with you wherever you go.

4. *Personal preferences are accounted for.* Are the words you are currently reading too small? Too **large**? Too…**ANNOYING**? Paperback books cannot be modified according to personal preferences, but e-books can.

5. *Innovation.* The way you read a book is not the only advancement the Information Age has gifted the literary community with. There is also the factor of what you can read. Ellora's Cave Publishing will be introducing a new line of interactive titles that are available in e-book format only.

6. *Instant gratification.* Is it the middle of the night and all the bookstores are closed? Are you tired of waiting days—sometimes weeks—for online and offline bookstores to ship the novels you bought? Ellora's Cave Publishing sells instantaneous downloads 24 hours a day, 7 days a week, 365 days a year. Our e-book delivery system is 100% automated, meaning your order is filled as soon as you pay for it.

Those are a few of the top reasons why electronic novels are displacing paperbacks for many an avid reader. As always, Ellora's Cave Publishing welcomes your questions and comments. We invite you to email us at service@ellorascave.com or write to us directly at: 1337 Commerce Drive, Suite 13, Stow OH 44224.

Discover for yourself why readers can't get enough of the multiple award-winning publisher Ellora's Cave. Whether you prefer e-books or paperbacks, be sure to visit EC on the web at www.ellorascave.com for an erotic reading experience that will leave you breathless.

WWW.ELLORASCAVE.COM